Chark's Bones

For
Leilani

Salman Smith

Chark's Bones

A 'Chark and Beane' Mystery

⅋⅋

HOLMAN SMITH

To order additional copies of this book, contact:
Xlibris Corporation
1-888-7-XLIBRIS
www.Xlibris.com
Orders@Xlibris.com

Chapter 1

Private Ben Stewkley struggled to keep his eyes focused on the black streak of sweat down the tunic of the soldier in front. God! he was tired. No time to fall by the roadside and sink into that sweet, painless sleep. He lifted his eyes and looked ahead at the steel helmets of the other columns of soldiers among the hedgerows as they moved slowly along the sunken, winding French road.

It was summer 1940 and the Hamptonshire Regiment was retreating to the coast ahead of the Germans. With every step Ben and his companions came closer to the English Channel and safety. Through the drifting, acrid smoke and the whine and crackle of gunfire they could smell the sea. For five hot days they had survived on water from horse troughs, vegetables from the gardens of deserted farm houses and fitful sleep under wet blankets.

"Keep moving!" called the tall, gaunt sergeant from the head of the column. His right arm hung splinted and bloody. "Keep your eyes on the man in front. Only two more miles to go."

A hollow-eyed private marching next to Ben hitched up his pack on sore shouders. "Only two more miles," he mimicked. "Fucking idiot's been sayin' that all morning. We goin' round in fucking circles?"

"The navy'll be there to pick us up," continued the sergeant "Then we'll have lots of rum and roast beef with mashed potatoes and gravy."

"Oh, yeah?" called out Ben. "Should've joined the navy when I had the chance. Nobody told me I'd wind up in a lousy French ditch with an old rifle and a wet arse and no food. I only joined up to get three meals a day."

Some of the column laughed but the sergeant looked back over his shoulder and fixed Ben with baleful, unsmiling eyes. At the back of the column a soldier started to sing a marching song but his lone voice faded away leaving only the irregular scrunch of marching feet.

Artillery shells screamed in from the left and burst across the road ahead. The column broke up and ran for cover. Ben leaped for the ditch and lay flat with his hands over his head as the earth shook, trees splintered and earth and rocks showered down. The shelling stopped and the smoke began to clear. Ben looked around furtively before climbing out of the ditch onto the road and lining up again with the rest of column.

They marched wearily on and soon reached the place in the road where the shells had hit. The sergeant called them to a halt while the medics tended to the wounded and carried the dead away to a small clearing in a nearby apple orchard. Ben gratefully dropped his rifle and pack on the ground and sat with his back against a low, stone wall. He turned his face up to the sun and drifted off into a half-sleep.

"You. Private." The sergeant leaned over Ben and poked him with his swagger stick. "Get up. Work to be done."

"Why me?"

"Because I say so, soldier. So pick up your gear and move."

Ben didn't move. "Find someone else. I'm tired."

"Not too tired to make smart-assed remarks?" The sergeant drew a deep, hissing breath. "On your feet, country boy."

Ben looked up at the red-rimmed eyes and slowly, deliberately stood. He hitched up his pack and shouldered his rifle. All the time looking at the sergeant with cold, unblinking eyes.

It was a short walk to the clearing where the dead were laid out in a neat line under gray blankets. There were five of them.

"Get on with it."

"With what?"

"The paybooks, man," said the sergeant taking a drag on a tattered cigarette. "Get their paybooks. We'll need them for identification when we get home. If we get home. With dimwitted bastards like you for soldiers we'll be dead or prisoners before night. Hurry it up."

Ben took a deep breath and pulled back the first blanket. He stared at the bloody, mangled corpse. Nausea rose in his empty stomach. He took out the man's paybook and went on to the next. As he lifted the blanket from the last body he gave a gasp and stepped back.

"That one too," said the sergeant with a dry laugh.

"But he's got no head."

"He did a little while ago. He won't miss it. Just get the poor bastard's goddamned paybook and let's get out of here."

Ben's hands shook and he sobbed quietly as he felt inside the bloody tunic. There were letters in there. Letters with hand-written names and addresses and one with a fancy picture printed in one corner and a typed address. Ben had had no letters since he left England and here was a dead soldier with letters to spare. He took the letters and paybook and stuffed them in his own pocket. Then he vomited dryly on the grass.

"You through?" demanded the sergeant "Let's go."

Ben took one last look at the bodies and stopped to think. All the injustices, slights and slurs in his life became personified in the sergeant. He called him quietly. "Sarge."

The sergeant turned painfully and faced the muzzle of Ben's rifle from an arm's length away.

"What the hell?"

Ben smiled. He squeezed the trigger and shot him through the heart. He dragged the sergeant's body by the feet over to the others and laid it next to the headless man. He pulled the blanket over them both.

Ben dropped his pack, took his rifle and threw it in a high, twirling arc among the trees. He marched off across the open fields into the smoke and flames and bullets. As he marched he sang a joyful hymn he'd learned at school. Ben was free at last.

Chapter 2

Fairport was Ben Stewkley's home. He had been born there and lived with his widowed mother in isolated, genteel poverty in a terraced house with lace curtains and a polished brass doorknob. It was a mean-spirited little town sandwiched between the forested hills of Hampton County and the pebble beaches of the English Channel. A gray and brown place with a population of impoverished, retired civil servants, pensioned navy petty officers and laborers who worked in the dockyard across the harbour in the city of Hampton.

Ben attended a church school from whose violent discipline he sometimes escaped by playing hooky on sunny days and riding the country lanes north of the town on his bicycle. The bike had been his father's legacy to him. To his lonely and embittered wife, his father left the house, a small widow's pension and a closet full of books. In the evenings while his mother complained of her station in life and made clothes on an old Singer treadle sewing machine, Ben read and reread the books. He fantasized about the future and how to escape the cloying misery of his existence.

His future was made clear to him one evening as he sat reading 'Treasure Island'. Lost in the apple barrel with Jim Hawkins.

"Close the curtains, Benjamin." It was the signal for his mother to get to work sewing clothes. "It's a good job your poor father can't see me now. Sewing like a slave. Making clothes for people who are no better than I am. For pennies. Just so I can keep up decent appearances."

"Yes, Mum," said Ben without looking up. "I know."

"He never made any money, you know, your father. Could've done, of course. No push. That was his trouble."

Ben nodded and turned a page.

"You take after him. Always had his head in a book too. No profit in that."

Ben closed his eyes tightly and fought the resentment which rose up in him. It was the same old catechism of complaint. Then she came up with a new one that turned Ben's muscles to stone.

"You'll be leaving school soon," she said as she snipped a thread. "Get you a job in the dockyard. If the war comes again there'll be good wages paid and the money will be welcome."

Confirmed. Ben was to follow in his father's footsteps into that ugly, dirty, sweaty world of smoke and noise. Small wages and no prospects of advancement. A tear fell on the page of his book as his mother's voice faded into a monotone. He wiped the tear away with a finger. Somehow he must get away. Somehow.

In the early summer of 1939 Ben fell in love. She was the daughter of a dour, religious fanatic of a dairyman who lived in a mud-beseiged cottage on the fringe of the northern forest. Ben had ridden his bicycle farther than he had intended that Sunday. He stopped to beg a glass of water at the farmyard gate. A short, blackhaired girl in a faded dress and oversized wellington boots handed him a tin ladle of cold well water and smiled up at the handsome stranger with his fair hair hanging over his eyes. And Ben was lost.

The Sunday rides became a regular habit. On sunny days and rainy days they met shyly at the old barn where the chickens roosted and the winter feed was stacked. But anything more than the briefest of conversations between them was prevented by the girl's father. "Time to get back to the house, my girl. There's work to be done," he would command from the barn doorway and she would walk dutifully away giving Ben that smile over her narrow shoulders.

One Sunday evening after he had visited the farm, Ben climbed off his bicycle and wheeled it through to the back of the house to find his mother standing in the kitchen, her hands on her hips eyes blazing with anger.

"And just where have you been?"

"Out for a ride. Why?"

"That's not what I hear."

Ben stood his ground and said nothing.

"I hear you been seeing some slut up in the hills."

"She's no slut. You've no cause to speak like that!"

"So. You've been seeing some girl. I heard from the women at the church that she lives in that disgusting place over Skellmer's End way." She leaned forward and peered into Ben's face. "They're dirty people. Live with animals all the time. They're not our kind. What made you think of such a thing?"

Ben took a deep breath. "She's my friend and I'll see her as often as I like. You can't stop me."

His mother stepped forward and jabbed him in the chest with a bony finger. "We'll see about that."

A week later on a Saturday morning, when Ben went to check the tyres for his Sunday ride the bike was gone. Sold for a few precious shillings to the owner of a junk shop.

That night, Ben lay awake looking out at the stars through his bedroom window. Then, as the first wash of daylight cast shadows across the wall, he quietly packed his few belongings in an old canvas bag, crept silently down the stairs and stepped out into the cold air.

It was a long walk to the farm at Skellmer's End. The handles of the bag were thin. They made his shoulders sore. His thin shoes rubbed blisters on his heels and by evening hunger made him light-headed. When he arrived at the farm, the family were at prayer over their supper by the light of kerosene lamps. Ben waited in the darkness behind the barn until the black-haired girl walked out to scatter feed for the chickens. She stopped and stared as Ben signaled to her.

"I couldn't leave without seeing you again," he said. "Going into Hampton to join the army. Sign up with the Hamptonshire Regiment."

"That's a long way," she whispered. "I'll miss you, Ben."

He nodded.

"You can't ride all that way tonight," she said firmly. "Stay in the barn. Father won't know. Least, not 'til morning. Where's your bike?"

Ben explained about the bike.

"You walked all the way from Fairport?" she asked wide-eyed. "And you're going to walk to Hampton?"

"No choice."

"Wait here," she said and left. Minutes later she appeared again and handed Ben a piece of bread and a slice of ham. She watched as he ate. Then she took something from her pocket and handed it to him.

"What's this?"

Two shiny half-crowns. "Take them. For the bus. It's my own money. From the eggs."

Ben shook his head.

"Take them, Ben." Her eyes were fierce and compelling. He put them in his pocket. "And here's another." She reached in her pocket again gave it to him. "Keep it safe and bring it back to me one day. I'll be waiting." Then she reached up and kissed him as the lantern swung in the cottage door and her father called her name.

Ben slept uneasily in the straw. He woke next morning before the sun rose, picked up his bag and made his way to the country bus stop down the lane from the cottage. The moon hung in the eastern sky as he waited until the first bus of the day rumbled around the corner and stopped for him.

At noon, Ben presented himself at the army recruiting office in

Hampton. He stood before a wooden table and waited for a heavy sergeant with a red sash and peaked cap to acknowledge him.

"Name?"

"Benjamin Harold Stewkley."

"Age?"

"Seventeen,"

Hesitation by the sergeant."Address?" Ben gave a fictitious address in Fairport.

"Religion?"

"Church of England."

"Next of kin?"

"None."

The sergeant looked Ben up and down. "Another bloody orphan. Seems like the whole county is peopled with orphans this month." He pointed to a row of desks across the hall. "Over there. Medical. Get undressed."

When it was Ben's turn, the young medical officer looked him over, prodded and tapped, looked into his ears, eyes and mouth and checked his reflexes. "You're more than ten pounds underweight, son. When did you last eat?"

Ben's eyes turned down.

"Get some food at the canteen," said the medic. He pointed to a door and turned to prepare for the next recruit.

"Does that mean I'm in, sir," asked Ben.

"Yes, you're in," And as Ben walked away the medic added; "God help us if we have to fight a war soon."

A week later, Ben Stewkley was marching and countermarching the parade grounds of Aldershot as a private in the Hamptonshire Regiment.

Chapter 3

While the Hamptonshires struggled homeward from France, two small boys in England tried to understand the great wave of change that was enveloping their world.

Solomon Chark and his son David lived in London above the antique shop and workshop which was Solomon's business. It was a busy part of the city north of the river Thames

"Eat up, David," said his father wiping soup off his red and gray beard with a linen napkin. "It's not for ever. We'll be together again soon. And I'll be visiting you as often as I can."

"It's not the same," muttered David. "You're sending me away."

"Solomon put his spoon down and placed his hand over David's. "Yes, David," he said quietly. "Because it's not safe here. Your mother, God be with her, and I ran to London ahead of the terror. Now you have to go where the bombs don't fall. Me, I have to stay. Some day you will understand."

But David did not understand and he cried into his pillow that night as Solomon paced the floor until daylight.

They ate breakfast in silence next morning and when the time came to leave, Solomon helped David dress. Then he crushed him in his arms and wept. They walked slowly, hand-in-hand together to the schoolyard. A young boy in his gray topcoat and green cap, the tall, older man in a long black coat and homburg hat. He carried his son's suitcase in his free hand.

"Come on David, over here," called a plump, kindly teacher as they stood together just inside the gate. "You're over here with the rest of your class." She bustled over, put her arms around his shoulder and led him away.

Solomon watched with the other parents as the chattering and pushing children were lined up and seated in the waiting buses. He watched the bus drive slowly out of the schoolyard and when it turned a corner and David's waving hand was out of sight, he walked sadly back to his shop.

*

They had tied a label reading 'Marsh Farm, Fairport' on David's coat collar. After a bus and train journey he stood, bewildered, on the Fairport station platform clutching his suitcase and a brown paper bag full of groceries for his new guardians. After a lot of confusion, the tired and cranky children were sorted and packed into taxis and deposited one or two at a time on the doorstep of their new home.

At Marsh Farm David looked up at Mrs Darley. A large, gray-haired woman missing one front tooth and wearing a black linen dress and rubber boots. She looked down at the small, pale boy with wavy, black hair and big brown eyes. His clothes were rumpled and the string handles on his grocery bag had broken so that he held it to his chest with one arm and the heavy suitcase in the other.

"David?" Mrs Darley's voice was warm and she smiled as she said his name.

"Yes, ma'am."

"Come on in. You must be tired and hungry. All that way from London." She pronounced it 'Lunnon'.

The interior of the house seemed to be one large room. There were sagging old chairs, a scrubbed whitewood table and several cats and dogs sleeping in the shadows. A welcoming smell of cooking wafted from the coal-fired stove.

"Sit ye down, David," said Mrs Darley taking his coat and luggage. "We'll have something to eat. Mr Darley gets in late from the packing plant over in Hampton."

She busied herself at the stove and placed a large plate of beef, mashed potatoes and gravy in front of David. He looked at it for a moment.

"Go on. Eat. 'tis good country food you'll be eating from now on."

He was hungry and ate until he was full. As Mrs Darley hovered over him with more, there was a knock at the door and a woman equally as large as Mrs Darley strode in. She was loud and flowery with dyed hair and a heavy stroke of red lipstick.

"Evenin' Flo," she called. "That your evacuee?" She pointed at David and sat in one of the shapeless chairs by the stove. Flo Darley handed her a cup of tea and sat in the other chair.

"Yes, Mavis," she replied proudly. "Arrived today. Nice lookin' lad aint he?"

David's eyes moved from one woman to the other as they spoke.

"This is Mrs Privett, David. She lives next door." Mavis ignored the introduction.

"Mine came yesterday. By taxi, if you please. Never been in a taxi meself." She sipped her tea. "Had to laugh," she continued. "First thing the little tyke wanted was the toilet. Shoulda seen his face when my old man gave him a flashlight and pointed down the yard." Mavis-from-next-door threw back her head and roared with laughter.

"What's 'is name then?" Mavis Privett spoke of David as though he were one of the Darley's mute pets.

"David. David Chark. He's from London."

Mavis' eyes narrowed. "Chark, eh? That's a funny name. What's your Dad's name, then?"

"Solomon. Solomon Chark."

"Solomon Chark," repeated Mavis slowly her voice rising with each word. "Jewish gentlemen is he? You Jewish?"

David stared at the table top in embarassment.

"Don't know, ma'am," he whispered.

"What's he do, this Solomon Chark?"

"He's an antique dealer."

"Oh, one of those. Rich is he?"

David was silent and wide-eyed at the onslaught of questions. But Flo Darley came to his rescue by picking up Mavis' cup as a signal that it was time to leave.

"His label says he is 'Church of England'," said Flo. "Darley will be home from work soon."

Mavis stood up. "Church of England," she mused. "Good. He can go to church with my Phil. We need more choir boys. There must be one or two voices among those London kids." Mavis laughed. "Mind you, with those god-awful accents you can't understand what the little buggers are talking about. Well, I'll be off then. Thanks for the tea."

When the door was closed behind her Flo turned to David.

"Don't you worry about her," she said kindly. "She means well but she's got no manners. Comes from Hampton. You'll like her son Phil though. See him tomorrow." Flo's voice softened. "Darley and me don't have no children of our own. I hope you get to like us."

David smiled for the first time that day.

Flo Darley took David by the arm, led him up to his bedroom and waited until he fell asleep. Then she sat by the kitchen stove knitting and listening to the radio while she waited for her husband to come home. And thinking. How could a mother willingly give up a child like that? How many of those London kids are lucky enough to get good homes? Pity the poor little mites that get stuck with the likes of Mavis Privett.

*

Paul Lovedean lay on his belly on the salt marsh south of Fairport. Gulls shrieked and the wind off the sea rustled through the coarse grass swirling up eddies of fine sand. He was two years older than David Chark and lived in an eighteenth-century red-brick house with a walled garden and mullioned windows in a part of Fairport known as Old Town. The Old Town was the original village of Fairport and defined by a crossroad with the 'Duke of York' pub (commonly known as 'The Duke'), the post office, general store and Town Hall on the corners. The Lovedean house was on Hamm's Lane which ran south from the pub towards the salt marsh.

"Paul? Paul?" His mother's voice was faint against the wind.

In the haze across the gray water of the English Channel, Paul could see wisps of smoke. Somewhere out there his father commanded a rust-streaked old destroyer herding wallowing freighters carrying food and fuel from America. Captain Charles Godolphin Lovedean was a broad, bearded, blue-eyed professional sailor who came home to Fairport bearing exotic gifts and telling tales of strange places and stranger people. The brief periods of togetherness with his son Paul and wife Mary were full of laughter and country walks and Sunday dinners in their warm house. Then he would be gone and the waiting started again.

"Paul! Paul! Lunch is ready!"

His mother's voice interrupted his thoughts again from beyond the line of elm trees. She stood at the edge of the marsh shading her eyes from the bright sun.

"Paul! Paul! You there?"

Paul stood up and waved to her. Then he brushed the dead grass and twigs from his sweater and with a last, longing look out to sea, set off back to the house, lopping the heads off tall grasses with a stick as he went.

*

On a gray morning in September, the vicar of Fairport presided over a memorial service in St. Ethelred's church for those who had died in the Battle of France.

"Shove over," demanded Phil Privett as he squeezed into the pew beside David. "You see they put those prepschoolers at the back? Best place for 'em. Rotten snobs." There was much jostling and complaining as the row of boys accommodated the latecomer.

The Preparatory School deputation sat together in the dark apse where the baptismal font stood massive and ancient. They shared a contraband bag of extra-strong peppermints that Michael had smuggled past the watchful deacon at the door. Paul Lovedean scanned the congregation.

There's my mother," he said pointing to a covey of straw hats halfway down the nave. But nobody was listening.

"Sit down!" hissed the deacon.

The portly, white-haired reverend Tweed climbed ponderously into the pulpit and leaned out over his flock. The noise diminished to nothing. He coughed before picking up his notes and began his eulogy.

"My friends, we are gathered here in the sight of God..." He paused and shook his head lightly "to pay homage to those who gave their lives in the defence of freedom in the fields of France." His voice droned on for another twenty minutes while husbands, whose heads had begun to droop, were elbowed in the ribs and fidgety children were shushed. When he stopped, the mayor stood to read in solemn voice the names of the fallen. Among them was Private Benjamin Stewkley of the Hamptonshire Regiment.

Mrs Stewkley sat alone and silent in her seat. Her face gray with pain. Her clothes hung limply on her bent and frail body. The outward fire of her hatred of the world was cold now. Only her eyes betrayed it as she stared down at her yellowing cotton gloves tightly clasped around her precious bible.

David and Phil became close friends during the weeks after the memorial service. They spent their days walking the fields and lanes around Fairport, playing football and listening to the radio in Phil's house.

As he promised, Solomon Chark visited his son at the Darleys as often as he could get away. He would arrive at the Darley's door carrying a bag of strange London delicacies that made Mr Darley's eyes narrow with mistrust and Mrs Darley coo over the boxes of chocolates from the growing underground economy of the city.

Solomon arrived late the day after Christmas. The bombing in London had increased that week and the trains were delayed. He stepped stiffly down from the bus and walked to the Darley's in dry, frigid air that hurt his nose. He shook hands with Mr Darley and dropped the package on the kitchen table, made small talk for an hour and then took David for a walk along the lane and stopped at a fallen tree. They sat, huddled in coats, hats and scarves their breath mingling in the cold air.

"David," he started, "It's time to come home, son."

"But Dad, I just got on the football team and Phil's the goalkeeper. We play the church school next week."

Solomon smiled to himself. How quickly the young adapt.

"David. I've sold the house in London. We're going to live in the country. There's a town not far from here called Eastchester. I went there and found some old cottages that were going to be demolished. I made an offer to the owner and he accepted. They're not much but we can work on them and I can move my workshop there. What do you say?"

David shrugged and looked away. "Can we take all our things. Like mother's books and pictures?"

"Of course, anything you want."

"Can Phil come to visit?"

"As often as he wants."

"And will we see Mr and Mrs Darley?"

"Yes,"

"OK," said David after a minute's pondering. He jumped down from the tree. "When can I see the cottage?"

Solomon eased down and walked beside him back to Marsh Farm.

"Actually, it's four cottages. Small ones. We will knock down the walls and make them into one."

"They'll have to have a name," said David. "All the houses around here have names. Not numbers."

"Good," said Solomon. "And you can choose the name."

"That's easy. 'Aurora Cottage.'" It was his mother's middle name.

Solomon drew David to him. "Of course. That's perfect. Aurora Cottage. Now let us the Darleys tell."

Chapter 4

In February 1941 the army commandeered the horse pasture behind the 'Duke of York' pub and the broad swath of salt marshes that led down to the sea. The shoreline was sealed with barbed wire and a minefield and anti-aircraft gun emplacements were built along the low cliffs above the beach. Then, with much pomp and circumstance, a company of the Hamptonshire Regiment marched down from the railway station to make camp on the pasture.

They formed a long column headed by Colonel Ford in his World War 1 uniform and brown boots and Sergeant major Bullock in his new battledress and red sash. The column swept down the High Street past St Ethelred's church and turned into Hamm's Lane.

"Left, right, left, right," chorused Paul Lovedean and his friend Michael as they aped the soldiers, striding along on the sidewalk swinging their arms high in imitation. Then they raced ahead to claim a ringside seat in their elm tree on the edge of the pasture where the soldiers were to make their camp.

The column approached the 'Duke of York'.

"Eyes right!" bellowed Bullock and several hundred grinning faces snapped towards the "Duke" in unison. The assembled barmaids and cellarmen cheered their potential customers.

"Eyes front!"

High up in an ancient elm tree Paul and Michael watched as the army reached the pasture. Colonel Ford and the Sergeant Major were first through the five-bar gate. Paul pointed and giggled. "Colonel Ford looks like the doorman at the theatre in that uniform." He ducked his head as Michael swung at him with his fist.

"That's my uncle you're talking about, Lovedean"

"My Dad says he's nuts," said Paul.

"That's because of the war. My Dad says it addled his brain. Now he talks to himself a lot," said Michael. "Here they come."

The column reached the elm tree below the boys and the scrunching cadence of nail-studded boots on the paved road gave way to a soggy squelch as the first rows of soldiers stepped into the soft turf of the pasture. As they slowed, the following rows cannoned into the first and the Hamptonshires dissolved into a struggling, cursing horde. The boys in the tree cheered and hooted. Colonel Ford was beside himself with anger. He raged up and down, his face purple, slapping his swagger stick on his trouser legs.

The muddy and embarassed soldiers moved to higher ground and waited for their equipment to arrive. The trucks had been requisitioned from an unwilling Albert Hoff, a local building contractor. They sported a new coat of brown and green camouflage paint and a bulging load of boxes and canvas tents. The trucks slithered to a stop in the mud on their cheap, bald civilian tires. Paul and Michael listened from above.

"Well, what do we do now, Colonel Ford, Sir?" Bullock accentuated the "Sir" and thrust his chin forward, eyes bulging.

"We'll have to haul the big, ugly bastards ourselves, I suppose," snarled the Colonel glaring up at the tree where Paul and Michael were now laughing uncontrollably and in danger of falling off their perch and breaking a bone or two.

"Very well, sir," said Bullock in a mock pedantic tone which did little to conceal his contempt. He walked away across the muddy field.

*

By midday the trucks had been hauled to higher ground by sweating soldiers. The cooks had set up a temporary field kitchen beneath tarps tied to the trees. Oil-fired stoves were lit and rough tables set out in lines. Fragrant steam rose from the soot-blackened pots simmering on the stoves.

The cooks made hot, sweet tea and laid out trays of food on the tables. Weary soldiers lined up to heap their metal plates and fill their mugs. Paul and Michael climbed down from the elm tree and timidly approached the camp. Soon they were sitting with a group of cheerful soldiers eating thick corned beef sandwiches and listening to the mens' good-natured bickering laced with traditional soldiers' epithets and insults.

Along Hamm's Lane the crowds of Fairporters had drifted away as the evening closed in. Harry Osborn and Fred Cummins; who had served with the Hamptonshires in the First World War, watched the show in the manner of old soldiers who, stricken with morbid nostalgia, felt it necessary to make odious comparisons.

"Christ, Harry! What a shambles. At least, in the First War we 'ad 'orses to do the pullin'. I heard Germans got tanks that'll do sixty mile an hour in mud like that."

"Yer right, Fred," said an equally disgusted Harry, "How about I buy you a pint in the "Duke"?"

"Drown our sorrows, eh?"

The two old soldiers pushed open the door of the "Duke", stepped into the familiar, smoky haze and found their way to the comfort of the crowded bar.

*

After sundown, khaki tents had been erected in lines and oil lamps flickered warmly in the cooling evening air. The bugler sounded "Lights Out" and the defenders of Southern England settled back into their coarse blankets to sleep or talk while the sentries smoked and gossiped among the trees.

It was dark when Paul and Michael parted. Paul reached the kitchen door where his anxious mother waited.

"Where have you been?" she demanded "I've been worried sick. It's dark."

"Down the Lane."

"Doing what?"

"Watching the soldiers set up camp on the horse pasture. We got to stack rifles like Cary Grant in that movie about India. Then a fat cook gave us tea and sandwiches. I'm glad my dad's not in the army. He'd hate all that mud and marching about. Is he coming home soon?"

Paul chattered on as he washed his hands at the kitchen sink while his mother set the table for supper.

Mary Lovedean was a short, trim woman with bright blue eyes and thick brown hair. Her woolen skirt and cotton blouse were covered by a white apron tied firmly around her waist. She spoke with the rounded lilt of the West Country where she had been born and where she met her husband Charles when he was newly-commissioned in the Royal Navy.

"I suppose you'll not want supper tonight after all that heavy army food?"

"Not really, Mum," said Paul "Those army sandwiches are really big."

"All right, then. Off to bed with you."

As Paul stood up to leave, Mary waved an envelope at him. "Letter came in the afternoon post," she said with a little smile. "From your Dad."

Paul tried to snatch it away but Mary playfully waved it over his head. "A letter? Why didn't you tell me? Why didn't you tell me? What does he say? Is he coming home?" Paul hugged his mother fiercely as she rumpled his hair and smiled down at him.

"I don't know, son. He can't say when but I know it won't be long. I can tell by the way he writes. Here, you read it."

Sleep did not come easily to Paul. He lay on his bed, hands clasped behind his head, looking through the many-paned window at a thin sliver of moon that raced through black patches of cloud in a navy-blue sky.

Soon his father would come striding down the Lane and scoop him up in those strong arms and swing him around as he always did. Across the hallway in her pink and white bedroom, Mary Lovedean read and reread the precious words of love and hope that were scrawled in that large, familiar hand. She turned out the light and slid down between the cold, lonely sheets. A distant train howled into the night and a few revelers at the "Duke" quavered the notes of a bawdy song.

Beyond the horse pasture at the edge of the salt marshes it was getting cold. The anti-aircraft gunners shivered and leaned back into their unpadded metal seats.

"Another day over," said a gunner to his mate as he packed away his binoculars.

"Yep. They'll be back tomorrow. It's the Air Force stations they're after. Poor bastards are getting plastered."

"Well, so long as they're after the airfields and not the great sinful metropolis of Fairport. God! What a dump. I suppose we're safe enough in this bloody swamp. But I'd rather be up there in the Big Smoke anytime, bombs or no bombs. Wouldn't you?"

His friend laughed. "I suppose so. Right now I'm too tired to give a shit."

At the order to 'stand down', the gunners walked back to their wooden huts and lay down fully-dressed on camp beds.

"Goodnight."

"Goodnight, mate."

Chapter 5

"We've got to get those damn horses out of the pasture and close off the vegetable gardens near the church, Mr Mayor." Colonel Ford stood in front of Mayor Cecil Temple's desk in a cloud of cigarette smoke. He peeled off his gloves and dropped them in his uniform hat.

"Oh, so it's Mr Mayor, is it, Colonel?" said the mayor irritably. It was morning and he hadn't had his tea yet. "What happened to Cecil and Titus? You going all official on me? And why do we have to clear off the pasture?"

"Need to dig trenches from the church to Hamm's Lane."

"What for? For God's sake. You planning another World War One? What use will trenches be? It's bombers we need to worry about."

"Look, Cecil," said the Colonel staightening his back and jutting out his jaw. "My sector starts and ends in Fairport. I'm responsible. The manual says dig trenches. So I dig trenches. You want me to invoke military necessity or are you going to move those people out before I start to dig?"

"They're not going to like it, Titus."

The Colonel shrugged his shoulders.

"Christ!" said the clerk of the court on the morning of the public meeting as he peered out of the mayor's office door "Look at that crowd. Bloody unusual. We usually have to pressgang bodies out of the "Duke" to make a quorum for a public meeting."

By nine-thirty the big room above the council offices was full and those unable to take a seat were crammed in the aisles and doorway.

At ten o'clock the clerk bawled for silence and the town councillors filed in to take their places at the long table. They sat on hard chairs. A device employed by a former councillor to ensure a greater customer turnover in her tearoom. It also worked to keep Council meetings short.

The mayor held up his hand for silence. "Ladies and gentlemen. There are only two items on the agenda. You've all been given a fact sheet so I'll start by calling the first speaker. Mr Allnut." He lifted his glasses and scanned the crowd. "You out there, Sydney?"

"I'm 'ere."

Sidney Allnut, the owner of the horse pasture, stumped up the aisle to the long table and confronted the mayor at close range. He spread his stained and calloused hands on the varnished surface. The mayor leaned back in his chair to avoid the onslaught of tobacco-laced breath. Sidney was a plump, balding man of middle years wearing a shiny black suit and celluloid collar normally reserved for Sunday service at St Ethelred's. He waved the offending piece of paper in the mayor's face.

"It's one thing to have the bloody government plough up the best parts of me pasture so people can grow vegetables. For no compensation I might add," he shouted. "I can see that, Mr Mayor, 'cos there's a war on. But it's another thing to have the bloody army dig damn great holes all over it. My poor horses will break their bloody legs and then how will you get the milk delivered to all those little children and those kids from London that's been sent down here?"

The mayor looked around at the murmuring crowd of voting-age Fairporters.

"But Mr Allnut," he said in his lawyerly voice. "This is a matter of national emergency. The army authorities, represented by Colonel Ford—" He raised his palm upwards toward the Colonel sitting on his left "—say they must dig the trenches around the town to defend us if the Germans land on the coast." He nervously smoothed back his black, oiled hair and looked imploringly at the Colonel who stared steadfastly down at the table. The mayor switched his attention to the other members of the council but they all squirmed in their seats and avoided his eyes. Finally, as the crowd grew restless and ribald comments shot out from the back rows, all eyes turned back to the Colonel. He cleared his throat and adjusted the tight little knot on his regimental tie.

"My men need to dig a pattern of trenches so that we can move about without exposing ourselves to the enemy. Do you understand that, Sidney?"

"No!" roared Sidney. "I'm in the milk-and-vegetable delivery business. You're in charge of soldiering. So dig your bloody trenches somewhere else. My horses is valuable animals. You might need them to pull your trucks out of the mud some day."

There was a wave of laughter from the crowd. The insult was not lost on the Colonel who, while visibly purple with anger, repressed his urge to grab Sidney by the throat and slowly strangle him. He also realised he had another problem. Much of the produce from the Ford family farm north of town was sold on Allnut stalls at the market and hauled cheaply to the railway station on Allnut horse carts.

"Well, Colonel? What's your decision?" asked the Mayor.

The Colonel rose, smiled broadly and gestured magnanimously to the crowd. "I think it's possible that the British Army can rearrange its plans for the defence of the country to suit Mr Allnut," he said with heavy sarcasm. "I will look into the matter. Perhaps the trenches can be moved closer to the elm trees. After all, Mr Mayor, the destruction of private property is something we expect from the Hun, not from British people." He sat down to a mixture of applause and derision and it took the mayor several minutes to regain order. The council moved more comfortably in their chairs.

"If that's acceptable?" The mayor looked along the row of councillors and got a nodding response. "We will now proceed with the rest of the morning's agenda which is the volunteer duty roster for the air raid wardens and blackout patrol."

At that, the crowd quickly dissolved through the doors into the High Street and filled up both bars in the "Duke".

*

The Army Pioneer Corps arrived a few days later with backhoes, tractors and trucks and got to work digging the trenches. They burrowed into the yellow clay and filled sandbags with the tailings until they had scored the pasture from one side to the other.

One overcast and drizzly day, when the digging got close to the patches of ground set aside for the townspeople to grow vegetables, Tom Rydal leaned on his walking stick and looked down into a trench. Several soldiers were doing something sweaty with picks and shovels. Tom had been Fairport Postmaster for many years and had a seat on the town council. By seniority he had claimed a choice piece of the pasture for his vegetable garden.

"Water table's only two foot down, son," he said in his slow, soft brogue.

"Aw, pipe down, Pop," replied a Cockney private with thick, black wavy hair which he pushed back from his eyes with dirty hands. "If the Germans come over and bomb us we'll need 'em. Best go home and dig a hole for yourself before they get 'ere."

The men continued shoveling dirt.

"Them trenches will be full of water by morning."

"Shaddup fer Gawd's sake."

"Get lost, Pop. Go get us some beer if you want to do something useful."

"Come on down and help instead of whining you silly old bugger."

Cheerful insults rose up from the hole. Tom Rydal shrugged and turned away. He walked slowly towards the trees, his leather gaiters and boots squeaking in slow rhythm.

He was right about the depth of the water table. Days after the Pioneer Corps left to dig more holes on the beaches, the trenches were full of stagnant water and green algae. Children sailed their boats and dangled their feet in them. Several fell in and had to be rescued by the soldiers until finally, the excavations were sealed off and abandoned.

Two weeks later a life was lost in the trenches. But it wasn't a child's. A German bomber returning from a night raid on an Air Force station was caught in the searchlights and hit by naval gunfire over Hampton. The crew struggled to fly the crippled plane back to France but it crashed and burned on the beach below Fairport. The only survivor baled out and landed on the salt marsh. He was in pain from burns on his hands and face. In the distance he could see the lights of Fairport. He struggled out of his parachute harness and stumbled across the marshes towards them. He was almost at the trees and a few yards short of the trenches when he died.

Next morning, a long ball from a scratch game of soccer on the pasture got lost and one of the boys went looking for it. The ball had rolled into a trench where it floated in the water just out of reach. The boy spent several minutes on his knees trying to reach it with twigs broken off a tree. The other players saw him suddenly straighten up and wave his arms at them.

"Here!" he called. "Look here!"

They ran over and stood in silence looking at the body of the airman. He lay face down in the water with one booted foot on the lip of the trench.

"It's a German," said someone in hushed, reverent tones.

The boys backed away warily, turned and ran to the police station to fetch Constable Walker.

Nobody questioned the circumstances of the airman's death. It was war. He was an enemy. And like all good Germans in England in 1941, he was dead. It was enough for Constable Walker, the coroner and the rest of Fairport. Nobody questioned how, with his head crushed on one side, he had managed to walk two miles from the place where they found his parachute. Or why he carried no identification. It would be more than forty years before that question was answered.

Meantime, he was buried in a discrete corner of St Ethelred's church-yard and recorded on his white wooden marker as "Unknown German Airman. Killed in the battle over Southern England 1941."

Chapter 6

The sun had risen in a pink and blue sky. It was cold on the salt marshes and the morning watch at the anti-aircraft gun sites on the cliff blew into their mittened hands or clasped warm mugs of tea. The air lay still over the sea and mist rose off the water.

One of the gunners slowly scanned the southern sky with powerful binoculars. He suddenly reversed direction. With a shout, he dropped them and reached for the red alarm button. Sirens wailed along the coast and in the town.

The gunners in the dugouts dropped their tea mugs, grabbed their helmets and in various stages of undress, raced to the guns and made ready for the onslaught.

"Oh, my God," said one. "There's hundreds of the bastards."

The black specks on the horizon flowed towards the coast, grew into airplanes and came slowly within range. The noise shattered the morning quiet and hot, smoking shell cases flew from the gun breeches and piled up on the green grass. The roar of airplane engines grew deafening. The barking guns swiveled to follow the bombers as they flew over in steady formation and then fell silent as they passed out of range. But no bombs fell on Fairport that day. The bombers had a bigger target in mind. London.

The gun crews wiped the sweat from their eyes and leaned back in their seats. Grim and silent.

"My old lady and the kids live in London. Near the docks," said one man through clenched teeth.

"Mine too. Stepney way."

When the alarm sounded in Fairport High Street, Paul Lovedean was idly throwing a tennis ball against the side of the house. At first, he ignored the warning as was the custom among Fairporters. When the guns started firing he looked into the sky and saw the mass of bombers approaching. He raced into the kitchen and took a steel helmet from its hanger and climbed onto the garage roof where he stood entranced at the sight. His mother pleaded with him to come down. But her words were lost in the roar of airplane engines.

"Look! Look at them! There must be hundreds of them!. You can see the swastikas on the tails. I can see the pilots." Paul danced on the roof holding the oversized helmet on his head with one hand.

It was all over in minutes. The throbbing roar reached a crescendo and then faded away to the north. The guns were silent after the last straggler disappeared over the rooftops.

"Did you ever see so many airplanes at one time?" asked Paul breathlessly as he climbed down. There was a pause and then Mary answered through tight lips.

"They were German planes, Paul," she said. "On their way to bomb London. God help those poor people."

*

The Old Town's community air raid shelter had been on and off the council's agenda since the war started in 1939. In the early days there had been some urgency about allocating the money and contracting with Albert Hoff to build it but apathy had drained the urgency away. The massive show of force over the town by the Luftwaffe had changed things and Mayor Temple was besieged by scared, angry Fairporters demanding action.

Another council meeting was called. Not public this time. It was held in the small council chamber next to the mayor's office. It was called for nine o'clock in the morning and Albert Hoff was summoned to attend.

The councilors took their seats and the clerk poured tea and passed it along the table. The council chamber was a dusty room filled with heavy, varnished furniture lit by what little light could penetrate the layer of nicotine-stained dirt on the panes of its narrow clerestory windows. Outside, workmen were busy piling sandbags against the lower windows and doorways.

The mayor polished his glasses and looked around the room. "All here?" The clerk nodded. "This is a special meeting and the only subject is the community air raid shelter. Is Albert Hoff present?"

"Yes," called Albert from the back of the room. He stood up and walked up to the table. He was dressed in a light gray double-breasted suit and two-toned shoes. A "snappy dresser" according to his friends. His thin red hair was brushed back over his head and his pink skin shone.

The mayor cleared his throat and leaned forward.

"Mr Hoff, according to our contract you were supposed to have started the construction of the shelter months ago. So far as we can see you haven't lifted a shovel yet." There was a mutter of agreement among the councilors.

"And what's more, we made a substantial downpayment," said Miss Phillips the sharp-faced principal of the Church School who served as treasurer and secretary. Albert Hoff lifted his chin and faced the council hands-on-hips.

"If Colonel Ford," he began, pointing at the man. "If Colonel Ford had not requisitioned my bloody trucks and ruined them and if Sid Allnut had let the army dig their damn trenches where they belong instead of across the only gap in the trees big enough to let my tractor through, I could have got started."

The mayor was not amused.

"Mr Hoff. There is no need to use foul language," sniffed Miss Phillips. "The council only wishes that you live up to your obligations. I am quite sure you understand the importance of the matter? The Germans are bombing London and all the other big cities, including Hampton. It could be our turn tomorrow." There was a growl of support from other councillors.

"Alright, Albert," said the mayor wearily. "Now, just tell us when you intend to start."

"Tomorrow," said Albert "Assuming my nephew Ted is out by then."

"Out? Out of what?" demanded Colonel Ford.

"Out? What do you mean, out?" The mayor was losing his temper and an unusual tinge of pink was rising above his collar.

"Jail. He's inside again. Nicked by Constable Walker last night. Drunk and disorderly outside the "Duke". He says."

"Can't you get along without him for a while?"

"Oh, no, Mr Mayor," said Albert with deep conviction. "Ted is the only one who can read the architect's plans. Very technical they are. Oh, no Ted is essential for this job."

Miss Phillips began to contest Ted Hoff's ability to read at any level but the mayor raised his hand for silence. He leaned over confidentially to councilman Noble, the magistrate, who was dozing off in the warmth of the crowded room. After a few whispered words the magistrate nodded unhappily and sipped cold tea with a grimace. The mayor raised his eyebrows at Colonel Ford and got a grudging nod of assent.

"Alright, Albert," he said. "Your worthless nephew will be released into your custody. Now, will you get started on the shelter before the Germans come back and blow us all to hell?"

"If he pays his fine," squeaked the magistrate who was now thoroughly offended by being forced to take part in the proceedings.

"Yes, yes," replied the mayor testily.

Albert took a roll of notes from his pocket, peeled off several and dropped them in front of Miss Phillips with a smirk.

"First thing in the morning. Just you see. Have that shelter built in no time."

"I hope so. I hope so."

Albert walked briskly out of the chambers, along the High Street and into the saloon bar of the "Duke". It had been open for at least fifteen minutes and there was drinking time to make up.

The "Duke" was a plain, rectangular building with small windows and a heavy, black door which opened onto the sidewalk. Inside, the ground floor was divided into the saloon and public bars by a flimsy partition of wood panels and frosted glass which adequately separated the drinking classes. Gladys, the barmaid served both bars but the beer was a penny a pint more in the saloon side.

Albert pushed open the door and hung his hat and coat on a peg on the wall.

"The usual, Albert?"

"Yes please, my dear." He leaned over the bar and whispered in Gladys' perfumed ear. "Anybody in the public?"

"A few regulars." She pulled a pint of best bitter and placed it before Albert. He handed her a pound note and carefully counted the change before turning to carry it to his favourite seat near where Tom Rydal was sitting looking down into an empty glass.

"Mornin' Tom."

"Mornin' Hoff."

"Didn't see you at the council meeting this morning," said Albert. "They got onto me something awful about that air raid shelter."

"I heard." Tom Rydal picked up his glass and peered into it as though surprised it was empty. Albert screwed up his eyes thinking how the hell old Rydal gets to the pub before him every day and knows all the latest gossip without, apparently, leaving home except to potter in his vegetable patch and scrounge drinks in the "Duke".

"Get you another?" asked Albert.

Tom nodded and Albert waved at Gladys to bring two more beers.

"So how's the shelter coming?"

"Very well," lied Albert "We start excavating the hole tomorrow. After we get some planks laid over the useless trenches that old fool Titus Ford dug."

The postmaster took a deep swig at his beer, belched and wiped his mouth appreciativly on his sleeve.

"So what's it going to be like down there?"

"Well," started Albert leaning back in his seat to see, if by chance, he had a larger audience. "We'll dig a hole six feet deep, line it with concrete and set steel arches across it. Then we'll cover it with curved, corrugated sheets. You know, like the ones we used in the last war."

"I was too old for the last war."

Albert paused to drink another inch of beer before continuing. "Then we adds three feet of dirt over the whole thing. Supposed to stand anything but a direct hit."

"A direct hit?" Tom peered slyly over the rim of his glass. "You trying to tell me the Germans are such good shots that they can hit one little air raid shelter from way up there in the sky?"

Albert paused. He tried to figure out if the old geezer was just stupid or making fun of him.

"How do we get into this shelter? My wife's old. She can't climb stairs, you know."

"No problem," beamed Albert. "There'll be a ramp at one end so the old people and babies can be wheeled down there as quick as a flash after the siren sounds. Me and Ted have thought of everything."

"Have you, indeed?" mused Tom with the faintest of smirks. "Lavatories?"

"Two. The chemical kind."

"Lights?"

"Lights too."

"The electric kind?"

"Of course. What else?"

"The kind that goes off? Like when the power fails in an air raid?"

Albert looked down into his glass and frowned.

The "Duke's" bars were rapidly filling up. The noise behind the partition suddenly increased as several young men entered the public bar, their boots clattering on the bare wooden floor. Ted Hoff, fresh from the town jail behind the police station pushed his way to the counter. His suit was rumpled after a day in the cells and he had two days growth of wispy beard on his chin. His thick red hair was uncombed.

"What'll it be, young Ted?" asked Gladys.

"Pint of mild, love."

"Not so much of the 'love' if you please. Name's Gladys to you."

Ted and his friends laughed.

"We should drink in the saloon bar, she don't mind them calling her soppy names in there," said one youth with hair hanging in his eyes.

Gladys pulled the beer and took the money. "Your uncle's in the saloon," she said quietly. You want me to tell him you're here?"

"Nah," said Ted, "I'll tell him." He pressed his nose against the frosted glass partition. "Uncle Alf. You buyin' today?" There was a snort of indignation from the other side.

"No, I'm bloodywell not," called Albert. "After payin' your fine, I'm too broke to pay for your damn beer too."

There was laughter from the other patrons in the public bar until Gladys shushed them firmly.

"Regular chip off the old block," said Tom Rydal as he savoured the last inch of his beer, rose stiffly and left the "Duke" to walk back to the Post Office for his lunch.

The following day, the task of building the shelter began. Albert Hoff supervised getting the backhoe in position watched by four day-labourers who stood in the doorway of a flimsy, temporary wooden hut provided for the purpose of brewing tea and sheltering from the rain. Ted was in the truck trying desperately to manouver it and the hoe through the trees and over the water-filled trenches. Albert stood on a little hump of ground gesticulating grandly.

"Left a bit. Now, right a bit. No! Right, I said. Left. Right. Now straighten 'er up. Straight, you idiot!"

After much sliding and crashing among the piles of timber and steel, the hoe was finally in position and the labourers reluctantly picked up shovels and began to work.

Over the next few weeks, while the German Air Force passed over-head on its way to London, Hoff and Nephew (Construction) Ltd. scoured out the pit, poured concrete and welded steel ribs together. Then the labourers leaned skillfully on their shovels while the mechanical equipment poured tons of dirt on the finished structure. When the whistle blew for the last time, the childen descended on the site and made it their playground.

Chapter 7

The people of Old Town went dutifully to the air raid shelter when the sirens sounded the alarm. For a while. They became impatient with sitting in its cold, damp confines with nothing to do for hours at a time but drink tea from flasks and watch the rowdy, bored children. Slowly, they began to ignore the warnings and go about their business as usual and the shelter fell into disuse and neglect.

On a windy morning in April when the first hint of spring came with the sound of bird song and blossom on the plum trees, Paul Lovedean and his friends Michael Ford and Joe Mishkin were enjoying a half-term holiday from the Prep school. Joe was the son of a local greengrocer who had joined Paul and Michael in St Ethelred's choir much to the amusement of his father who had never set foot inside a Christian church (or any other church for that matter) for many years.

The three boys walked over the horse pasture in search of something to do. Kicking a football around had lost its appeal and Joe's homemade kite was lodged somewhere up in a tall elm tree, beyond recovery. They stood looking at the air raid shelter. It was now a large lump on the pasture. Grass and weeds had covered it.

"What's that sticking up from the end?" asked Joe pointing to what looked like a garbage can with a hinged lid.

"Can't be a chimney," said Paul. "They wouldn't put a fireplace down there, would they?"

Michael ran towards it. "Let's go and find out." he called to the others.

They laboured up the muddy mound, lifted the heavy steel lid of the emergency exit and peered down into the blackness.

"Sure is dark."

"There's a ladder."

"Bet you won't go down." Joe stepped over the sill and put his foot on the first rung. With wave and a whoop he was gone. "Come on!" he called from the echoing depths. "You're not scared are you?"

Michael hesitated for a moment. Then he followed Joe down the steel runged-ladder.

"Come on, Paul. You frightened of the dark?" Laughter rose from the shelter as Paul teetered on the edge. Then he took a deep breath and plunged downwards to join the others in the dark space below. The boys ran shouting through the dark shelter towards the small rectangle of light at the other end and out into the daylight again. Then they did it all over again with variations on the whooping and hollering in the dark.

The game got boring after a while and they wandered off to a little clearing among the bushes under the elm trees. They lay looking up at the sky chewing stalks of long grass. The previous summer, after seeing a Robin Hood spectacular at the local cinema, they had used the piece of ground to build a secret camp and pretended to be Robin's Merry Men. The blackened patch of earth around the campfire was still there. Last year's autumn chill and damp had taken all the excitement out of being forest-dwellers so they had stashed the old cooking pot in the fork of a tree and retired until summer.

"What d'you want to do?"

"Dunno. What d'you want to do?"

"Light a fire and cook some vegetables? I've got matches," said Paul.

"OK," said Joe. "You start the fire. Me and Mike'll scout out some stuff from old man Rydal's garden."

Mr Rydal's carefully-tended vegetable patch was a hundred yards away towards the church and the two boys set off across the pasture in exaggerated caution pretending they were commandos raiding the Germans and Mr Rydal was their sinister objective. They ran from tree to tree and slid on their bellies as they reached the plot. Then they filled their sweaters with onions, potatoes and carrots and retreated.

Paul collected twigs and dead leaves to pile on the black earth and started a fire. It took most of his matches and a lot of blowing before a flame took hold and white, steamy smoke billowed up among the elms. Joe pulled the cooking pot down from the tree, filled it with water and they waited for it to boil.

The boys sat around the fire warming their hands, scraping the vegetables with Michael's penknife and dropping them into the water. The pot had been boiling for a while and the fire had reached a red, smokeless state when a shadow fell across the scene. Their conversation stopped abruptly and they looked up. A man in a khaki battle dress stood over them, arms crossed against his chest, feet spread apart. The soldier's face was pale with dark, deep-set eyes that stared unblinking from beneath bushy, black eyebrows. A frightening, threatening face. He looked at each boy in turn and then into the cooking pot. When he spoke the words were like a slap in the face. Menacing and cold.

"Now, what the hell is going on here?"

Michael let out a whimper of fear as he stood up. The soldier pointed at him.

"Enough of that whining, boy!"

Michael clamped his mouth shut and retreated back a step.

The soldier grinned, crossed his arms over his chest again and pointed at the cooking pot with the tip of a highly-polished boot.

"Where did you get that food?" He lowered his head and leaned towards the boys.

"From the garden over there," said Paul pointing to Mr Rydal's plot. His voice cracked a little.

"You mean you stole it?" hissed the soldier. There was silence. "Well, did you steal it or not?"

"I suppose so," whispered someone.

"You suppose so," mimicked the soldier. "You know there's people starving over there in Europe? I know, I've seen them." He stepped closer to the fire and kicked over the cooking pot in a cloud of steam. The ashes and dirt spoiled the shine on his boots.

"Now," he growled. "You little bastards put those vegetables back where you found them."

The voice brought another whimper from one of the boys and keeping one eye on the soldier, they picked up the remains of their feast and stood helpless before him. Suddenly, he gave a mirthless laugh and swung away from the boys for a moment. With a playfull roar, he spun back and reached as though to grab one of them with outstretched hands. As the boys jumped back in fear, he gave a high-pitched shout and walked away across the pasture slapping his thighs and laughing at some unshared joke.

With speed born of fear the boys plunged through the bushes and ran as fast as they could until they reached the safety of the Lane. In the distance they could hear the demented laughter ring out again as the dark figure strode off towards the salt marshes and disappeared. But it was the look of torment in the man's eyes that Paul Lovedean was to remember most clearly years later.

Chapter 8

Captain Charles Lovedean rubbed away the condensation with his sleeve and peered through the salt-encrusted window of the bridge of the destroyer HMS ELSON.

"Tug approaching from the starboard bow, helmsman. Hold her steady."

It was early in the morning of Wednesday June 17th 1941. The weather was calm as the destroyer moved slowly through the narrow harbor entrance between Hampton and Fairport. Seven knots was enough to create a gentle bow wave which lapped at the seawall. An orange sun was rising above the smoky rooftops of the dockyard and mist lingered among the navy ships anchored in the harbor. The work-worn tug bumped and pushed the rust-streaked ELSON into a berth alongside another destroyer already tied to the jetty.

Dockyard workers caught the lines thrown to them by the seamen on the deck and secured the ship to the bollards. The engines stopped and silence invaded the ELSON for the first time in three weeks. The morning shift clambered aboard carrying their toolboxes and immediately began the job of refitting the destroyer for another tour of duty in the cold, treacherous waters of the Atlantic.

"Electrical cables aboard?" asked Lovedean.

"Yes, sir. We're connected to the landlines," replied Chief Petty Officer Robinson.

"Good. Clear the bridge, gentlemen".

The officers and seamen turned to each other with smiles of relief and shook hands before making their way carefully down the ladder to their respective quarters. After three weeks at sea on a pitching, rolling deck the stationary ELSON felt strange and the men joked with each other as they negotiated the narrow gangways holding onto the rails.

There was a knock at his cabin door. Captain Lovedean opened it and accepted a mug of hot coffee from a young sailor already dressed in his best blues, shaved and shining with anticipation.

"Port watch got first shore leave, Smith?" said Lovedean

"Yessir,"

"Enjoy yourself and keep out of trouble,"

"Yessir," grinned the young man who had every intention of enjoying himself. Keeping out of trouble was in the lap of the gods and the shore patrol.

Lovedean's cabin was small. Just enough room for a bed, a desk, two ugly chairs and a clothes closet. He threw his hat on the bed, fell into a chair and gratefully sipped the hot coffee. God! It would be good to slide into a hot, soapy, full-sized bath and lay there until the water got cold.

Lovedean was a powerfully-built man of forty, of average height with pale blue eyes. The heavy wool sweater under the blue uniform jacket was beginning to irritate his neck as the temperature in the destroyer rose with the sun. It reminded him that he needed a shave. The creased face and red-rimmed eyes in his mirror showed he could use several nights of undisturbed sleep too.

There was a knock at the door and Lieutenant Wickam, his second in command, entered hat-in-hand. He was younger than Lovedean by ten years and tall and blond. The strain and fatigue of the past few weeks had left its mark on him too. The normally healthy pink skin was now gray and lined, the bright eyes tired.

"Port watch is ready to go ashore, Captain. Will you say the usual words of fond farewell and sober return?"

Lovedean nodded.

"I told Chief Robinson to collect all the crews' hatbands. The ones with the ship's name on them. And replace them with the blank ones."

"I remember," said Lovedean as he stood up and picked up his hat. "Security."

"Admiralty orders," said Wickham. He held out his hand. "But I took the liberty of keeping some. Sentimental reasons. Thought you'd like to keep a couple yourself."

Lovedean took the roll of black silk ribbons with the name "HMS ELSON" marked in gold letters. "Thanks, Wickham. I'll take one home for young Paul. He saves stuff like this."

Lovedean carefully folded them and placed them in his wallet. "Now let's see the port watch off on leave."

Chief Petty Officer Robinson had assembled the watch on the quarter deck. The other half of the crew would remain on board under the command of Lt Wickam and be replaced by Lovedean and the port watch after their leave was over.

The chief called the watch to attention and turned to the captain with a salute. "Port watch ready to go ashore, sir."

"Thank you, Chief," said Lovedean. He jumped up on a hatch cover to be better seen and called the crew to "Stand easy."

The men relaxed.

"You have seven days leave ahead of you," began Lovedean. "It's not much. But there's a war on so use it carefully. I don't want any of you carried back on board full of beer and incapable. Some of you have families and will be with them. To you others planning visits to the houses of ill-repute in this fine old town I must give the customary warning. Don't bring back your medical problems, slap them on the doc's table and say "Cure this," as though it were a common cold." There was a burst of laughter. "It not that easy and you'll get scant sympathy from the Navy. Remember. Roll call is at seven in the morning one week from today."

Chief Robinson called the crew to attention and saluted the Captain as he jumped down from the hatch.

As the sailors filed ashore down the sloping gangway, the dockies were already lowering cases of food and ammunition into the depths of the destroyer. The electric pumps hummed as fuel oil filled the tanks. The brilliant white light of welder's torches flashed and sputtered in competition with the morning sunlight as they repaired the damage on the superstructure caused by the mountainous waves of the Atlantic.

*

The telephone in the hallway of the red-brick house on Hamm's Lane jangled. Mary Lovedean wiped the flour from her hands and picked it off the hook.

"Hello?"

"Mary? It's me. Charles. I'm home."

*

"Thank you, sir. Have a good leave, sir." The Royal Marine guard handed Captain Lovedean his pass and snapped a salute. He opened the judas gate to let him out of the dockyard and into the busy streets of Hampton.

There were no taxis at the curbside so Lovedean decided to take the bus and enjoy his first day ashore by looking at familiar landmarks. There were fewer cars than on his last leave and convoys of dark blue navy trucks rumbled slowly along the city streets. People went about their business but without the usual bustle and animated conversation. The bus stop was a short walk away and green doubledeckers were waiting in a line. Lovedean hoisted his suitcase under his arm, ran stiffly across the street and boarded a bus marked "Ferry" He climbed upstairs and took a window seat.

"Tickets please." The bus conductor swayed up the aisle grabbing the backs of seats for support. He collected coins from each passenger and dispensed colored tickets and good humour to each one.

"Town Hall, Jack?" he said to a young sailor. "That'll be threepence." He punched a red ticket for him.

"Fish Market, love?" He took the coins offered by a stout woman in a shabby topcoat and soiled headscarf. "Change at the railway station."

He grinned widely as he got to Lovedean. "How about you, sailor? Got some leave 'ave yer?"

Lovedean nodded and handed him his money.

"Ferry please."

"Right, guv'. That'll be fourpence. Don't do anything I wouldn't do." The conductor nudged Lovedean with his ticket holder and sang his way down the stairs.

Lovedean wiped the condensation off the window with his handkerchief and went back to looking at the familiar sights. Things were not the same. As the bus neared the ferry dock Lovedean noticed some gaps in the rows of little houses. There were piles of rubble in open spaces. He turned to a grizzled dockie who was sitting across the aisle engrossed in the sports page of the Hampton Chronicle.

"I see the council have finally begun to clear out some of those old slums."

There was an unfriendly silence.

"Wasn't council what cleared 'em. Was bloody Germans. Lot of good people got killed that day." The dockie returned to his paper and sucked noisily on his pipe.

"I'm sorry, I didn't know," said Lovedean. "Been away for a while." The dockie grunted.

The bus drew up at the ferry terminal. Lovedean picked up his suitcase and clambered down the narrow stairs. He bought his ticket for the ferry at the booth and walked down the ramp to a waiting boat for the short trip across the harbor to Fairport. The ferry had seating on the uncovered upper deck and a cabin below where the coal-fired boiler provided both steam power and heat for the passengers. But Lovedean preferred the upper deck. He watched the spray hiss up from the bow as the squat little ferry bobbed across the busy waterway.

There was a full load of passengers. A small girl and her mother squeezed beside Lovedean on the wooden seat.

"Sorry," said the mother.

For a while the little girl studied Lovedean intently. He turned to get a better view of the Fairport landing dock and felt a light tug at his sleeve.

"Are you an admiral?" asked the girl pointing at the gold rings on his sleeve.

"No, my dear. I'm only a captain."

"My daddy is a gunner on the Hood."

"You must be very proud of him."

"Yes," she said "He's coming home soon."

Her mother whispered to her and she quickly withdrew her hand from Lovedean's sleeve.

"That's alright, madam," he said, smiling down at the girl. Got a boy of my own about her age. What's your name?"

"Ethel. Ethel Witherstone. I'm eight and I miss my dad."

Tears welled up in her big, blue eyes. She hunched her shoulders and leaned back into the seat. Lovedean struggled for a suitable reply to lighten her unhappiness but nothing came. Then he remembered the hatband that Wickham had given him.

"Ethel, I have something you might like. It's not much. Just a hatband with the name of my ship on it. I have another to give to my son. His name's Paul."

He took it from his wallet and handed it to her. She took it gravely and showed it to her mother. At that moment the ferry bumped the dock and the deckhands secured it with ropes. Then the passengers poured off and Ethel smiled and gave Lovedean a wave of her hand before she and her mother disappeared in the crowd making for the line of Fairport buses.

Taxis were waiting. Lovedean walked over to the rank where an elderly driver took his suitcase and stowed it on the luggage rack.

"It's Mr Lovedean isn't it?" he asked, peering through thick lenses. "Remember me? Harry Benson. I used to fix your car down at the garage. They got me driving a cab now. All the young fellers are called up and nobody's got petrol for their cars no more. Makes a little money and helps the war effort, I suppose."

"Of course," said Lovedean. "Harry Benson. How's your wife?"

"Fair to middlin'. War's got her real nervous."

Lovedean nodded his sympathy and climbed into the cab.

"Where to, Mr Lovedean?"

"Church school, please Harry. I think I'll walk across the horse pasture and up the Lane. Surprise Mary and Paul. Maybe even see Paul in the pasture."

"OK," said Harry and the taxi whined away from the ferry dock into Fairport. Lovedean looked for signs of bomb damage like those in Hampton. Apart from the taped-up windows and walls of sandbags, there was none. The town looked much as it always did.

The cab stopped at Church School. It was ten o,clock.

"Here we are," called out Harry. "You sure you want to get out here? It's a long walk across that pasture."

Lovedean nodded. "Yes, I'm sure, Harry. Need the exercise. Been at sea too long. Need to feel the grass under my feet again." He made to take his suitcase down but Harry restrained him. "You leave that with me, sir. I'll drop it off at the "Duke". It's right close to your house. You can pick it up there any time. Save you lugging it all the way across that field. No charge. It's on my way back."

After a moment's deliberation Lovedean handed his case back and thanked Harry. Then he paid him and set off over the spongy grass towards the distant line of elm trees. It took fifteen minutes to reach the trees and the air raid shelter. Through the trees he could see the gray slate roof of his house and the curling wisp of smoke from the chimney. He stepped onto the gravel path that Albert Hoff had laid between the shelter and the Lane.

As Lovedean passed the wall of sandbags protecting the shelter entrance, he heard a grunt and a rush of air above him. The blow landed on the back of his head and his dead body fell into a heap on the ground.

*

As Captain Lovedean lay dead on the gravel path, Private William Brown woke in a ramshackle wooden shed on the other side of the horse pasture. The shed was used by Tom Rydal to store tools and bags of fertilizer. Brown sat on a heap of empty sacks on the dirty floor with his back against the wall.

After a long night alone with nothing but his army greatcoat and muffler to keep out the chill, his anger at the army was cooling. The thought of the warm barracks and hot food down there on the salt marsh was tempting him back. He was AWOL, but only by a few hours. Through a crack in the wall he could see that the sun was up and there was a faded advertisement painted on the wall of a building a short distance away. It read "Duke of York-Fine Ales and Good Food." Brown pulled his pocket watch from the depths of his coat and was surprised to see how late it was. The pub would not be open for at least an hour and he did not want to risk being spotted by an MP patrol before he had chance to get a beer and something to eat. So he settled down again to wait.

William Brown was a son of a poor farming family which made a lean living from the shallow, sandy soil of Salisbury Plain.

"Mum, I'm going to join the army," he had announced one morning after the war started and the meagre harvest was over. "Maybe I can help finish off what Dad tried to do in the First War."

His mother had cried but the broken man lying in his bed close to the fire turned his hollow eyes towards William in knowing silence.

"But, Billy," said his mother. "Who will tend the farm if you're gone?"

William took her hand gently and sat beside her. "You have the other boys, Mum. They're a mite young yet but strong as horses. You'll get a good price for the oats and beans now because there's a shortage of everything. Anyway, I'll be one less mouth to feed and they won't call up the boys in the army because you need them here. Don't worry. I'll be back soon. War can't last for ever."

He turned his lean and tanned face towards his father and crossed to his bedside. He leaned his hand on the castiron headboard. "You understand, don't you Dad?"

"Yes, son." His father's voice was small and he wheezed as he struggled for breath through lungs half-destroyed by chlorine gas. "When you go I want you to take something. It will remind you of home when things get bad." He searched in the drawer of his bedside table and held out his hand. William took something studied it.

"But, Dad. This is your watch with the regiment's name on it. The one the General gave you personally in the hospital. You swore you'd never part with it. It's got your name and rank on it."

"Same name as yours 'aint it?" said his father "Take it. I want you to have it. No good to me now." He collapsed back on the pillow in a fit of coughing and Mrs Brown bent low to whisper something in his ear. William Brown pocketed the watch and turned his head away to hide his tears.

Soon afterwards, William said goodbye to his family and left the farm. He caught the train to Aldershot where the army gave him a perfunctory medical examination and literacy test. It was noted that his occupation was "farm laborer" and they directed him to the Pioneer Corps. After six months of digging ditches and pouring concrete for coastal defences, Private William Brown had had enough.

"My God," he complained to a friend as they sat in a bare barrack room polishing their boots by the light of a kerosene lamp. "We was poor on the farm. But we could hire old codgers to dig the ditches in the spring. I joined the army to fight not fill bloody sandbags and clean mud off me boots every evening so some fuckin' officer can inspect them in the morning before I get 'em covered with mud again. I've had it. I'm going home to do a real job."

"They'll catch you and bring you back, Bill. Probably put you in the jail."

"Bollocks!" snorted William.

That evening, William got a pass, walked through the compound gate and set off inland to find a railway station. As he crossed the pasture on his way into Fairport it got dark and his sense of direction failed him. Tom Rydal's shed appeared by chance and he pushed open the sagging door. He arranged the sacks to make a bed for himself and lay down to sleep.

It should be time for the pub to open. William took out his watch again and saw it was past ten. As he closed the watch to return it to his pocket he read the inscription again.

'Pvt William Brown Hamptonshire Infantry Regiment 1918'

He studied it for a moment and pictured the old man dying slowly by the fireside. With a sigh of resignation, he made up his mind. He walked into the morning sun and closed the shed door behind him. He turned in the direction of the salt marsh to head back to his duty in the construction site on the beach. But he was hungry and the bloody army could wait. Private William Brown strode off towards the "Duke". As he approached the elms and the air raid shelter he felt the need to relieve himself and stood behind a tree to unbutton his trousers. There were footsteps behind him and he half-turned in embarassment. There was a grunt of effort and a black object descended on him. The blow caught him at the base of the skull and he was dead as he hit the ground.

Chapter 9

Paul Lovedean had dressed quickly on Wednesday morning. He clattered downstairs to find his mother already working in the kitchen. She was kneading bread dough and watching saucepans simmering on the stove.

"Visitors coming?" asked Paul with a grin.

Mary playfully flicked a towel at him. "For that you can get your own breakfast. And if you're going out this morning, be back before twelve o"clock. Your father said he'd be home for lunch."

"OK". Paul ate hurriedly and left at a run for the horse pasture.

He found Michael and Joe and they kicked a ball around for a while. Until the novelty wore off. Then Joe picked up the ball and they climbed onto the five-bar gate at the entrance to the horse pasture and pondered their options.

"What shall we do now?"

"Dunno."

"Want to go over to the "Duke" and talk Gladys out of some lemonade and crisps?"

"Nah," said Paul. "My mum's cooking up a storm because my dad's coming home today. Anyway, we got warned off last time by that pot boy of theirs. Miserable bugger."

There was a minute of silence as the gate swung gently on its ancient, creaking hinges.

"Bet you won't go down the shelter," said Michael giving the gate a shove which caused the other two to teeter and struggle for balance.

"What for?" asked Paul. "It's dark down there. Anyway it stinks. Those old gardeners piss down there."

"You're both scared." Michael gave the gate another push and Paul and Joe jumped down in confusion. Joe faced Michael nose-to-nose.

"No, we're not!"

"Prove it."

"OK," said Joe. "We'll line up at the escape hatch and go down the ladder and out the other end. Twice."

"Three times," countered Michael.

"OK. Three."

Michael led Joe and Paul up to the top of the mound. He opened the hatch with a clang of metal on metal.

"I'll go first. You follow me," He dropped into the black hole.

Michael was halfway down with Joe right behind him when he stopped to call out to Paul who was lingering on the first rung of the ladder.

"Come on, Paul! You're not still scared of the dark are you?"

"No, of course not." With an effort, his legs shaking, Paul stepped onto the next rung and climbed down the ladder to join the others.

The three raced towards the exit in a frenzy of excitement, shouting and screaming as they went. The cavernous shelter rang with noise. Then they climbed back and did it all over again. By now, Paul's fear of the dark was submerged by the noise of their hysterical laughter and he willingly lined up at the hatch again for the third run through.

"Once more!" cried Michael as he plunged down the ladder followed by Joe and Paul.

Paul reached the bottom of the ladder at the same moment the sun's rays broke through the clouds and slanted down the hatch. It illuminated the concrete floor at the base of the ladder. The light shone there briefly before being extinguished by another cloud. But long enough for Paul to see a pair of boots, a crumpled khaki greatcoat and a man's head half severed from his neck, hanging grotesquely to one side. The wide-open eyes stared at nothing and blood covered the shoulders and sleeves of the coat. The dead man's hands lay on the floor beside him, palms upward.

For a second, Paul stood motionless. Powerless to move. Then, with a scream, he ran towards the exit and into the daylight ignoring the whooping and hollering of the other two boys. He continued to scream and shake in the sunlight as the others stared at him.

"Shut up, Paul," said Joe in disbelief. "The game's over." But Paul couldn't stop.

"What's wrong, Paul?" Michael took him by the arm and shook him roughly. Paul stopped screaming and stood in wild-eyed, silent hysteria. Then he ran.

Constable Walker was riding his bicycle down Hamm's Lane to the police station at the end of his morning shift when he saw Paul running towards him. The boy was sobbing. Walker jumped off the bike, let it fall to the ground and intercepted him in full flight. Walker was a big man and he scooped Paul up like a toddler. For a moment, Paul struggled in his strong arms.

"Easy, boy. Easy. What's the matter?"

"There's a man in the shelter. I saw him. I saw him!"

Walker put Paul down on his feet and straightened his helmet. "You boys been playin' in that shelter again?" he said sternly. "Haven't I warned you about that place?"

Paul nodded.

"It's dangerous down there. What if you gets hurt? Could be days before we find you."

"Yes, sir," said Paul between sobs. "But I really did see him. He's dead. There's blood all over. Really." He looked up at Walker, his eyes pleading for him to believe him.

"You're young Lovedean aren't you?"

"Yes."

"You've given yourself quite a fright." Walker reached down, picked up his bike and took Paul gently by the arm. "Come on, lad. Let's get you home. I'll have a word with your mother."

They walked together down the Lane. P.C.Walker leaned the bike against the wall before rapping on the front door of the Lovedean's house. Mary opened it and with a gasp, clamped her hand to her mouth.

"It's alright ma'am," said Walker. "Your boy's had a bit of a fright, that's all. They been playin' down at the shelter again. I know how it is. Kids' imaginations sometimes runs away with them. 'Specially now with all the talk of bombing." He pushed Paul towards his mother. "I reckon some hot milk would help. But keep him away from that place in future. It's not safe."

With a deferrential touch of his fingers to his helmet, Walker walked to his bicycle and pedaled ponderously back the way he had come and turned into the High Street towards the police station.

*

"You're a bit late today. Anything to report?" asked the duty sergeant.

"Not much, sarge," said Walker taking off his helmet and laying it on the counter. "Someone's stealing milk bottles from doorsteps again and some drunk's smashed a window at the "Duke". Got his name so I'll drop by and lean on him when he's sobered up. And the Lovedean kid scared himself playing in that damn air raid shelter. Told me some story about a dead body. Hysterical, he was. Had a word with his mother."

The sergeant laughed and pushed the day book over to Walker. "You'd better make a note of it before you go off duty. Keeps the pages full."

Walker started to write. He glanced up at the Smith's clock on the wall. It was 11.47.

*

At 12:20, the gunners on the salt marsh were in their positions waiting for the punctual arrival of the Luftwaffe on its way to London. The sound detectors, protected by walls of sandbags and looking like an array of over-sized Victrola horns, slowly scanned the sky listening for the rythmic beat of two-engined bombers. The radar operators sat in their dark, underground room peering intently into the screens on which a green lines showed the height and direction of incoming bombers. It was a radar operator who saw them first and his calm voice echoed through the loudspeakers to the crews.

"Here they come."

"Fifty miles."

"Fifteen thousand feet."

"Two seven oh degrees."

"One eighty miles an hour."

"Looks like fifty of them. No, make that seventy five."

The sound detectors and gun barrels rotated slightly and zeroed in on the approaching squadrons.

"Got 'em!" called the victrola man.

"Ready," called the gun captains as the barrels stopped moving.

"Usual time. Usual place. Regular as bloody clockwork," muttered a gunner to his mate as he squinted through his gunsight. "You'd think the bastards'd know better by now. We got two last week. Hampton got six."

The sergeant stabbed at the red warning button with a stubby finger. Sirens sounded in Fairport and along the coast.

At the first sound of the monotonous song of the siren the people of Fairport stopped their daily routine to look up into the sky and wonder if they should make a run for the shelter or not. The bombers were flying higher now thanks to the gunners and the Royal Air Force. Apathy had settled onto the town. Nobody went to the community air raid shelter. A few took their children by the hand and went casually down to their cramped garden shelters. The schoolchildren were led, complaining, to the narrow, brick shelters in the schoolyards where lessons continued by the dim light of naked electric bulbs. In the streets things looked relatively normal and people went about shopping and gossiping as usual. Constable Walker put on his helmet, mounted his bike and pedaled out of the police station and up the High Street towards his home to get his lunch.

At the gun battery, the radar operator's voice boomed out again over the Tannoy speakers.

"Attention. More contacts." There was a pause as he made calculations on a piece of paper.

"Nine oh degrees. Descending rapidly."

The gunners glanced warily at each other. This was unusual. Sweat began to trickle down their faces as the realisation grew. They were the target. The radar towers stood out like beacons on the coast and many had been attacked by dive bombers. Tension rose. Then the radar operator's voice had a different tone. A tinge of excitement.

"Looks like fighters."

Oh, Christ!. Now we're for it. The gunners steeled themselves and waited for the order to depress the guns and shoot at the fighters as they came in fast and low. But the sergeant waited and sweated.

"It is fighters," called out the radar man. Then his voice rose. "They're ours! Spitfires and Hurricanes! They're ours!"

Cheers rang out along the marsh and the crews leaned back thankfully into their hard metal seats and watched the furious action develop above them.

Out over the English Channel, approaching landfall over Fairport, the regular formations of German bombers flew on towards their primary target as they had done most days for weeks. Below them, the crews could see the pattern of green and brown fields and the waves breaking slowly along the yellow beaches. Farm houses and barns dotted the peaceful countryside and sharp steeples of churches thrust up among the trees. Ahead lay the gray mass of London where yesterday's fires poured a smoky pall across the sky.

The German pilots watched warily for the pattern of black and white anti-aircraft fire that had become more effective lately. As they looked down, the fighters pounced on them from above. Spitfires swooped out of the bright morning sun through the ranks of black bombers, their guns chattering. Within seconds the sky was filled with a whirling, chaotic mass of wings, smoke and condensation trails. The bombers broke ranks under the onslaught and soared off in every direction.

Below, in Fairport, the people looked up in open-mouthed silence as the battle raged over their heads. The guns on the marsh were silent. The gunners laughed and cheered at the death of the bomber crews as their planes splashed into the sea or roared down to earth and exploded in orange flame.

Six Heinkel IIIs had left their station near Cherbourg that morning with a full bomb load destined for London's dockland. They reached the rendezvous over Spithead safely and then turned northeast towards London. When the Spitfires caught them they were over Hampton Harbour. Bullets thudded into the fuel tanks of one Heinkel and there was a flash of orange. The bomber disintegrated and debris fell towards the water. Another belched smoke and rolled over slowly as it fell. The heavily-laden bombers rolled and weaved in desperate attempts to evade the nimble fighters. The panic-stricken voices of the young German crews crammed the radio frequencies as they called each other for help. This was not what they had been prepared for. Not failure and a fiery death on a sunny day. Until now it had been easy. Just ineffective anti-aircraft fire...

The Heinkel leader kept his head. He turned sharply left over Fairport and dropped altitude in a last, desperate attempt to lose the Spitfires. Another Heinkel followed him. Their wings shuddered under the load of bombs and fuel.

For a moment, the leader and his follower were free but from the horizon, more fighters closed in. He made his decision to flee and live to fight another day. The Heinkels jettisonned their bomb loads, the planes leapt free of the weight and accelerated south over the Channel. And ran for the safety of France

The first of the jettisonned bombs straddled Fairport High Street at 12.36pm and opened up a row of huge craters. A row of red-brick houses between the Church and the Post Office were demolished in an instant. The front wall of the Duke was blown off exposing the interior like a child's doll house.

Gladys and her customers were killed. Some died in their accustomed places, lungs and hearts collapsed by the blast. Others were hurled against the back wall under the mirror and died in untidy little heaps, their blood splashed across the dingy, flower-patterned wallpaper. Animate and inanimate debris showered down on the town and fires erupted among the broken buildings. Across town, other bombs lifted cars and buses onto the roofs of buildings like blown straw.

Harry Benson's taxi lay burning in the crater outside the Duke. Fractured pipes gushed great fountains of water and gas mains ignited like giant blowtorches and set light to the asphalt of the roads. Somewhere in the distance there came the tinkling sound of emergency vehicles but it was too late for hundreds of Fairporters who, in their apathy, had died and were incinerated in the white-hot fires which roared upwards in the brick shells of their little houses.

Across the harbour, white phosphorous incendiaries and high explosives rained down on the rows of ships moored at the Hampton dockyard jetties. The smoke from the burning destroyer ELSON rose high into the sky and mingled across the harbour with the smoke from the burning town of Fairport.

The clang and rattle of fire engines and ambulances could be heard all day as they rushed in from outlying districts to augment the overwhelmed and frantic locals. Men and women worked to exhaustion in the searing heat to pull to safety anyone they could find. The streets of Fairport Old Town had virtually disappeared and the rescue teams clambered over piles of hot rubble in their desperate search. The flames burned late into the night and cast a red glow that could be seen for a hundred miles. Some say it could be seen in London.

Next day, the fires were out and the grimy, exhausted emergency crews, tired beyond sleep, sat at their vehicles silently sipping tea provided by women in green hats and coats. The homeless survivors were temporarily housed in the Church School and the injured taken to the county hospitals. Constable Walker's bicycle and helmet were found high up in a splintered oak tree. His body was never found and it was

assumed that he was riding along the High Street when the first bomb
fell.

The Lovedean's house was wrecked by the blast which tore off the
front of the Duke. But the house did not burn. The rescue crews found
Mary Lovedean in the shattered remains of her kitchen the morning
after the raid. She was dead. Crushed by the weight of the collapsed
chimney. Two hours later, a police dog found Paul alive under the
stairs, trapped in a tiny space between the two heavy wooden beams.
His left arm was crumpled beneath him, broken in two places and cut
by glass. The rescuers carefully lifted the beams from him and placed
the unconcious boy on a canvas stretcher. Then they carried him gently
across the littered streets to the overcrowded Fairport Memorial Hospital where overworked, gray-skinned doctors and nurses worked without sleep or rest.

When Paul woke he saw the sun shining through unfamiliar tall,
undraped windows. There was a sharp, astringent smell. His bed was
different. The blue coverlet was tucked in as tight as a drum skin across
his legs. A plump nurse in a starched white and blue uniform and black
stockings sat beside him. She wore a little white hat and was reading a
book.

"Hullo," she said, putting her book away in her pocket. "You're
finally awake."

"Where am I?" Paul's throat was dry and his voice hurt.

"In the hospital." She wetted his cracked lips with a little water on a
towel. "They fixed up your arm and it's going to be fine." She pointed
somewhere to Paul's left. He turned his head painfully and saw a bulbous, bandaged object hanging there in a metal cradle.

"Is that my arm?"

"Yes."

Paul's head began to clear of the anaesthetic and the memory of
the explosion that had thrown him down the stairs returned.

"Where is my mother?"

There was a moment of silence as the nurse lowered her eyes and
gathered all her young courage to answer. Paul stared at her with pained,
pale blue eyes.

"I'm sorry Paul. I'm afraid she's dead."

"And my father? Did he come home?"

"We don't know, Paul."

"Oh," said Paul in a little voice. He turned away to stare at the blue sky through the window. "He said he was coming home today." His grief would come later. It was the nurse who cried and a doctor took her tenderly by the arm and led her away.

Chapter 10

By 1950, the rubble that once had been Fairport's town centre had been dumped in a green field beyond the town. 'Hoff and Nephew' (Ltd.) built a new council school on the site in the ugly-cheap style of the period. The asphalt playground undulated with the decaying rubbish beneath it. New generations of Fairport children intoned their multiplication tables in its cold confines.

The dead of 1941 were commemorated on a plaque fixed to the wall of St Ethelred's church and children played on the empty spaces along the High Street. The Duke had been repaired. Outside the pub on the sidewalk, it sported plastic tables and chairs with umbrellas proudly advertising 'Heineken Beer' 'Campari' and 'Stolichnaya'

During those years after the war, Fairport languished in comfortable but impecunious isolation while Hampton flourished frantically with the industrial boom. New roads and automobiles carried the Hamptonites north and east into the country looking for *lebensraum*. They built rows of identical red-brick houses with attached garages. Ersatz country pubs sprouted on land from which sheep and cattle had been evicted. In the 1970s, the more prosperous citizens, to avoid the stigma of suburbia, rediscovered Fairport and began to bid up the price of land between St Ethelred's church and the ferry dock.

By 1981, there were fashionable boutiques and restaurants among the lawyer's offices, real estate agents and supermarkets along the rejuvenated High Street. On the board outside a new concrete and glass building was a sign reading: 'Edward A. Hoff Esq. Estate Agent'. Ted Hoff had taken over the management of 'Hoff and Nephew' and was now engaged in developing tracts of 'exclusive' and 'executive' homes on the horse pasture. Albert Hoff had bought the pasture from Sidney Allnut's widow for pennies after the war. He retired to Brighton where he lived in a white bungalow with plastic garden ornaments. Within walking distance of the local pub. He died of cirrhosis without realising some of the wealth that Ted was now accumulating selling 'desirable' property to wealthy clients.

Ted Hoff was middle-aged. He had thinning, sandy hair and a beer belly which was partly hidden by an expensive, if loud, double-breasted suit. He sat at his glass-topped desk in the office overlooking the High Street with a telephone clamped between ear and shoulder cleaning his nails with a toothpick.

"Yes, Mr Stamshaw. Of course, Mr Stamshaw," he said, looking bored. "I can offer you an exclusive site. About half an acre. Give or take a few square feet. Price?" Ted sucked in his teeth and counted to five. "Let me see. Perhaps we'd better discuss that later after you've seen it? Best bit of property on the south coast, is that. Come by in the morning?"

He hung up the phone and smiled to himself. He'd come a long way since he and uncle Albert had built that old shelter during the war. Ted called out to his decorative secretary in the inner office.

"Vanessa, I'm off to Ocean View. Back about lunchtime."

Sure, thought Vanessa. More like a session with the other boozers at the 'Duke'. She waved a diffident hand and picked up the phone to make an appointment at the beauty shop.

Ted walked out into the street, climbed into his cream Jaguar and drove the quarter mile to the old horse pasture behind the Duke. The pasture had been renamed "Ocean View Estates" (on a clear, fine day, with glasses, you might see across the marshes). A pair of imposing, tastless gates with a stylised golden fish and the name written in flowing blue script guarded the entrance.

He pulled up inside the gate and admired his creation. The winding, black-topped streets were complete and a few houses were already occupied. Instant lawns and birdbaths flourished in the fenced front gardens. To his right, on the northern extremity of his estate, was the line of ancient but protected elm trees.

The town council, finally aware that the southern part of Fairport was fast becoming a sea of concrete driveways and slate roofs, had decreed that the remaining trees should be preserved. But with Ted Hoff's luck still holding, that action had only served to increase the value of the remaining land. On that land was the decayed remains of the old air raid shelter and Ted was pleased to see that a contractor was at work removing it. The site was the only one which could honestly claim the title of "Ocean View", however fleeting that view was. With its row of old trees separating it from the other houses, it would make an ideal spot for Mr Stamshaw's fake Tudor house with a swimming pool and three, detached garages.

The shelter was an untidy hump on the ground. Its emaciated, curved steel ribs stuck out of the top of the mound of earth. The decayed wooden retaining wall had broken in several places. Many years before, the town council had ordered the entrance sealed off with plywood and the escape hatch welded shut. Up to that time, the shelter had been a storehouse for black market goods, an aromatic trysting place for lovers and a mushroom farm. Now the fetid interior was being exposed to sunlight for the first time in more than thirty years.

Ted got out of his car and picked his way through the clutter of broken concrete and splintered wood. A yellow backhoe with a Japanese name on the boom growled and squealed as it pushed and pulled at the rusty steelwork. Ted acknowledged a wave from the operator as the hoe dropped mangled pieces of metal in the bed of a truck with a clang and a cloud of ochre dust. The hoe pounded on the ribs of the shelter, the earth around it collapsed and flowed into the hole.

As the hoe scoured out another load of earth, a large part of the retaining wall collapsed causing a minor avalanche of dirt and rotten wood. The back hoe stopped growling as Bill switched off the engine. Ted started forward, curious to know what the delay was. It wasn't tea-break time yet. Bill climbed down from his cab and walked through the loose dirt. He stood staring down at something at his feet and pushed his cap back on his head. He slithered down deeper into the hole. Then he straightened up and struggled back up the side of the hole.

"Better take a look at this, Mr Hoff," he called."There's something down there. Something 'orrible."

Harry slammed the door of the dump truck impatiently and joined Bill at the hole as Ted made his way towards them.

"What's wrong?" "What is it?" asked Ted

Bill pointed a dirty finger. "Skeleton," Mr Hoff. "Where the 'ell did that come from?"

Harry climbed down and looked carefully at the site. "Not a skeleton, Bill. There's two of 'em. See? Two skulls."

The weight of the three men dislodged more dirt and the two skulls, which were close together, were plainly visible. The blood drained out of Ted's face and he reached out to steady himself on Bill's arm.

"You OK, Mr Hoff?"

"I'm fine," said the pallid Ted. "Better call the cops."

"I'll do it," said Bill and he walked away to use the phone in the 'Duke of York'.

Harry leaned down and picked something up from among the bones.

"What you reckon this is, then?" It was a rusted piece of flat metal.

Ted stared at it trying to fight off the nausea that had gripped him. "It's a spade, Harry. Handle's rotted away."

"You think it belonged to one of those?" Harry pointed to the skeletons. "Maybe they was labourers when they built the shelter?" He wiped the dirt off his hands with a handkerchief.

"No," said Ted. "I knew all the workmen in those days. None of them was ever missing. Never knew a labourer to not pick up his wages at the end of a job."

Ted walked back to his car and sat waiting for the police to arrive. God! What a thing to show up after all these years.

*

Inspector Phil Privett and two uniformed constables from the Fairport police station arrived at the shelter in ten minutes. Privett was tall and bulky with a thick waist and jowls that rode on his shirt collar. His cropped, coarse hair was streaked with gray. He staggered heavily over the soft, heaped dirt and looked down at the morbid scene. Ted Hoff had regained his composure and walked over from his car to join the policemen.

"Now, what have we here, Mr Hoff?" It was "Ted" in the 'Duke' of an evening but this was business and the proprieties have to be observed.

"Two skeletons," he turned to the hoe operator. "Bill here turned them up. Don't ask me how they got there. We was just breaking up the old shelter and they just appeared. Called you right away."

"Touched anything?" Privett took out his notebook and licked the end of his pencil.

"No," said Ted. "Not me. But Harry found what looks like an old shovel near the skeletons." He pointed to where the rusted piece of metal lay. "Must have been buried with them."

Privett raised his eyebrows. "You sure?"

"It was lying close to the skulls," said Harry.

Privett pointed to the shovel. A constable picked it up, tied a label on it and placed it carefully in a plastic bag. Then Privett took Harry by the arm.

"Show me exactly where you found it." Harry pointed at the spot and Privett tore a page from his notebook and put it on the spot with a rock to hold it down.

By now, a small crowd of workmen and residents had gathered and pressed close to see what was going on. Privett called for their attention.

"You'll have to move away," he shouted. "Constables Bray and Alver here will take charge." The crowd dutifully dispersed partly because from their viewpoint, there was nothing to see anyway. But Ted Hoff remained.

"Here, Phil," he said indignantly. "What about my backhoe? Can we move it? We can get on with some other work."

"No, Ted," said Privett quietly as he stuffed his notebook and pencil into his jacket pocket. "I'm calling this a crime scene. We have to call the scene of crime boys in to make sure. Nothing gets moved in case it destroys evidence."

"Oh, shit," said Ted. He sat down on a block of broken concrete and studied the toes of his two-toned brown shoes.

*

Two hours later, the area had been cordoned off. Yellow plastic tape marked the site and a blue plastic tarp suspended from the trees and tied to metal posts secured it from the weather and curious onlookers. Bill and Harry had given their statements at the police station and gone to the Duke to tell their story over pints of bitter.

Dr Brightman, the police surgeon from Hampton, arrived with his assistant and cases of equipment and began his preliminary investigation of the skeletons. He was a short, portly man well past retirement age with bushy white hair and a lined face. His assistant, an eager intern from the Hampton Infirmary, was thin and dark-haired.

Brightman kneeled in the dirt, brushing at the partly-exposed skeletons with a paint brush and dictating notes to the assistant as he progressed. Then he rose stiffly, pushed his spectacles back up on his nose and peeled off his latex gloves.

"What do you make of it, Doc?" called Privett from above.

"Better call the homicide boys from Eastchester, Phil. There are two bodies here. Each has a massive skull fracture. Been here a long time. By the way the bodies lay, they didn't just fall down, they were placed here. Forensics at the county lab will have a better idea." Brightman struggled out of the hole disdainfully refusing the outstretched hand of his assistant. "You'll get my report in the morning."

With a flourish of his hands, Dr Brightman walked back to the van followed by the assistant lugging equipment in both hands.

Chapter 11

Chief Inspector David Chark, C.I.D, stopped reading a blue-covered file and impatiently dropped it on his desk. He stood up. The window of his office in the Hamptonshire County Constabulary Building looked out over the rooftops of Eastchester. He turned and picked up the report to try again. Trying to summon up real interest in another Friday night's violence in the video arcades and pubs in the sleazy backstreets of the town.

How is it possible to communicate to undereducated, malnourished and unemployed teenagers that sticking someone with a switchblade during a drunken argument is, at best, simple assault and at worst, attempted murder? Not a private argument between friends and ..."none of your fuckin' business, you stupid bitch." as the suspect was reported to have said to the policewoman at the scene.

The years hung well on Chark. His hair was still thick and wavy with just a hint of gray. His face was angular with few lines. He wore bi-focal spectacles which continually slid down his nose. He closed his eyes and leaned his brow on the cool glass of the window.

Oh, Solomon Chark, he mused. What a problem you left me when you died. Enough money to live almost any way I want. You sly old fox! All those years pleading poverty. You even bought identical cars each year so that the neighbours wouldn't suspect you had money to spend. Never could shake off those old fears, those old habits, could you?

The telephone interrupted his thoughts. Chark ignored it.

You were right about one thing, Solomon. I should never have become a policeman. A position in public service? Too exposed, you advised. But I was young and what did I know?

The phone burbled again. Chark hated the phone when it did that. Old-fashioned phones had a healthy jangle.

Maybe Miriam was right after all. I should have retired and lived it up like she wanted. Back to France or Italy. But I said no. So she left me and took Rebecca with her. After twenty years she leaves me for a second-rate musician from Los Angeles. Am I that dull? Don't answer that, Solomon. I don't want to hear.

The phone rang again. Chark grabbed as though to strangle it and sat at his desk.

"Chark."

"Dave Chark?"

"Is there another one?"

"It's Phil. Phil Privett."

Chark relaxed back in his chair and began to laugh. "Sorry about the welcome, Phil. I was just gearing up to write my resignation speech."

There was a chuckle from Privett. "Every year at this time. Every year. What you want is some real police work to stimulate the old intellect."

Chark and Privett had maintained their friendship since they were boys together during the war years in Fairport. The kind of friendship that could fade for years and then be taken up as if only days had passed. They had done their National Service together in the Navy and then gone on to join the police.

"So what's happening down in Fairport? How's your mother?"

"Mother's fine. Very old now but always asks after you, Dave. Looks forward to your cards at Christmas and her birthday. Says she wants chocolates next time."

"Good. Glad the old girl's still feisty," said Chark. "Now, what's the real police work you had in mind?"

"We need your help, Dave. Got a murder on our hands. The first in twenty years."

"You local people can't handle it?"

"No, Dave. It's a little unusual because the bodies have been in the ground for a long time. We've asked for the forensics people from the county crime lab. And for you."

Chark took a gold pencil from the pocket of his London-tailored suit, opened a notebook and listened as Privett explained the circumstances of finding the skeletons in the Fairport air raid shelter. When he finished, Chark gratefully dropped the blue file into his OUT box and looked at his watch. "It's one o'clock. I'll be there by four. There'll be some daylight left so you can show us the crime scene." He buttoned his jacket and stretched the phone cord to its limit as he pulled his raincoat from the peg on the wall and hung it over a chair. "You've secured the crime scene?"

"Yes," said Privett "Got two constables standing guard twenty four hours. Nothing's been touched since Doc Brightman left. His report came in an hour ago."

"And how long did Doc say they had been buried?"

"Long time. Maybe thirty or forty years, he says. Can't be sure until forensics have had a chance to check."

"I'll be damned," said Chark. "They must have been there about the time we lived in Fairport."

"Could well be, Dave. Something to think about, eh?"

"Yes. I'll see you in a couple of hours. Oh, and Phil, you better book us a couple of rooms somewhere. I'll be bringing Beane along with me. Detective Sergeant Hume Beane."

During the next fifteen minutes Chark checked with the forensics team to make sure they were on their way to Fairport and had the records clerk pull all the files on criminal activity in Fairport for the last fifty years. It was not a very thick file. Then he summoned Hume Beane to his office.

"Yes, Chief?"

Hume Beane was a tall, sandy-haired man of thirty. He wore a tweed suit which was a little too large for him and coloured somewhere between brown and green. His accent was Glasgow Scot. He had a degree in criminology, another in computer science. And permanently baggy trousers.

"Sit down, Beane. We've work to do..."

"If you want that computer run on the teeage gang members in Eastchester, it'll be ready tomorrow," Beane interrupted. "Takes time to print them off." He turned to go but Chark stopped him with an impatient wave.

"No, Beane. This is real detective work. Suspected murder down in Fairport. I want to be there by four o'clock. How soon can you pick me up at my place?"

"Bloody hell! Chief," said Beane. "I've got a date tonight. Already stood her up twice because of overtime. Why me?"

"Because you're the best detective sergeant in the county. That's why," said Chark as he handed Beane the pile of Fairport records.

"You tell her that," grumbled Beane.

"Ah, yes," said Chark with a grin. "The delectable Fiona. She'll understand."

Beane looked at him in wonderment. "Like hell she will," He hit the doorpost with his clenched fist. "She's single, beautiful and her father owns an Italian restaurant. Took me months to get a date." But Chark wasn't listening. "What's this?" Beane finally recognized that Chark had thrust something in his hand.

"All the reports filed with Eastchester relating to criminal activity in Fairport since 1933."

"1933? Holy Hogmanay! What kind of a murder is this? Sounds more like an Ellis Peters novel."

Chark laughed. "That's what we are going to find out, old son. Pick me up at my place in half an hour. And pack enough socks and underwear for a week."

Beane growled and stomped off through the outer office.

Chark drove home along winding country roads and pulled up in the half-circular, gravel drive of Aurora Cottage. The four cottages that Solomon Chark bought during the war had been remodeled into a spacious house with all the comforts of the twentieth century. The garden was a minor masterpiece of traditional English landscaping. It was presided over by a retired farmworker named Smith whose wife was Chark's housekeeper.

Chark pushed open the kitchen door and found Mrs Smith in front of the television set drinking tea. She was a plump, comfortable woman with a wraparound pinafore and thick ankles.

"Afternoon, sir" she said "Wasn't expecting you 'til evenin'. Shall I make some more tea?"

Chark declined. "I'll be away on business for a few days, Mrs Smith. Came by to pack my bag. Can you take care of things here for a few days?"

Mrs Smith beamed her "of course" and settled back to the soap opera and a plate of cream crackers.

Chark changed his suit for a more comfortable tweed jacket and slacks before packing a suitcase. He was snapping shut the clasps when the doorbell rang. Mrs Smith greeted Beane and showed him into the living room.

"Right on time," said Chark. "Did you bring that computer thing with you?"

"Never leave home without it. It's in the car."

They took their leave of Mrs Smith and walked to the unmarked police car Beane had checked out of the motor pool.

"I'll drive," said Chark as he lowered himself into the driver's seat and adjusted the mirrors. "It'll take about an hour to get there. You can read the Fairport crime reports to me on the way. Just the important bits."

Chark reached out and switched on the radio as the car left the driveway. He recoiled in horror at the blast of noise that filled the car.

"What in hell is that?"

"Rock and Roll, Chief."

"Sounds more like a bad muffler." Chark hastily searched and found more soothing sounds.

"What's that?" asked Beane with a grin.

"Mozart. A horn concerto."

"Sounds more like a wornout clutch pad."

Chark pointed to the sheaf of papers in Beane's hand. "Read on, McHaggis."

Fairport's crime register was mostly cases of fraud, wife-beating, grand theft and drunk driving. The only murder, in 1956, was a case of jealousy over a girl which resulted in one brother killing the other with a rabbit gun. There was a dance hall full of witnesses and the guilty brother got twenty years. Served twelve. Beane closed the files and let his head droop.

Chark slowed down as they approached the Hampton exit from the motorway and took the westbound road around the harbour to Fairport. As the car swung, Beane jerked awake against his seatbelt and the sheaf of papers on his knees slid onto the floor.

"We there yet?" he mumbled stretching out and looking around at the trees and farmlands which spread away to the south. A knot of gray roofs and the stubby spire of St Ethelred's church appeared among the trees.

"Close," said Chark. "Be there in a few minutes." He slowed down again and signaled a turn into a landscaped exit ramp with a signboard reading 'Welcome to Fairport–Home of Ocean View Estates'.

"I can smell the sea'" said Beane as he scooped up the papers from the floor. "Reminds me of Rothsay when I was a kid."

"The coast here is flat," said Chark. "When the tide goes out it uncovers a mile of mud and sand. That's what you can smell."

"I was forgetting, Chief. You know Fairport well, don't you?"

Chark nodded and drove slowly through the town as pedestrians wandered back and forth in front of the car. He braked sharply at the intersection of the High Street and Hamm's Lane.

"My God! It's a pedestrian mall," he said, half-amused. Short, white pillars and heavy chains barred the entrance to the High Street. A uniformed police officer with a radio strapped to his chest and a bulge in his tunic approached the car cautiously.

"Can I help you?"

The policeman leaned down and looked in at Chark. He scanned the interior of the car and took the ID wallet that Beane held out. The policeman checked it briefly and handed it back.

"Thanks sergeant. Can't be too careful these days."

"How do we get to the police station?"

"Back up. Take the next left and first right. Parking lot is behind the station. Can't miss it. It's the big, ugly building with the aluminium windows."

There were a dozen black and white patrol cars filling the police parking lot but Chark found a space with a number painted on it near the rear entrance. He stepped out of the car and stamped his feet.

"I'm bloody stiff. That car's got wooden seats. Next time you drive, Beane. You slept all the way."

"It was the music," said Beane as he heaved his computer out of the back seat. "Couldn't keep my eyes open".

Chark set off towards the station carrying his briefcase followed by Beane with his computer. Beane mused sadly. About now he would be getting off shift and getting ready for his date with Fiona. Maybe he should call her. She did sound a little disappointed when he said he had to work tonight.

The Fairport police station was a warren of small offices and corridors. Phil Privett's office was near the front of the building. Chark rapped on the door and pushed it open. The office was predictably small and lit by a single, white regulation globe suspended from the centre of the yellowed ceiling. There was one small window set high up on the wall and the afternoon sun slanted through the panes and shone brightly on the row of green regulation file cabinets. Privett was searching through one of them as Chark entered.

"Dave!" He took his pipe out of his mouth and reached his hand out to Chark. "It's good to see you again." They shook hands warmly.

"This is my assistant, Sergeant Beane. Hume Beane to his friends."

Beane gratefully placed the heavy computer on the floor and shook Privett's hand. He saw that Privett was a slow-moving, heavy man with thinning black hair and a pale complexion. He had a resigned, contented, middle-aged manner.

"Tea?" suggested Privett. He mimed to someone through the door of the office and motioned Chark and Beane to sit down in old straight-backed chairs. "We've cleared the office next door for you. It's not very big but knowing you, you'll not spend much time in it."

Beane groaned inwardly. Chark wouldn't but he would.

Privett took a folder from his desk drawer and pushed it over to Chark. "Medical Examiner's report. Both victim's skulls were fractured by a sharp blade. In both cases the blade had nearly decapitated them. The shovel found near the bodies is almost certainly the murder weapon."

Strong, milky tea with two sugar lumps in each saucer arrived on a tray carried by a policewoman in a light blue blouse, black skirt and sensible shoes. While they sipped, Chark and Beane read the report through. The sun was lower when they finished and the first shift was clattering down the corridors on their way home. Chark looked at his watch.

"There's still time to visit the crime site before the light goes," said Chark. "Is it far away?"

"Back of the 'Duke of York'. You know the place. We'll drive there in your car." Privett picked up his gloves and hat and they followed him out into the parking lot.

"Damn it!" said Privett as they emerged from the gloom of the building. "Somebody's parked in my place again." Chark laughed as he opened the door of the offending vehicle.

"Talking of the 'Duke'," said Privett as they drove away, "They call themselves a motor hotel now. Converted the upper floors into bedrooms years ago. I reserved two rooms there. That OK with you?"

Chark nodded.

"Sounds good to me," said Beane with a smile. A room over a pub. Things were looking up.

*

At the air raid shelter site, the forensic team were already at work photographing and measuring. Bright lights illuminated the ground under the tarp and a wooden table had been set up using saw horses and sheets of plywood supplied by Ted Hoff. Plastic bags containing objects and soil samples were being catalogued by a man in light blue overalls. Chark peered over the shoulder of another man who was delicately brushing the dirt from a leg bone with a paintbrush.

Chark turned to Privett. "The bodies were not inside the shelter?"

"No," said Privett. "The shelter has a concrete floor and walls set deep in the ground. The bodies were buried outside in the space between the retaining wall which surrounded the shelter and its curved, metal roof. Dirt's about six feet deep. The wall was needed to prevent the dirt from sliding off the roof."

"I see," said Chark thoughtfully. "And the bodies were laid one on top of the other?"

"Yes," said Privett. "According to Doc Brightman. Head to head."

Chark walked to the evidence table and spoke to the investigator who was writing labels for the plastic bags.

"Evening, Jim."

Jim looked up and shook Chark's outstretched hand. "So they got you in on this one? Good."

"What's happening?"

"Nothing much to report yet, Chief Inspector. I think that one of them was a soldier. See this?" Jim held up a bag with a piece of rotting material inside. "Quite distinctive. What's left of an army boot. World War two vintage. British army issue. Steel studs and heel tips." Jim put the bag down carefully and picked up another. "Not sure about this yet but I'm halfway certain this is a naval officer's hat badge." He pointed at a fibrous mass with a pencil. "See those wiry things? I think that's gold wire. All the organic material has rotted away but the shape is roughly correct. We'll be sure when we have stabilised it in resin and had a closer look. Should be through here by tomorrow. Have more for you later."

Chark thanked him and walked back to where Privett and Beane were watching the photographer pack up his equipment and load it into the van.

"Let's go, Phil," said Chark. "Light's fading and I'm hungry. Beane here will dry out and curl up at the edges like a British Railways sandwich if we don't get some beer into him soon."

Privett laughed and took Beane by the elbow. "Come on sergeant, I'll buy you both a pint at the Duke. It's been a long day."

The light faded from daylight to dusk as they drove away from the shelter. Chark parked behind the 'Duke' and Chark and Beane checked in at the reception desk. Then they carried their luggage up the narrow stairs to their rooms while Privett waited in the bar.

Privett found a table and placed his peaked cap under the seat to announce to all present that he was off-duty.

"Evenin', sir." Charley Frater wiped the table over with a damp rag. "The usual?" Charley was a short, wiry man in his sixties. His short-cropped gray hair matched the colour of his shirt and apron.

"Yes please, Charley. Expecting two more in a minute or two."

"Those city cops you told me about?" he said with an air of distaste "Yes."

"Put them in the front rooms like you said," said Charley and he walked off to pull a pint of Best Bitter into a dimple mug.

The bar of the "Duke" was a large room. The partition that had separated the saloon and public bars was gone and there was only one price for drinks. A polished wood counter and the ornate Victorian mirror, which had miraculously survived the bombing, occupied one side of the room. Neon beer signs flickered on the walls and at one end of the counter was a glass showcase full of sandwiches, pork pies and shiny, red apples.

"Rooms alright?" asked Privett as Chark and Beane came into the bar.

"Small," said Beane. "I'll have to sit on the crapper to take a shower."

The others laughed. "Well, it beats having to run down the hall dressed in your bathrobe every time you need to take a leak," said Privett beckoning Charley over to take their orders. He turned to Chark. "You could check into one of those chromium palaces out on the motorway. They have suites."

Chark shook his head much to Beane's relief. "The Duke's alright, Phil. It's close to the police station."

Charley arrived at the table and took Privett's empty glass. "Three more?" he asked. Privett nodded.

"Who's that?" asked Chark.

"Charley Frater. Been here a long time. Ever since we were kids together. You remember. He was the pot boy Gladys used to yell at all the time. Matter of fact, he was in the 'Duke' when it got bombed in '41. Maybe you should talk to him about it."

Chark glanced at Beane and nodded. Beane made a mental note to add Charley's name to the list in his database in the morning.

After Privett and Chark had reminisced about their boyhood over another drink, Privett retrieved his hat and stood up. "Well, I'll be off now. See you both in the morning?"

Two beers and a plate of thinly-sliced roast beef sandwiches later, Chark left Beane in the bar talking to a couple of local women. He climbed the creaking stairs to his room. The bed was soft and cool, Fairport High Street was silent and in five minutes he was asleep.

Chapter 12

The next morning Beane was sitting at a table with a plate of fried eggs, bacon, kidneys and bread before him. The bar had been transformed into a dining room by the addition of checkered tablecloths and single flowers in little glass vases.

"Morning, Chief. I just love these country breakfasts."

Chark sat down opposite him and stared. "You going to eat all that stuff?"

" 'course I am. Why?"

"Have you no mercy on your arteries?"

"What?" said Beane with his mouth full.

"Never mind."

Chark ordered coffee, toast and the fresh fruit plate and they ate in silence until Beane wiped the last vestige of yellow egg from his plate with a piece of bread and pushed it away.

"What's the plan for today, Chief?"

"What's to plan?" said Chark draining his coffee. "We've got two forty-year old corpses, a rotten army boot and a shovel." He pushed away from the table. "Come on. Let's walk back to the station and see what forensics have dredged up."

The High Street was bathed in watery sunlight. It had rained during the night and the shaded side of the street was still wet. Shopkeepers were gathering in little groups to discuss the morning's business. They turned to stare at the two policemen as they strode down the centre of the mall towards the police station.

"Morning, Chief Inspector. Sergeant," said the duty sergeant at the front desk. "Mr Privett is in his office, sir. Regular morning briefing. Be over soon."

Chark picked up the morning edition of the Eastchester Chronicle and sat in the front office while Beane checked out their office.

"One desk, two clapped-out chairs, a telephone and somebody's messed with my computer," complained Beane. "Wish people would leave it alone". He sat down at the desk, rearranged the computer carefully. Switched it on and waited for the screen to light up. With a grunt of satisfaction he pronounced it healthy.

A group of uniformed and plainclothes women and men carrying notebooks trooped out of Privett's office

"Mr Privett's ready now, sir."

Chark and Beane walked in to find a young man with long fair hair and rimless spectacles seated in a chair smoking a cigarette. He stubbed it out in an ashtray and stood as Chark entered.

"This is Dr Overton," said Privett. "He's from Hampton and is doing the pathology work on the two corpses." Dr Overton shook hands with Chark and Beane. It was a firm, confident shake.

Chark and beane sat at Privett's desk and accepted a copy of the preliminary report.

Dr Overton opened his folder and looked around at the others. "Ready?"

Chark nodded.

"Victims were men. Oldest aged thirty five to forty. Youngest was in his middle twenties. Both killed by a single blow with a broad, sharp instrument. Spinal cords were severed at the base of the brain in each case." He hesitated as he turned a page.

"Would the wounds be consistent with shovel like the one found at the site?" asked Beane.

"Yes. We're putting the shovel under microscopic examination to confirm it but the shape and angle of the wound is consistent with the shovel. And, by the way, the murderer was right-handed."

"A woman possibly?" asked Chark.

"If she was over five seven and strong. Yes, it could be a woman. A shovel is a hell of an axe if wielded right." Overton continued from his files. "The younger man was about six feet tall. Strongly built. However, there is evidence of ricketts at an early age. Definite curvature of the legs. Malnourished too, by the evidence in the teeth. They were really bad."

"Then it could be concluded that he came from a poor background?" said Chark.

"Could be," said Overton. "And a hardworking one. According to the condition of the skeletal remains his muscular development indicated a lot of heavy lifting."

Overton turned to his report again. "The older man was shorter by three inches. Well-developed with no signs of malnourishment. Teeth were well cared for. His right arm had been broken earlier in life. Probably as a child or teenager."

"Any personal effects?," asked Beane stretching his legs.

"A number of coins. About three pounds worth. Can't say who they belong to. They all fell from the clothing and were mixed together. All dated 1940 or earlier. A pocket watch was found and I suspect it belongs to the younger man because we found a wrist watch with a metal strap on the wrist of the older corpse. The pocket watch is a cheap silver-plated type with an inscription the back—'Pvt William Brown. Hamptonshire Regiment 1918'. If it wasn't for the date on the watch I'd say you had a tentative ID there."

"Anything else?" asked Chark.

"Yes. A ring. With a single diamond. Large one. On the middle finger, right hand, of the older man. One large penknife, owner uncertain, and some metal buttons from a battle dress. Nothing more yet except for the cap badge and boot you already know about. Jim was dead right about both. According to our specialists, a British army boot circa 1940 and a naval officer's cap badge. There are some scraps of fabric from the clothing but nothing in detail yet. Take a few days to identify them."

Dr Overton closed his file. "That's it for now, gentlemen."

Chark thanked him and asked "Where is the evidence?"

"We've set up an incident room in one of the interview rooms," said Privett. "We have to share it with the museum I'm afraid. Short of space, you know."

"Museum?" echoed Chark. "What's that?"

"I'll show you," said Privett and led the way.

They filed into the incident room. It was small. One scarred wooden table, two hard chairs and a glass cabinet that had once displayed ladies lingerie in a long-gone department store. Inside the case was a collection of Fairport police memorabilia including the rabbit gun used in the only other recorded murder in Fairport, Constable Walker's helmet, a collection of whistles, pieces of shrapnel, several decaying maps and books.

The evidence collected at the air raid shelter site was bagged and labeled and laid out on the lid. Except for the skeletal remains. They were at the Eastchester C.I.D Crime Lab.

"Dr Overton," said Beane. "Did the investigators come up with any identification of any kind?"

"No," he replied thoughtfully. "Funny thing. You would expect something. But, considering the time the bodies had been lying there, any paper items could have decayed away. Good point, Sergeant, I'll have the boys do a thorough analysis of the soil samples."

"What's that?" Chark pointed to two bags containing dark material cased in plaster.

"We don't know yet. That's the fabric remnants I told you about.

There's something there which looks like silk with fine metal wire in it. Something like the hat badge. Jim, the technician, wants to look at it again so I said I'd take it back today. Incidentally, I'm pretty sure it belonged to the older man. There's another piece of fabric which looks like it and I'm ninety percent sure it's blue in colour."

Something about the two relics stirred Chark's memory. "Can you leave them here for a while?" he asked. Dr Overton paused and chewed his bottom lip. "Yes, I think so," he said "If you need them. But just for looking at? Don't mess about with them. OK?"

Beane had been writing in his notebook. He stopped and rubbed his chin thoughtfully. "If this was robbery why didn't the murderer take the coins and the ring and watches?"

"Maybe he was disturbed?" suggested Overton.

"No," said Chark firmly. If he, or she, had time to bury them, there was time to collect the valuables. There wouldn't be much paper money in a private soldier's wallet. No, robbery wasn't the prime motive. Something else was."

After Dr Overton left to return to Hampton, Chark and Beane returned to their cramped office and sat drinking tea. Chark was thoughtful for a few minutes while Beane entered data into the computer.

"First thing to do is identify the victims," he said, half to himself. "Not much to go on." He leaned back in his chair and turned to Beane who was leaning forward earnestly over his screen, tapping at the keyboard. "Any ideas, Beane?"

"About what?"

"Identifying the victims."

"Same old routine, I suppose. I ask a million questions and get a thousand answers. You fill in the blanks with guesswork. And we hope this thing..." he pointed at the computer..."helps. If there's a pattern it will find it quicker than we will."

"Right," agreed Chark. "You start with the Town Hall. Get a list of all the residents of the town in the war years and check if any of them are still alive. Then we'll interview them. The voter's lists should help." Chark got up from his chair and buttoned his jacket.

"While you are at the Town Hall, I'll be checking out the infallible source of town gossip.

"What's that?"

"The church. See you at the Duke for lunch."

Chark walked out of the police station and pulled up the collar of his raincoat as he headed into the breeze that carried a fine rain. In the High Street, groups of elderly men and women stood gossiping and smoking among the stalls set out on the mall in front of the shops. Stall-owners were arranging their goods on trestle tables protected from the capricious weather by canvas awnings.

Fairport seemed smaller than when he and Phil had run and shouted through these same streets during the war. Then, the streets were almost deserted and the shop fronts empty. The files they had brought down from Eastchester contained black and white "Before and After" pictures of the High Street. They gave a drab impression of Fairport. Today, Chark could see faded but familiar shades of red and yellow in the brickwork of the old houses that had survived. There was bright paintwork and gaudy advertisements on the new shopfronts. The carefully-pruned young trees in the mall wore a delicate haze of green leaves.

There were still a few gaps in the rows of buildings. One was now a fenced playground for children. It had a sandbox and plastic things for them to climb on and slide down. Another gap was a municipal parking lot for shoppers. Most of the remaining cottages had been converted to some other use; a video arcade, fast food restaurants a wine bar and a delicatessen. Chark smiled to himself at the thought of what the Darleys would have made of the place.

He reached the west end of the High Street, climbed over the low chain barrier and crossed the street to St Ethelred's church. He walked through the lych gate into the quiet greeness of the churchyard.

An old man who was busy sweeping the brown gravel path between the gate and the church door greeted him. "Mornin' sir." He was short and wiry. Not much over five feet with a deep brown face lined from exposure from the weather. He wore a crumpled, brown corduroy suit and a striped shirt without a collar. Around his stringy neck was a red kerchief knotted at the front under an unshaven chin.

Chark stopped. "Good morning to you, sir."

"You lookin' fer the vicar?" he wheezed, leaning on his broom.

"I was admiring your old church."

"It's old alright. Part Norman part Victorian. We don't get many people at services any more. We got more folks in town these days but a smaller congregation. Folks got no time for church. Not like the old days." The old man pushed a greasy cap back on his head and scratched his bald head.

"My name's Chark. David Chark."

"Oh, aye. Policeman. My name's Henry Purvis. Everybody calls me Purvis."

Fairport might have more people today but the news travels just as fast as it always did.

"You've lived in Fairport a long time?" asked Chark.

"Yes, sir. More than sixty years now. Used to work at old Colonel Ford's farm. Took care of the cows and suchlike. Retired now. He left me a hundred pound when he died back in sixty five. Lot of money then." Purvis coughed harshly and spat in a pile of leaves.

"Then you were here during the war?"

"Yes. Reverend Tweed was vicar then. Funny old geezer. Used to talk to hisself a lot. Liked to shoot rabbits and squirrels and birds in the woods up north of here before they built all them new houses. Used to run the locals off because they disturbed the birds." Purvis cackled at the memory. "Loosed off a load of shot at me once when I was rabitting there during the war. Hit me in the arse. My old woman didn't stop laughin' for a month."

"What became of the Reverend Tweed?"

"Old Tweedle D.D?" Passed away in fifty six. We got a new vicar then. They appointed Reverend Batley. He were assistant vicar at the time. He's lived here since just after the war and set to retire himself now. Means I got to break in a new vicar." Purvis picked up his broom and continued sweeping. "Better get back to me chores, sir. Nice chatting with you."

Chark turned and walked up to the heavy, iron-clad door of the church and pushed it open. Inside, it was cool and still. His footsteps rang out on the stone floor and echoed around the austere, high-vaulted chamber. Light from the circular stained-glass window over the altar spread coloured patterns on the white walls. Pictures of sombre saints and memorials to past, forgotten battles filled the tall, narrow windows above the rows of pews. It was in this church, in the seats in front of the altar, that Chark and Phil Privett had congregated with the other children of Fairport on Sunday mornings, dressed in starched surplices, to sing in the choir. Memories of their journeys of discovery through the dark and dusty corners of the church, up the tower and down into the crypt flooded back as he looked around.

Chark stood in the opening of the wooden screen which separated the nave from the church door and baptismal font. The church was empty. As he turned to leave, a door opened behind the elevated pulpit and a man dressed in clerical black stepped out and began changing the hymn numbers in the wall bracket. He noticed Chark.

"Can I help you?" he called down.

"Reverend Batley?"

"That's me. Denis Batley. Vicar of St Ethelred's. All dressed up in his best blues waiting for the noontime action. That is, if any of my flock show up." He stepped down from the pulpit and walked along the aisle towards Chark and extended his hand.

"Chark. David Chark. Chief Inspector. County Constabulary."

"Ah, yes," said Batley after a little hesitation. "I've been expecting you to call. You've come about the bodies in the shelter. God rest their souls. We plan a memorial service as soon as they are released for burial. Have you any idea when that will be, Chief Inspector?"

"No," said Chark. "I can't say."

The vicar was about average height but stooped. His thick, white hair was brushed straight back and clipped short on the sides. His face was lined and very pale. Sad and somehow lifeless. He looked older than Chark had anticipated.

"Is there something I can do for you, Chief Inspector?" asked Batley sitting down on a pew and gesturing Chark to join him.

"It's possible, vicar. I need to identify the deceased. To do that I may need the help of people who were living in Fairport during World War II."

The vicar raised his shoulders and turned his palms upwards. "I'm afraid I would be of little help, Chief Inspector. You see, I came here straight from Hampton Theological College in 1948. Spent eight years as assistant vicar to Reverend Tweed. We had a big congregation then."

"Yes, I know. I spoke to Henry Purvis on my way in."

"Really?" Batley's eyes focused on Chark's for an instant. "And what did that old reprobate have to say?"

"Not much. Said your predecessor liked to shoot things and you were about to retire."

"Well," said Batley. "That much is true. The diocese has made it clear they want a younger man in St Ethelred's. Can't say I blame them." He rose stiffly. "Why don't you come over to the vicarage for a glass of sherry? I'm about to take a break. If you're going to interview all the people who lived here during the war, you could do worse than start with my housekeeper, Mrs Walker. She's been a resident all her life. Husband was killed during the war. Place was badly bombed, you know. They never found his body. Hard on a religious woman like that."

Batley pulled the door of the church closed behind them and walked with Chark in the churchyard.

Purvis had finished sweeping and was sitting on a toppled head-stone drinking cold tea from a stained milk bottle. "Mornin', vicar," he called with a saucy grin. He touched his cap.

"Purvis," responded Batley and hurried on with Chark.

"You've been here for a long time, Mr Batley," said Chark as they walked up the path between the church and the vicarage. "Did you never consider moving on? Seems unusual for a vicar to stay that long in one place these days."

Batley thought for a while. "No," he said. "No, I won't leave. Too many things to do." He dismissed the subject with a wave of his hand and led the way through a garden gate set in a high brick wall.

"What do you think of the place?" asked Batley. The decaying, Victorian vicarage stood alone in two acres of lawns and shrubs. Within the wall was a row of ancient beech trees.

"Fascinating, aren't they?" said Reverend Batley when Chark stopped to look. "The whole of the British Isles were covered in trees like these a thousand years ago. Those few that remain have gained a mystical aura. Like ghostly apparitions from our past. Now, it would take an Act of Parliament to cut them down but only a nod from that idiot town council to demolish this old house."

He led Chark up four worn steps to the ornamental door of the vicarage. He opened it with an effort and waved Chark inside.

It was a gloomy place. Chark sensed the chill and dampness in the dark living room. Perhaps the living was a poorer one than it appeared and there was not enough money for heating.

They were seated in the dimly-lit living room sipping sharp, pale sherry which Batley poured from a decanter on the ornate sideboard. As his eyes got accustomed to the light, Chark became aware of the oil paintings of the stern-faced men which hung on the walls above him. Dennis Batley's predecessors. Men with bushy side whiskers, clerical collars and ample bellies. Faded photographs and illuminated biblical quotations filled the spaces in between the dark picture frames. Batley noticed his interest and rose.

"There," he said with pride, pointing to a framed photograph. "Class of '48. That's me on the left end of the back row. A small but distinguished group."

Chark stood and moved closé. He looked at the fading, cracked black and white picture of a dozen young men seated stiffly in rows. They wore dark, ill-fitting suits. World War 2 demob suits without a doubt.

"They put me in the back row because I was wearing boots," said Batley. "All the others had shoes. Wouldn't look right for a Doctor of Divinity to be seen wearing boots on his graduation day."

Batley reached out and pulled an old-fashioned bell rope beside the unlit fire. A thin woman dressed in a flowered pinafore wearing her hair in the tightly-rolled fashion of the forties entered.

"You called, vicar?"

"Yes, Mrs Walker. This is Chief Inspector Chark. From Eastchester. He's investigating the incident on the horse pasture. He wants to hear from people who lived in the Old Town during the war. Can you spend a little time with us?"

Mrs Walker stared at Batley for a few seconds and then at Chark before nodding her head. She accepted a glass of sherry without a word. Chark guessed her age at about seventy. Perhaps more. When she spoke it was heavily accented with soft vowels. The shiny, black eyes never left Chark's.

"What do you want to know?"

"Any thing that might help me understand the people who lived here. Gossip. Scandal. That sort of thing."

Mrs Walker was slow to respond but as the sherry warmed her, she became less inhibited and she spoke more freely.

"During the war young people had all kinds of temptations to resist," she said. "What with all those soldiers about the town and girls going to dances and smoking and drinking." She gave a little shudder of disgust. "Then there was young Ted Hoff with his black market cigarettes and whiskey and silk stockings what he kept in the air raid shelter." Chark leaned forward.

"The shelter? You mean the one in the horse pasture?"

"Yes. Everybody knew about it. He kept stuff down there. Put a big brass lock on the door and told everybody to keep out. Said it was unsafe." Mrs Walker lowered her voice. "But we knew better. They say he started his new estate agent's business with the profits."

Chark made a mental note to talk to Ted Hoff and find out from him when his enterprise had started.

The vicar poured more sherry for them and Mrs Walker rambled on about the debauched nature of today's youth and the sex, violence and nudity on television which, on Christian principle, she never watched. Then she lowered her hands primly to her lap and said quietly, "Then there's Nora Priddy, of course. Beggin' your pardon, vicar." The vicar glanced quickly at Chark.

"That's all right Mrs Walker, go on," said Chark firmly.

"Well, young Nora was a barmaid at the 'Duke of York' public house in the war. About seventeen then. Trouble was, she couldn't resist a uniform. Used to go around with servicemen from the camps around Fairport. Local boys got jealous and called her all kinds of dirty names. Didn't do no good though. She just laughed it of in them days."

"As I remember," interrupted the vicar. "Charley Frater had quite a crush on Nora, didn't he?"

"Yes, nice boy was Charley. But she wouldn't have anything to do with him, of course. Him being only a pot boy and too young to wear a uniform. You know Charley he used to pick up all the dirty glasses and wash them. Lived with his mother in a cottage on the Ford Farm. Never took a drop of liquor."

"Chark opened his notebook and turned back a few pages. "Charley Frater. Yes. He's the barman at the 'Duke' isn't he?"

Batley laughed. "You could say that. Mr s Walker's right. Charley Frater and his mother lived in a charity cottage on the Ford farm before and during the war. His father died when he was a baby leaving nothing but debts. Consequently, Charley's education was minimal and I believe people treated him badly. Now he owns the pub. Paid cash for it, they say."

"On a pot boy's wages? Or did he take up some other job?" said Chark.

Mrs Walker leaned forward in her chair, her face close to Chark's. "He went to Canada on an assisted passage. Government paid his fare. Made a lot of money. Says he was in the insurance business." Her voice became more conspiratorial. "If you was to ask me, I'd say you should take a close look at our Charley Frater."

Chark studied his notebook for a second as Mrs Walker settled back in her seat with an air of minor triumph.

"And what happened to Nora Priddy?"

She answered quickly as if to get the offending words out as quickly as possible. "Got pregnant and married a Pole."

Batley continued the story. "One of those airmen with an unpronounceable name. Michael something. Fighter pilot, I think."

Chark turned to Mrs Walker. "Anything more?"

"Not much more to tell you, sir," said Mrs Walker smoothing her hair and rising to leave. "Not many of us left now. Got to get back to my baking."

"Just a few more questions, please, Mrs Walker." Chark raised his pencil briefly. "Do you know a Mr Purvis?"

"There was a stiffening in Mrs Walker. "What's that dirty old man been saying?" she demanded.

"Just giving me some background on the town back in the war."

"Well, you just don't take any notice of what he says. Nasty trouble maker he is."

"Last question, Mrs Walker. What happened to Nora Priddy and Michael?"

"They still lives in Fairport. Out on the Aldershot road. Can't remember the address.

Chark stood up and thanked her. "That's alright, we can get it down at the station."

As Mrs Walker left, Chark turned to Batley and handed him his glass. "Thanks for the information and the sherry, vicar. That will be all for now. If anything occurs to you that might shed some light on what went on back in the war years, give me a call at the station, will you? Leave a message."

The Reverend Batley smiled an "of course" and showed Chark out of the front door.

As he walked back to the High Street and the Duke, Chark tried to arrange the bits of information gained at the interviews into some logical form. But it wouldn't fit. More information was needed. Maybe Beane had come up with something.

*

The bars and restaurants along the High Street were filling up and impatient drivers lined up at the parking lot barriers eager to pay their fifty pence for a one hour stay and a chance of a seat near their friends. Chark pushed open the door of the 'Duke' and found that Beane had already staked his claim at the bar with a plate of sausages and french fries covered in tomato ketchup. Chark looked at it and lost his appetite.

"What will you have, Chief?"

"Large scotch and water, please."

Beane beckoned Charley Frater over with a fork and ordered the drinks.

"What did you find at the Town Hall?"

Beane pointed to his notebook and a sheaf of copies on the counter. "More than I expected." The spiral-bound book was open at a page with a handwritten list of names. There were cryptic marks against some of them. "Got the names from the voter's lists from '39 to '43. They ran copies for me", said Beane through a mouthful of chips. "I've compared them with the latest one. About forty names. That's all." Beane ran a ketchup-stained finger down his list. "Thirty nine to be exact. Lot less than I expected."

"Good," said Chark as Charley placed his drink on the bar in front of him. "We'll start interviews this afternoon. You take half, I'll take the others."

"Right."

"Matter of interest," added Chark casually. "Is there a Nora Priddy on the old list?"

"How do you spell that?"

"P-R-I-D-D-Y,"

Beane took up the old voter list and ran his finger down to the Ps. "No. What year was she born?"

"Probably 1924 or 1925."

"She would have been too young to vote in '43. Why?"

Chark counted the reasons on his fingers.

"According to our Mrs Walker at the vicarage; she was young and attractive, she was attracted to men in uniform, she worked right here in the 'Duke', close to the air raid shelter. The local boys were jealous of the local talent and she caused hard feelings among them,"

There was a pause.

"And both our victims were men in uniform," added Beane.

"Right," said Chark as he reached out and speared the last of Beane's sausages with a fork. "Curiouser and curiouser."

Chapter 13

"Let's call it a day, Beane," said Chark. "We're getting nowhere with this." They had spent the evening reading and and re-reading their notes from the interviews with the few ageing residents of Fairview Old Town who had survived the war years and still lived there. None could provide information that would help in identifying the bodies buried in the air raid shelter. Nobody could remember a missing soldier or navy officer. The official records had accounted for everyone. Beane had entered the lists and the reports of each interview in his computer and tried to find a common thread. There wasn't one. Not even a coincidence to resolve.

The temperature in the office was dropping fast and the noise of activity in the outer office had stopped as people headed home for the day.

"I can't stand any more of that pub food," said Chark standing up and putting on his jacket. "How about trying one of those restaurants in the High Street? I'm buying."

Beane switched off the computer and put on its plastic cover.

They walked down the cooling and darkening High Street in search of a restaurant offering something other than steak and chips or fish and chips. Beane would have been happy with either but since Chark was going to pay, he grudgingly walked the length of the High Street and back again to let him choose. They had almost agreed on a wine bar with salty snacks when Chark noticed a hand-painted sign for "Bizzano's Restaurant" pointing down a narrow, cobble-stoned alley between two closed shops. A menu sheet was clipped on the doorpost by a clothes peg. Chark adjusted his glasses and read it.

"Good," he pronounced and pushed open the door. "Italian food and not a pizza listed. Let's give it a try."

The restaurant was warm and smelled of garlic and hot olive oil. Its decoration was artfully composed of glassless old window frames suspended on wires and highly-coloured fake washing hung on clothes lines. Each table had a red and white checkered cloth and a vase with two red flowers. They were greeted and seated by a dark-skinned waiter wearing a faded black suit and a white apron. Chark ordered a bottle of Orvieto Classico with antipasto followed by a pasta dish with broiled fish. As they sipped wine and munched on the antipasto the subject of conversation returned to the case of the two corpses.

"First thing we need is a positive identification," said Chark."That much is clear. Without that we can't do anything." He peered thoughtfully into his wine.

"The inscription on the watch," said Beane who quietly craved a glass of beer in place of the tart, dry wine. 'Private William Brown- Hamptonshire Regiment.' That's about as close as we've got."

"William Brown," mused Chark. "Just our luck to have a Brown. Couldn't be Ramsbottom or Shapiro. Oh, no, it's 'Bill Brown'. Timing's all wrong too. Our victim was too young to have been in the army in 1918. He could easily have bought that watch at a pawn shop. Or found it." Chark dipped his fork and retrieved an olive.

"Or stole it," said Beane. "Or maybe inherited it?"

Chark lowered his fork. "Beane. That's a real possibility. Good deduction on your part."

"Stole or inherited?"

"Inherited," said Chark, "Tomorrow, you get over to the Hamptonshires' regimental headquarters and get them to check their records. They're in Aldershot. Records go back to the Crimean War. Can't be many William Browns who served in the First World War." Chark grinned as Beane grimaced at the inevitable. "At least, not too many."

"Right, Chief. No more than a couple of hundred."

The waiter hovered again and offered more wine. Chark shook his head. To Beane's relief.

"Chief," said Beane, changing the subject. "Is it true that you and Phil Privett were in the navy together?"

"Yes. We were close in those days. Kept in touch after the war. Got called up at the same time and did our national service at HMS 'Royal Arthur'. Climbed the mast at HMS StVincent together Why?"

"Nothing, really. Just can't imagine you in bell-bottomed trousers and a little white hat. That's all. Old Phil doesn't have the shape for it."

Chark laughed. "Phil was a skinny kid in those days. All arms and legs. We both were. We thought we looked sharp in our uniforms." Chark went silent for a while and held his hand up to stop Beane from interrupting his thoughts. "What was that you said?"

Beane started to apologise "I'm sorry, Chief. Didn't mean to-"

"It's OK, Beane," said Chark impatiently. "What was that you said about uniforms?"

"I said I couldn't imagine you and Phil Privett in bell-bottomed pants and a little white flat hat."

Chark slapped his hand on the table, bouncing the vase and alarming the waiter who ran towards them from the kitchen. "That's it! The hat. You remember that black thing set in a block of plaster among the evidence on the display cabinet? One of those things I asked Overton to leave for a couple of days? About an inch wide and four inches long?"

"Yes," said Beane. "What about it?"

"I know what it is." Chark drained his glass and stood up. "Let's pay the bill and get out of here. I want to look at the evidence again."

They left the restaurant after Chark overtipped the doleful waiter and assured him that their rapid departure was not a reflection on his service or food.

The High Street was nearly deserted now as they hurried back to the station where only the desk sergeant, two constables and the night cleaning crew were on duty.

Chark unlocked the door to the interrogation room and switched on the lights. He pointed to one of the packets on the display cabinet. "That's the one. I'll open it up. You bring the desk lamp over."

"Overton was adamant about not messing around with the evidence, Chief."

"If it bothers you, Beane, I'll do it myself."

Beane sighed, picked up the heavy, old-fashioned lamp and stood it on the cabinet next to the black object Chark had carefully tipped out of its plastic envelope. Chark looked at the object from several angles for what seemed like minutes.

"Yep, that's what it is," said Chark straightening up. "I'm certain now." He moved the block of plaster with its mounted strip of fragile black material and pointed with the tip of his gold pencil. "See that little bow? That and your remark about my little white hat gave it to me. This is a sailor's hatband. They had the name of the ship embroidered on it in gold thread. I had "HMS Royal Arthur" on mine. During the war they took the names of the ship off. With any luck this one might still have a name on it."

Chark lifted the block closer to the light. "There's a magnifying glass in my briefcase."

Beane brought the magnifier and watched as Chark lifted the block up to the light and moved it around.

"Something here but I can't make it out," said Chark. He lay the magnifying glass down and rubbed his chin for a moment. "Light's not strong enough."

A few minutes of searching in the maintenance closet with the help of the duty sergeant produced a high-wattage light bulb and Beane inserted it in the lamp while Chark waited impatiently.

"Let's try it another way." Chark lay the block on the desk and beckoned Beane to move the lamp. "Lower it towards the block." Beane brought the heavy lamp down to within a few inches of it as Chark kept his eyes on the black surface.

"Good," said Chark with a hint of excitement. "There are letters on the surface. Now move the lamp so the light shines at an angle."

"Be better if we had plane-polarized light," said Beane. "The lab boys have all the tools up in Eastchester."

But Chark ignored the advice and pushed the lamp closer.

The heat from the bulb was beginning to rise and the metal was getting uncomfortable. Sweat formed on Beane's forehead.

"That's it! Keep it still, Beane. Don't wave it about. I can see something."

"Hurry up, Chief. This thing's red hot and my arms are shaking."

"OK, OK. Hang on, hang on. I can see an "M", and an "S". Then there's an "E", and "L", "S", something and an "N"." The something looks round. Must be a vowel. An "O" or a "U"."

Beane's arm gave out at that moment and he let the lamp roll back upright. "Five to one it's an "O", Chief."

"HMS ELSON."

Chark put the block back into its plastic bag and pointed to another. "Take a look at the other thing Joe couldn't identify. Bring it over here and we'll do the same routine on it."

Beane lay the scrap of blue-black, plaster-mounted fabric on the desk and lowered the lamp at an angle while Chark peered through his glass again. It took only a few seconds before Chark dropped the magnifying glass and looked up with a grin of triumph. "I knew it. He was a three-ringer."

What's that?" asked Beane as he gratefully replaced the hot lamp in its place on the desk.

"Those fibres are gold thread. Like the hatbands. Three rings of them. Our navy victim was a captain in the regular navy. He pointed to the fabric again. "See that? That's a piece of the lower part of his sleeve and because the threads are straight it means he was regular navy. Reservists had wavy rings."

"So what does it mean?" asked Beane. "Captains didn't wear hat-bands with their ship's name on them, did they?"

"No," said Chark. "Sailors are a sentimental lot. With luck, it was a souvenir from a ship he had served on. Don't forget, it was folded. Fortunately, the words are on the outside. Funny thing though. What's a navy captain doing in a horse pasture in a little town like Fairport? And wearing his uniform, too?" He stood up and yawned. Then he made for the door. "Come on, Beane. A good night's work. The Duke's still open I'll buy you a beer to wash down the wine and pasta."

They switched off the lights, locked the door and said goodnight to the duty sergeant on the way out. As they walked towards the 'Duke' in the cold night air, Chark hummed a little tune and took Beane by the arm. "You make for Aldershot tomorrow, I'll tackle the Navy Records Office over in Hampton, they should have some information on an HMS ELSON or ELSUN. Navy ships are hard to lose track of."

But Chark's good humour was short-lived. As they pushed open the door into the smoke-laden bar and elbowed their way to the counter to order the drinks, a familiar, high-pitched voice rose above the buzz of conversations.

"Evening, Chief. What's news?"

A thin man with a fringe of fine black hair around his bald crown sat at a table with a pint of beer in his hand. He was wearing a dirty, belted raincoat.

"Sam Gilkicker," said Chark without enthuisiasm. "I might have guessed he'd show up here sooner or later."

"That's all we need," said Beane taking his glass from Charley. Sam Gilkicker was the crime reporter for the Eastchester Chronicle. A good reporter but a royal pain in the ass according to Chark. Sam stood at Chark's elbow.

"What have you got for me, Dave?"

"What the hell brings you all the way from Eastchester to Fairport,

Sam? Don't you have enough rapes, robberies and assaults back home to fill that miserable column of yours? And call me Chief or Mr Chark."

"You know me, Dave. Nose for an unusual story. If Chief Inspector Chark's on the case it might be good for an exclusive in tomorrow's edition." Sam sipped his beer and recognised Beane with a wink. "How about you, sergeant. Buy you another beer?"

Beane turned his eyes to Chark for approval but got no more than a narrow-eyed frown which translated as "No". But Sam Gilkicker was not dismissed so easily.

"Been talking to that Inspector Privett over at the station," he said taking a deep drag on his cigarette. "Said you're on the job so I reckon it's more than just an ordinary homicide case. So what've you got for me?"

Chark sipped his beer unhappily. The lull before the storm was over. If Sam Gilkicker got here first, the rest were on their way and the weekly tabloids were going to have a field day with this one.

"Alright, Sam. This is as much as we have." Chark led the way to a vacated table in the corner of the bar where they could sit in relative quiet. Chark described the events of the past few days sticking to the facts and divulging nothing that which could not be obtained by patient sleuthing by an averagely competent investigative reporter. He said nothing about their evening's work and the inscribed watch. When he had finished and Sam had hastily scribbled notes in his pad, Chark pushed his glass over the table.

"Another beer, Dave?"

"No," said Chark. "I think that little speech of mine is worth a brandy for me and my friend, Hume."

As Sam left to get the drinks, Beane leaned over the table. "So it's Hume now, is it?"

"Only in front of Gilkicker." Sam walked down the High Street to call in his copy for the morning edition.

Chapter 14

Chark woke early on Wednesday morning. He made instant coffee with the little plastic packets of powder and hot water from the stained electric kettle on the dressing table. He dressed in a blue double-breasted suit and a white shirt, Royal Navy tie and conservative, black lace-up shoes. Then he called ahead to Navy Records in Hampton and made an appointment for ten o'clock. He walked over to the police station where Phil Privett was already at work signing the day's report sheets filed by the night shift. He waved Chark to a seat and offered him tea and biscuits.

"Hear you were working late in the office last night," said Privett. "Find anything interesting?"

"Nothing that I want Sam Gilkicker to hear," said Chark over the rim of his tea cup fixing his eyes on Privett and waiting for a response. Privett leaned back and threw a sheaf of papers on his desk.

"OK, Dave, guilty as charged. Sam Gilkicker was in here yesterday digging around for information. He picked up your scent in Eastchester and called me. I spoke to him. Telling that old shark nothing just makes him more persistent and obnoxious. You know that."

"Yes, I know Sam," said Chark. And he also knew that Phil Privett couldn't resist a little attention and flattery from the press either. Which makes him talkative. "I don't want Sam Gilkicker or any of that tribe of scribblers thrashing around the town like a bunch of circus barkers. I need to get to know more about these people in Fairport. Can you keep him at bay for a few more days?" Chark stood up and placed his cup on the desk.

"I'll try, Dave," said Privett. "I'll try. But by tomorrow we'll have the rest of the press gang down here when they find out that Sam's found a real story."

"Do your best, Phil. A few days." Chark pulled on his gloves. "Now. What's the quickest way to get over to Hampton? Beane's got the car today."

"Quickest way is the old way. Over on the ferry. But you can have another car if you want to drive round the harbour."

"No, thanks," said Chark. "I need some fresh air for the little gray cells to work on. But you can have someone drive me to the ferry terminal."

"Where are you going?"

Chark smiled. "Just getting acquainted with the local scene, that's all."

Ten minutes later, the police driver dropped Chark off at the terminal where he bought a ticket and boarded the ferry for Hampton. The short journey across the water was not the same as when he had crossed it as a boy. There were sleek, modern warships anchored in the deep channel now. The old battlers of WW11 were long gone. White cross-channel ferries and a host of small boats were entering and leaving the busy port.

The passenger cabin of the ferry boat was large and airy. It had padded vinyl seats and windows crusted with salt. Spray fizzed up from the sharp bow and ran along the shiny hull.

"Not like the old days," said an elderly man dressed in an overcoat, muffler and peaked cap. "Old ferry boats had open decks. Coal-fired they were. When we were kids, we'd hang around the engine room to keep warm. It's better now. Folks can keep out of the weather."

Chark nodded. "I remember. Those old boats were in use during the war when I was a kid."

"Yes, guv. Never stopped running. Except for the big air raid in '41 when all the ferries stopped for a week when the docks got bombed. Some went to Dunkirk. You know that?"

"No, I didn't," said Chark truthfully and wondered if the victim in the navy uniform had used a ferry like this one.

With a squeal of tortured fenders, the ferry docked against the pontoon on the Hampton side and the passengers disembarked. The tide was low so Chark had to lean into the slope of the wide gangway leading up to the street. He was tempted to walk the couple of miles to the navy yard but it was an overcast day and there was a threat of rain in the air. He waited in line and took a taxi.

The main gate of the dockyard was open to all traffic but to enter the administrative section, Chark had to state his business and show identification to a Royal Marine guard in a kiosk. He confirmed Chark's appointment on the telephone and gave him a plastic pass to wear on his lapel. With a salute, the marine directed him to Navy Records.

They were in a handsome Georgian building on a quiet cobbled street lined with plane trees. Figureheads taken from old sailing ships were mounted on concrete blocks. The other red brick buildings lining the street had been restored and bore plaques describing their former purpose. Ship's chandlers' warehouses, once full of barrels of salted pork and limes, rum storage (a happy institution which Chark remembered from his navy days when the daily rum ration was still a tradition), sailmaker's shops, ropemakers and carpenters. All the paraphernalia of a lost age juxtaposed with the uncompromising starkness of modern technology. Gone were the hordes of labouring people going about their daily tasks. Now there were smartly-dressed men and women hurrying from one mellow building to the other carrying briefcases.

A breeze rustled the trees. There was a constant hum of electric motors and the gray mass of the superstructure of an aircraft carrier moored in the harbour loomed above the rooftops.

Chark ran up the stone steps of the Records Office building to its main door. He stepped into the semi-darkness of the lobby.

"Can I help you?" asked a pleasant, middle-aged, dark-haired receptionist. She glasses suspended from her neck on black cords. Chark showed his ID and she checked his appointment on her list. Then she directed him down a long corridor to a room with a heavy wooden door. He opened it and stepped into a brightly-lit office filled with rows of racks like a library. A young woman looked up from behind her computer screen.

"Can I help you?" Less welcoming. More businesslike.

"Yes," said Chark with a smile he hoped would crack her severe expression. "I've come to enquire about a navy ship."

"Which one?"

"I think its name was HMS ELSON or maybe ELSUN. I'm not sure if that's the full name or if they are the first five letters of a longer one."

"Sit down," she pointed to a chair. Chark pulled it over and looked over the desk as she tapped the keyboard. Green words flowed across the screen.

"OK, she said. "No ELSUN but there was an ELSON. Which one do you want?"

"There was more than one?"

"Not all at one time," she said "There have been seven altogether. First was a wooden ship laid down in 1816. The last is a guided missile cruiser commissioned in 1969."

"The one I'm interested in was in service in World War Two. Say 1940 or '41"

"1940. Let's see." She typed something and information flashed on her computer screen. "Yes. A destroyer. HMS ELSON. Laid down in 1918. Recommissioned in 1939. Destroyed on June 17th 1941."

Chark felt a surge of excitement. The ELSON had died on the same day as the air raid that had virtually destroyed Fairport.

"Destroyed? How and where?"

"Not a half mile from here, Mr Chark. Berth number twelve it says here." She scrolled down the file on the screen. "She was hit by bombs during an air raid and burned with several other ships that were berthed near her. Anything else?"

Chark nodded. "How about crew? Are there records of the ship's crew at the time the ELSON was destroyed?" The clerk swiveled away from the computer and pointed to another desk. "You'll have to talk to that woman over there. She handles navy personnel records."

The other woman was a startlingly beautiful Indian woman in a pale blue sari. Her brown eyes sparkled like the jewel in her nose. Chark showed her his ID.

"Can you give me some information about the crew of HMS ELSON in 1941? Just before it was destroyed in June of that year."

The woman nodded courteously and played the keyboard.

"Yes," she said in a lisping accent and looked up at Chark. "It's here. What exactly do you want to know?"

"Names and addresses. Anything you have."

"Of course." There was a buzz as the printer came to life and in minutes, Chark was holding a list of the ELSON's crew members in his hand. He thanked the women and sat for a moment on a bench in the reception area reading the sheets of paper. At the top was the name of the ELSON's captain. *Charles Godolphin Lovedean. Born 1903. Address: Hamm's Lane, Fairport. Missing June 17th 1941, presumed killed in action.* But Chark knew he had better information than that. Charles Lovedean was murdered within sight of his own home.

Chark ran lightly down the steps and whistled as he walked back to the guard gate. He acknowledged the marine's salute with a smile.

"Get your business done, sir?"

"Yes indeed. A very successful day."

*

That morning, Beane had driven out of the Fairport police station as Chark boarded the ferry for Hampton. He merged with the traffic on the motorway and accelerated towards Aldershot. He turned up the volume on the radio and leaned back in his seat. The motorway ran smooth and flat among the hills and spring flowers made splashes of colour on the grassy banks.

He reached Aldershot in less than an hour and slowly cruised the streets south of town town looking for the Hamptonshire Regiment's building. It was a large brick building with white-framed windows and a gravel forecourt that might have been a parade ground in earlier times. It was guarded by a pair of restored Second World War tanks and an array of antique artillery. Each piece had a brass plate attached to it describing its function and military history.

Beane parked the car and pushed open the glass-paneled main door. The building was meticulously clean and orderly. The ground floor housed the regimental museum. There were rows of glass cases containing the colourful uniforms of past years lining the walls. Red dominated the display.

A tall, angular man of about sixty years dressed in a gray suit with three rows of medal ribbons on the breast pocket came out of a small office behind the souvenir counter. His voice was strong and surprisingly youthful. Beane introduced himself.

"Detective Sergeant Beane, Eastchester County Constabulary."

"Glad to know you, sergeant. Sergeant Major Rowner. Jim Rowner. Retired now, of course. Been with the regiment since '39. How can I help you?"

Beane shook Rowner's outstretched hand and then explained his reason for being there.

"All the William Browns since 1914?" said Rowner scratching his close-cropped gray hair. "Christ! There might have been dozens of them. Can you give me something more to go on? Like his registration number, an address. Middle initial?"

"Beane shook his head. "Sorry. All we have is an old watch with an inscription on it."

Rowner raised his eyebrows. "Watch, you say? Can I see it?"Beane took the plastic envelope from from his pocket and carefully tipped the corroded watch into Rowner's hand. He studied it for a moment, smiled and beckoned Beane to follow him.

At the back of the museum were rows of glass-fronted display cabinets holding hundreds of personal objects donated by members of the regiment and labeled with their names.

"See those watches?" said Rowner pointing. All those in the cabinet were in good condition and despite the corroded condition of the one in Rowner's hand, they were identical.

"You're in luck," said Rowner. "Old General Brockhurst gave those watches to the wounded in field hospitals in 1918. There was a big counter attack that summer and we lost a lot of Hamptonshire lads. Some of them were gassed. The general toured the hospitals giving out watches and good cheer." Rowner dropped his voice and looked around as if to see if anyone was looking. "Stupid old bastard. What a deal. One cheap watch in exchange for a good pair of lungs." Rowner pointed to the office. "Let's look at the records."

Rowner took down several canvas-bound volumes marked "1918" and handed them to Beane.

"You're welcome to go through the records and find all the William Browns who were in the regiment that summer. Should save a lot of time." He pointed to a desk. "Make yourself comfortable over there while I take care of the front desk. If you find who you want, I'll try to find out what happened to him. If he got a pension it will be easier. Maybe even a last known address."

"Thanks," said Beane as he settled down in a chair at the scarred desk and opened the book at the first page.

It took him more than three hours to create his list. The entries were in chronological order, not alphabetical, and he had to read each of the three hundred pages. When Rowner closed the souvenir shop , he made tea and offered Beane a cup.

"Find what you want?"

"Would you believe eleven William Browns at the beginning of the summer of 1918 and only five at the end? What happened to them?"

"Dead, probably."

"That's greater than fifty percent. In less than a year? Jesus! What a war."

Rowner took the list of five William Browns and consulted several other books. After a while he looked up and handed the list back."

"You can forget three out of the five. No information. Been dead for years. You can tell by the little black marks against their names."

"How about the other two?" asked Beane "Any addresses or anything?"

"Yes," said Rowner. "One is listed as being in the Soldier's Hospital at West Lee, the other lives at a place called Draxford Farm. That'll be down near Hampton way. That's all I have. 'course, these addresses are years and years old." He handed the list to Beane.

"Thanks, sergeant major. You've been a great help."

"Any time, any time. Hope you find what you want. Those old soldiers are mighty ancient by now if they're still alive."

The car clock read two thirty as Beane sat writing a report on his visit to the Hamptonshire's headquarters. Then he pulled the map book from the glove compartment and started looking for the Soldier's Hospital at West Lee. He found it about thirty miles to the north of Aldershot; a black square set in a square inch of green. It could be reached by a meandering, B-class road that had many tributaries. But there was time left in the day to go looking, so Beane set off through the narrow streets of the town looking for directions to the road to West Lee.

After pulling over on the side of a country road to study his maps several times and doubling back to a place where he knew where he was, he finally found the road sign pointing to West Lee.

The Soldier's Hospital was a shabby building in the grounds of what had clearly been a large country estate. The gardens were uncared for and the hedgerows overgrown but there was a trimmed lawn in front of the solarium and a number of figures sitting in wheelchairs and wrapped in blankets were scattered over it. Beane rolled slowly up the drive and parked in the visitor's area. There were plenty of empty spaces. At the reception desk he spoke to a blue and white, starched nurse who was busy writing in a heavy ledger.

"Can you help me?" Beane smiled and straightened his unruly tie. Nurses always made him nervous. He was rewarded by a returned smile.

"I'll try. But first you have to tell me how."

Beane relaxed. "I'm trying to find a Private William Brown. Late of the Hamptonshire Regiment. I know it's been a very long time since he came here but you're my only lead. Must be more than eighty years old by now. By any chance does he live here?"

The nurse's face hardened. "Are you a relative?"

"No," said Beane taking his wallet from his pocket and offering it to the nurse. "Police."

"Wait here a moment, sergeant." She closed her ledger and walked off briskly, disappearing down a waxed and shining corridor. After several minutes, she returned with a gray-haired doctor wearing blue jeans and sneakers under a pale green surgical smock. He introduced himself and Beane showed his ID again.

"I'd be grateful for any information on a William Brown, sir."

The doctor thought for a moment before answering.

"There is a William Brown resident here, sergeant," said the doctor. "But I fail to see how the police can have any interest in him since he hasn't been out of the hospital grounds in ten years. Unless, of course, some relatives have magically turned up."

Beane shook his head. "We're investigating a case of homicide in Fairport. There's a chance he can provide information." He described the watch found by the body at the shelter.

"I see," said the doctor. "I must warn you that Mr Brown is very old and completely uncommunicative because of his deafness. I doubt that he can be of any help to you." Disappointment flickered across Beane's face. "He was severely traumatised. Shell-shocked they called it in those days. Mr Brown has spent most of his life in hospital."

"How about relatives?" asked Beane.

"None to our knowledge. He was nineteen when admitted. Nobody claimed him."

Beane stared. "Nobody? In all those years?"

"Nobody." The doctor showed eagerness to close the interview and get back to work. "That's all I can offer."

"How about personal belongings?" persisted Beane. "Maybe there's something among them that would help."

The doctor turned to the nurse who shrugged her shoulders.

"Can you look for me?" asked Beane. "Please?"

The nurse nodded. "You'd better take a seat, sergeant. This could take a little time." She walked off down the shiny corridor again.

"If that's all, sergeant, I must be off. Sorry I can't be of more use to you." The doctor held out his hand.

"That's alright, sir. Just a long shot, really."

Beane sat and read a magazine while he waited. The nurse reappeared carrying a shoe box.

"This is everything Mr Brown owns, sergeant."

Together they laid the treasured objects carefully on the desk. Beane moved them around reverently. There was a watch among them. In good condition but with one of the hands missing. He turned it over to find the same inscription on the back of the case. "Pvt William Brown, Hamptonshire Regiment 1918". If this William Brown still has his watch, likely he is not the owner of the one found at Fairport.

"Thank you," said Beane as the nurse put the things back into the box.

"Not much help I'm afraid," said the nurse.

"On the contrary. We are down to one possibility by elimination."

Back in his car, Beane sat for a moment and looked back at the hospital. The thought of spending his life in such a place appalled him. How could a nineteen-year-old be so completely lost to the world? He thanked God for doctors and nurses like the ones he had met there.

Beane drove out of the hospital grounds and made his way eastwards through a housing development that seemed to extend for miles along winding, concrete roads. According to the map, Draxford farm was only a few miles away as the crow flies but it took him half an hour to locate its position in the middle of the development. It was surrounded by half-finished roads and mountains of yellow clay heaped up from the sewer and water excavations.

Draxford farm was no longer there. There was a tilted, barely-legible sign on a post reading "DRAXFORD FARM". Its small fields were covered with cheap houses, the vandalised barn leaned and a few rusty implements lay buried in weeds and rubbish. What was left of the house stood surrounded by old apple trees, discarded tyres and dead cars.

The farmhouse windows were boarded up and vandals had scrawled graffitti on them. Beane leaned his shoulder on the door and pushed it open. Vermin scuttled. Weeds grew through the floorboards and strips of faded, red, flowered wallpaper hung from broken plaster walls. A rusted bedframe with a wrought-iron headboard lay near the crumbling fireplace. The sense of damp and decay was overwhelming. There was a feeling of poverty and desperation in this place where people had lived and worked and hoped and lost.

The contrast with the housing development with its shiny cars and well-fed children filled Beane with sadness. With a last look around, he got back in the car and drove through the development again to find the motorway. As the distance between him and Draxford Farm increased, his spirits rose and the prospect of a beer in the 'Duke' warmed him.

Chapter 15

When Chark arrived back at the Fairport police station a crowd had gathered outside to watch a TV mobile unit set up its equipment. He pushed his way through the crowd and found Privett's office full of newspaper reporters and cigarette smoke. As Chark opened the door the noise stopped and the newsmen pressed forward. Sam Gilkicker crushed his cigarette out in his teacup and elbowed his way to Chark's side licking the point of his pencil.

"Any progress on identifying the victims?" asked Sam. There was a buzz of questions from the group. Chark walked over to Privett's desk and sat on the edge with his legs outstretched, arms folded. Privett caught his eye and shrugged his shoulders in mute apology. Chark waited until the voices lowered again and spoke carefully and quietly as the newsmen wrote.

"Gentlemen. We have a lead on the identity of one of the bodies found in the air raid shelter. It appears that he was a naval officer. A captain. At the time of his death he served on a destroyer which was berthed in Hampton Harbour. And so far as we can determine, he was a resident of Fairport at the time." There was another rumble of questions.

"And the other victim?" asked Sam.

"No information beyond what you already know. He was likely a soldier. Private. That's all we know."

"You don't have a name for the Captain?" asked a woman from the back of the room. "Captains are not that common, even in Fairport."

Chark shook his head. "Not yet. We're still working on it."

The slight hesitation in Chark's voice was not lost on Sam Gilkicker who turned to Privett, winked and ostentatiously snapped shut his reporter's notebook. He grabbed his raincoat and made for the door and the public telephones. The other newsmen followed leaving Chark and Privett alone. Outside in the street, a TV reporter was talking to a camera in front of a crowd of Fairporters.

"Sorry about that, Dave," said Privett when they were finally alone.

Chark poured himself a cup of tea and relaxed in a chair. "That's OK, Phil. I expected it sooner or later."

"You hesitated over the question of the navy man's name. You got something you don't want the press to know?"

Chark stood up and paced the floor. "You ever hear of a Charles Godolphin Lovedean? He lived in this parish in the late thirties and early forties."

Privett screwed up his eyes in concentration. "Something familiar about that name. Seen it somewhere."

"Yeah, me too," said Chark thoughtfully. "Shouldn't take too long to find it among the records. Can you take care of that while I make a call at the vicarage? Another talk with our Mrs Walker might prove informative." Chark opened the office door and turned back to Privett. "When Beane gets back, ask him to wait for me here, will you? And Phil, not a word about Lovedean to the press gang? I don't want any embarrassment. I'm not certain yet that we've got the right name. Only a possibility."

Privett nodded his head.

It was raining gently as Chark walked over to the vicarage and rapped the heavy knocker on the front door. Mrs Walker opened it and stood back to let him enter.

"Afternoon, sir. If you wait here, I'll fetch the vicar for you. He takes a nap before evensong. Always does that." She started to move away.

"No," said Chark. "It's you I came to see, Mrs Walker. I need some more information about the town during the war and I think you can help."

"Me, sir?"

"Yes. Can we go somewhere to talk?"

Mrs Walker smoothed her hair with a bony hand. "Will the kitchen be alright? I have dinner started and I need to keep an eye on it."

"Of course." He followed her down a dark corridor to the back kitchen where the smell of damp was overlaid with the odour of food. The kitchen was a period piece from the last century. It was a large room with rows of plain wooden cupboards and a gray tiled floor. Against one wall was a massive cast iron range with a brick chimney and a brass hood. The heavy, wooden table dominating the centre of the room was scrubbed white. Tarnished copper pots and pans hung from an iron rack attached to the distant ceiling. Mrs Walker offered Chark a windsor chair and sat primly on the opposite side of the table.

"Now, sir. What was it you wanted to know?" Her black eyes gleamed behind her rimless glasses.

"What can you tell me about a family by the name of Lovedean?"

Mrs Walker sat stiffly upright in her chair. "The Lovedeans," she said. "Lived along Hamm's Lane. All gone now, of course. She was killed in the bombing. Lovely old house it was."

"She?" urged Chark.

"Mrs Lovedean. Mary her name was. Crushed under the chimney they say. We all sat under our stairs when the air raids came. They said it was the safest place in the house. Poor little boy."

Chark looked up from his notepad."Boy?" he said "What boy was that?"

"Her son. Paul was his name, I think. Yes, Paul. That was his name.

They pulled him out alive the next day. He was under the stairs like I said. She used to grow roses in their garden. Kept her busy, him being away at sea so much."

"You've a remarkable memory, Mrs Walker."

"Comes from being around a long time. Seen most of what happened in Fairport since I left home to work at the vicarage. We hear a lot up here."

Mrs Walker excused herself for a moment and poured two cups of black tea that had been simmering in a stained kettle on the stove. Chark laced it with milk and sugar and sipped. The sharp tannic flavour shrivelled the inside of his mouth and for a moment. He thought it had dissolved his teeth. Mrs Walker seemed amused.

"That's good farmhouse tea," she said. "Keeps you going, don't it?"

Chark recovered and smiled. "And Mr Lovedean? What happened to him?"

"Navy man. Officer. Never came back after the war. Lots didn't. I suppose when a battleship blows up there's not much to bury." She paused for a moment. "He and my Walker sometimes had a drink together at the 'Duke' on a Saturday." She lowered her eyes for a moment and Chark waited before asking his next question.

"And the boy, Paul." he asked "What happened to him?"

"He and the other boys in Hamm's Lane used to give Walker fits. Always getting into some trouble or other. Not like they do today, of course, not vicious, just boy things like stealing apples and climbing trees so the firemen have to get them down again. Walker was a policeman for ten years, you know."

"Yes," said Chark. "I know. Found that out at the station. Please go on about the Lovedean boy."

"They played silly games like climbing the air raid siren tower and running in and out of that old shelter after Walker told them it was dangerous. You know what little devils boys can be."

Chark agreed.

"Joe Mishkin was Jewish," she confided.

Chark pondered the age-old question. Being Jewish made him a different kind of devil? "Let me get this straight, Mrs Walker," said

Chark. "Paul Lovedean survived the bombing. Do you know what happened to him?"

"No. Dare say he was in the hospital after the bombing. I heard he was hurt bad. I was too busy looking for Walker. Never found him." She dabbed at a tear. "They put Walker's helmet in the museum at the station and gave me his medal. The old daybook is there too. His was the last entry the day of the bombing when the police station burned."

Chark made a note to check the display case when he got back to the station.

"Is there anything more you can say about the Lovedeans?"

"No. Quiet people they were. Not regular churchgoers but always a donation envelope in the box when they did. She sometimes helped at the church fete and baked cakes for the old people at Christmas."

Chark stood up and thanked Mrs Walker. Then she let him out of the vicarage and returned to her steaming saucepans.

It was while walking back to the Old Town that Chark remembered where he had seen the name Lovedean. He turned into the churchyard and walked up to the war memorial plaque set in the church wall.

Purvis stopped cutting the grass between a row of gravestones with his oversized clippers and walked over to where Chark stood. He squinted over Chark's shoulder as he read the names on the plaque.

"Watcha lookin' for, guv?"

"Lovedean."

"There." Purvis pointed with a dirty finger and read slowly. "Capt. Charles Lovedean and his wife Mary, June 17 1941."

Chark nodded.

"There's one of they time capsules too," said Purvis. "Behind the plaque. Put there in 1946 it was. To be opened in 2046. They put all kinds of junk in it." He cackled. "If I'm still around when they open it, I'll be able to tell them what it says. You knew them? The Lovedeans?"

"No," said Chark. "But I'm beginning to."

*

It was dark in the streets and the lights were on in the police station when Chark walked in. He went straight to the display case in the interrogation room and opened the lid. He lifted out the day book that Mrs Walker had told him about and read it. Then he carefully replaced it open at the last page. He walked back into the office where Beane was sitting in front of the computer nursing a mug of coffee.

"Get me one of those, will you?" said Chark throwing his coat on the back of a chair. "I just had the worst cup of tea in my whole life over at the vicarage."

Beane grinned as he stood and poured another mug. "Never let me introduce you to my old mam up in Glasgow, Chief. She keeps a pot boiling on the cooker all day. Takes the hair off your chest."

Chark took the coffee and they sat and compared notes.

"So, what did you find out in Aldershot?"

"Nothing. Not a damned thing. Do you know how many William Browns there are in this world? Half of them were in the Hamptonshire Regiment." Beane looked tired, his hair needed cutting and a day's worth of red beard glinted in the light.

"Bad day?"

"I found an old soldier in the hospital," said Beane angrily. "Been there more than sixty years. Only nineteen when he was admitted. Fought a bloody war, gets damn near killed and nobody claimed him. Nobody!" Beane leaned forward and put his head between his hands. "He had a watch just like the one found in the shelter."

"So that's not the William Brown we're looking for," said Chark. "Anything else?"

"There was another William Brown listed as living in a farm not far from here. When I got there it was all but destroyed. The only thing left of the farm is the old house and that's been empty for decades."

"Good work," said Chark. "Get onto the county people tomorrow and see if they have anything on him. Might be some old tax records"

Beane nodded wearily and drained his coffee. "How about you, Chief?"

"Bullseye," said Chark. "His name is Captain Charles Godolphin Lovedean. Missing in action, believed killed. All the facts fit. Dates, places, everything. I'll get Dr Overton to check if there are any dental records to make sure but I think we've got the right one."

"Hey! That's good news," said Beane. "Well done, sir."

Chark stood up and motioned Beane to follow him. "And that's not all. Come look at this."

They stood at the display case.

"What am I looking at?" asked Beane. "Something in the evidence I missed?"

"No. It's not on the cabinet. It's inside." Chark lifted the lid and took out the scorched day book. "Read the last page. The last entry."

Beane traced the faded, spidery writing with his finger and gave a low whistle. He looked up at Chark, his weariness gone. "Good God, Chief. You mean this has been here all the time. We were looking right at it? How did you find it?"

"Mrs Walker tipped me off. Her husband was on duty the day of the big air raid and wrote that last entry." Chark read it again.

"*Date: June 17th 194111.45 intersepted young Lovedean in Hamm's Lanereturned him to his home. boy histericalHe reported seeing a body in the air rad shelter.*

Warned him again about playingin shelter.12.15 inspected shelter. nothing to report12.30 shift end R.Walker P.C."

"What was the exact time of the air raid," asked Chark. "When did the first bombs fall in the High Street?"

"12.32 pm, according to the Town Hall."

"So Constable Walker signed off his shift at 12.30, rode his bike out into the street and was killed by the first bomb that fell." Chark paused for a moment. "How long do you reckon it would take for a small boy to run from the air raid shelter into Hamm's Lane?"

"Not more than two or three minutes."

"Then," said Chark. "If Paul Lovedean did see a body in the shelter at about 11.40, ran into Walker at 11.45 and Walker returned to check the shelter at 12.15 and found nothing, somebody removed the body, or bodies, in those thirty minutes."

"Assuming that Walker actually went into the shelter to check," added Beane.

"Right. In which case, if he didn't and the bodies were still there, the murderer had time to bury them later."

"In the confusion of an air raid when everybody else was terrified and totally concerned with staying alive," said Beane. "He was a cool one."

"But, wouldn't there have been people in the shelter? There was an air raid warning that day"

"Not necessarily," said Beane. "According to the people at the Town Hall, the shelter was almost unused. Fairport hadn't been bombed at all until that day. People ignored the warnings."

"I think we need to talk to Mr Paul Lovedean," said Chark. "You got anything in that computer of yours about him?"

Beane shook his head. "I doubt it. But I'll look."

Back in the office, Beane scanned through the database and came up with nothing as he predicted. He switched it off and turned to Chark.

"You realise that the body he saw could have been his own father's? And nobody believed him when he said he had seen it? Then he gets trapped in a bombed building and loses his mother. Jesus Christ! Can you imagine the state of mind that kid was in?"

"And what kind of a person is Paul Lovedean today?" said Chark. "If he's still alive." He stood up and stretched his arms. "It's getting late. How about a drink at the 'Duke'? Tomorrow's going to be another busy day."

"No thanks, Chief. I'm too tired. See you at breakfast."

Chapter 16

On Thursday morning Chark bought the Eastchester Chronicle from a vending machine outside the 'Duke'. He read the front page as he walked over to the police station. There was a six-inch double column about the Fairport murders.

FAIRPORT MURDER VICTIM WAS LOCAL HERO

One of the murder victims discovered
during the demolition of a WW2 air raid
shelter in Fairport has been identified
as Captain Charles Lovedean. He commanded
the destroyer "ELSON" out of Hampton during

the war and had been officially listed as
"Missing, Believed killed in action in
June 1941"

There was a blurred, war-time photograph of Lovedean in uniform that Sam Gilkicker had found somewhere.

Chark grimaced to himself. How many beers had it taken for Sam Gilkicker to get his exclusive out of Phil Privett? He brushed past the duty sergeant and strode into Privett's office ready to do battle with his leaky friend. Instead, he found it full of constables getting a briefing .

"Come in, Dave," called an animated Privett over the heads of the seated policemen and women. "Got a lot of calls from the citizenry as a result of the article in the morning's paper." No mention of Gilkicker. "Seems like everybody in the county knew Lovedean and who killed him! We're spreading out to interview the callers."

Chark waved him to continue and opened the door to the office where Beane was already at work entering data into his computer. He looked up as Chark entered and handed him a piece of paper.

"Old Sam really stirred things up today. We got a lot of calls this morning. Mostly cranks. But this one came in for you about ten minutes ago. Says she will only speak to you."

"Ethel Jordan," said Chark. "Number fourteen School Lane. Know anything about her?"

Beane shook his head. "Could be another crank call. What do you want me to do about it?"

"Nothing. Looks like you've plenty to do. I'll see her."

Beane grunted through the pencil in his teeth and picked up another message from the pile on the desk and began to play the keyboard again.

*

Ethel Jordan's house in School Lane was in the western part of the Old Town. It was a narrow dead-end lane leading up to the rusted and sagging gates of the elementary school which occupied a plot of ground

CHARK'S BONES | 127

next to the vicarage. School Lane might have been called "quaint" by a real estate agent with imagination. Each house had a small front garden and a bay window guarded by lace curtains, some of which twitched momentarily as Chark drove by looking for number 14. He parked his car outside the house and walked up a path lined with neatly-pruned rose trees. He rang the door bell.

The door was opened by a slim, middle-aged woman dressed in a conservative white blouse and black, pleated skirt. Her brown hair was softly waved and the house smelled of lavender. She smiled at Chark.

"Yes?"

"Chief Inspector Chark, County police, ma'am. You called."

"Of course," said Mrs Jordan. "How good of you to come so quickly. Do come in." She led the way along a mosaic-tiled hallway into the living room. It was a small room with french windows opening onto a manicured garden. There was a square patch of lawn with regular, weed-free flowerbeds around the edge. A yellow cat glowered at Chark from the back of a worn sofa and in one corner, a caged bird twittered.

Mrs Jordan sat primly in a chair beside the fireplace and offered Chark the one opposite. She brushed her hair back from her face and straightened her skirt.

"You called the station this morning to say you had some information for us, Mrs Jordan?"

"Yes. I hope you won't be disappointed with my little snippet, Chief Inspector. You must be very busy over at the police station. But I felt I had to call you. Can I make you some tea?"

"That's alright, Mrs Jordan," said Chark, the memory of the vicarage tea still fresh in his mind. "I had some at the station. Please continue," Chark clicked his pencil open and prepared to write.

"Well," she started, "First, my name was Witherstone, Ethel Witherstone, back in those days. I met Captain Lovedean when I was a girl. I didn't know his name until I read it in the paper this morning and saw his photograph." She picked up the paper and showed it to Chark.

"How can you be sure it's him?"

"I wasn't completely sure until I read the name of his ship, the ELSON. Then I put two and two together. You see, he was kind to me when I met him. I was a little girl and my father was away at sea. I didn't know what was going on in the war. People tried to shield their children from the truth but that only makes things worse when you don't know what's going on. Doesn't it? When I spoke to Captain Lovedean he answered my questions as though they were important. Children remember those things very clearly. Do you have any children, Inspector?"

"Yes, a daughter. She's grown now. At the university. Please go on. Where did you meet him?"

"It was on the ferry boat from Hampton. We, that's my mother and me, had been over to get my dad's pay and I sat next to this man in a beautiful uniform with gold things on it. I think I called him an admiral and he laughed and said he was only a captain. I must have said something about my dad being away and I cried. Then he took out his wallet and gave me something. I've kept it all these years."

Ethel Jordan reached up to the mantlepiece for a polished wooden box and opened it. She took out a black silk ribbon with the words "HMS ELSON" embroidered on it in fine gold thread. It was identical to the hatband found on the body in the shelter. "Is it important?" she asked.

Chark took the hatband and carefully laid it down on the table. He studied it for a second and then looked up, smiling. "Yes, Mrs Jordan, it's very important. Did Captain Lovedean say why he gave it to you?"

"I remember clearly. He said he was going home to see his family after being at sea and had another one to give to his son as a souvenir. Said he was about my age. It was a generous gesture and I tried to refuse but he insisted."

Chark took an envelope from his pocket and carefully placed the hatband inside. "I'll have to take this as evidence but you'll get a receipt for it," he said. "I'll make sure you get it back." He sat down and leaned forward in the chair. "Now, Mrs Jordan, we come to two very important questions. Please take your time answering."

She nodded gravely.

"First, what happened after Captain Lovedean gave you the hatband?"

Mrs Jordan thought for a moment. "The ferry docked and we all got off. There was a crowd."

"Did Captain Lovedean get off with you?"

"Yes. We went to get on the bus. I don't know what he did."

"He didn't get on a bus?"

"I didn't see him again. I don't think he went to the bus stop."

"Thank you," said Chark. He looked up from his notebook. "Now the other question. Do you remember the date when all this happened?"

Mrs Jordan smiled. "That's easy, Inspector. It was the day of the big air raid on Fairport."

Chark relaxed back into the chair. "Do you remember the time of day when you came back from Hampton on the ferry?"

"Must have been morning. We always went over to Hampton in the morning to get dad's pay. Can't be more exact than that. Sorry. Have I been of any use, Inspector?"

"Yes, " said Chark. "You have, Mrs Jordan. A very great help to us. A policeman will call on you to get a written statement of all that you've told me. In the next day or two."

Chark stood and offered his hand to Mrs Jordan who took it limply.

"I'm so glad I didn't waste your time," she said.

The lace curtains along School Lane twitched again as Chark drove away from number 14. He was in a good mood as he drove back to the police station. Things were beginning to fit into place and the timing of the murders was getting clearer. No need to confront Phil Privett about his loose tongue, it had worked out just fine.

The police station was unusually tense when Chark walked in. He found Privett in his office strumming his fingers on his desk as he spoke to two uniformed constables. Privett dismissed them and stood up as Chark entered.

"What's going on, Phil?"

"Incident over at the church. I'm glad you're back."

"What's happened?"

"Purvis, the old man who takes care of the churchyard has been attacked. In the hospital. Somebody bashed him over the head."

"Purvis?" said Chark. "When did this happen?"

"This morning about eight or nine. A boy delivering papers on his route found him lying on the ground outside the church. Wasn't lying there long, according to the doctor."

"Any witnesses?"

"Not yet. My people are investigating."

"No suspects?"

"No,"

"Any suspicions?" asked Chark.

Privett shook his head. "No, can't think of any reason for it. Unless it was just random viciousness. Poor old Purvis."

"What was Purvis doing when he was attacked?" asked Chark.

"Seems he was cleaning the war memorial." Said Privett. "You know, the plaque set in the church wall. Made of bronze, I think. There was a wire brush, some rags and a tin of Brasso lying on the ground beside him." Privett loosed his tie. "Now, who in hell would want to beat up an old man like Purvis. He wasn't a very attractive old geezer and he didn't have a penny to his name or, so far as anybody knows, any enemies."

Maybe, thought Chark, but he knows a lot of what goes on in Fairport and knowledge can be a dangerous thing sometimes.

"You seen Beane?" asked Chark.

"Over at the hospital, I believe."

Chark ran up the broad, stone steps of the Fairport War memorial Hospital two at a time. Inside the marble-tiled lobby he approached the reception desk and was directed to the second floor ward where Purvis was being cared for. A uniformed policeman guarding the door recognized Chark and opened the door for him.

Purvis lay as small as a child in the hospital bed. Only his stubbly, brown chin and hairy nose showed from the mass of bandages around his head. Plastic tubes were attached to his skinny wrists and stuffed up his nose. His breathing was scarcely discernable.

Beane sat beside the bed. He turned and shook his head slowly as Chark entered. A nurse and a doctor sat at the bedside watching the electronic equipment bleep rythmically. The green-robed doctor took off his mask and walked over to Chark.

CHARK'S BONES | 131

"We've done everything we can for the moment, Inspector. There's a compression fracture on the right side of his skull and we've been able to relieve the pressure on the brain. The next few hours are critical. My guess his chances are a little better than fifty-fifty."

"Then he can't talk to us?"

"No chance. Not yet. Even if he survives, the chances are he won't remember much."

"Thanks, doctor." Chark signaled to Beane and they left quietly. Outside in the corridor, patients in institutional gowns and carpet slippers shuffled carefully along the polished floors with the aid of zimmers and walking sticks. The smell of polish and antiseptics was making Chark queasy.

"What do you make of that?" said Beane pointing back at Purvis' room. "Any connection with the Lovedean case?"

"I don't know," said Chark. "There must be one somewhere. I hate coincidences."

"And they make a mess of my database, too"

"Well," said Chark. "Since we're here, the least we can do is some medical research on young Paul Lovedean. According to Mrs Walker, he was admitted to this hospital after the bombing raid of 1941."

The windowless Medical Records Department was in the basement of the hospital. Down several flights of concrete stairs and through a steel double door. The room was lit with white fluorescent lamps and filled with racks of aging cardboard boxes stuffed with manila folders. In an open space against a green wall covered with outdated calendars was a desk, a coffee pot and a gray-haired woman in a blue nylon coverall with a plastic "volunteer" badge.

She put down her magazine as the policemen entered.

"Morning," she said "What can I do for you?"

Chark introduced himself and Beane and learned that her name was Mrs Hathaway.

"We need to dig into your records, Mrs Hathaway. Back to June 1941. Do the records go back that far?"

She pressed her hands to her bosom and pretended to be offended.

"I'll have you know, sir," she said. "My records go back as far as the day the hospital opened in 1922. If I don't have records, it didn't happen."

"Well," said Chark with a grin. "Let's test your system. Can you find a record of a Paul Lovedean? Boy about ten years old. Admitted in June 1941." Chark crossed his arms theatrically. Mrs Hathaway punched his arm in a friendly way and walked off among the racks. In a few minutes, she came back with a yellow folder in her hand.

"Ask and ye shall receive," she said triumphantly.

Chark took the folder and opened it. There were three sheets of paper with faded, typed words and signatures and a set of misty x-ray pictures. It was all there. 'Paul Godolphin Lovedean. Admitted June 18th 1941. Contusions and cuts. Multiple fractures of the left arm and wrist. Released July 10th 1941.'

"Who was he released to?" asked Beane.

"Says here to a 'Mrs Edwina Mullion. Relationship-Aunt. United States citizen. Address: Pimm's Hotel, London WC1.'"

"Damn!," said Beane. "No permanent address. That's going to make it tough to find him."

The volunteer clerk reached out for her file. "Find what you want?"

"Yes," said Chark. "Can you make a copy of it for me? Not the x-rays."

"Of course."

Chark and Beane ate lunch in the Duke while Chark brought Beane up to date on his visit with Mrs Jordan and showed him the hatband she had given him.

"We've got to find Paul Lovedean, Beane," said Chark when Beane had taken a large mouthful of bread and cheddar cheese. "If his aunt Edwina was a United States citizen, there's a good chance he went back there with her. Lots of kids did during the war."

"Big place, the States," mumbled Beane through his mouthful.

"Yes. But if young Paul went there with her, he had to have a passport, didn't he?" Chark signed the bill and stood up. "Come on, Beane. Back to work."

"What about my sandwich?"

"Bring it with you."

Back at the police station, Beane got the duty sergeant to look up the number of the Passport Office in London and place the call. When the office phone rang, Beane picked it up and made the request for information. They'd call back.

Fifteen minutes later, the phone rang again and Beane answered. This time, he pulled his notepad towards him and began writing.

"He was what?" Pause. "When was that? "Destination?" Beane put down the phone and turned to Chark. "You were right, Chief. Paul Lovedean was issued a passport on July 10th 1941. There are duplicate pictures of him in their files. They're faxing copies."

"His destination?"

"Seattle, Washington State."

*

Was Paul Lovedean still alive? Did he stay in the States with his aunt after the war? Or did he return to England? Chark paced the floor of the office and pondered his options while they waited for the fax from the Passport Office in London.

The Passport Office search for Paul Lovedean in the U.K had produced an array of Lovedeans and Godolphins but no combination of facts that remotely resembled the elusive boy from Fairport. Eastchester had searched the telephone directories in Seattle and the surrounding towns but found no Mullions or Lovedeans. Edwina Mullion may have married. Or died.

A copy of Paul's birth certificate had arrived on Chark's desk an hour after he requested it. But it only confirmed his age, place of birth and the fact that Mary Lovedean (nee Mullion) and Charles Godolphin Lovedean were his parents. Edwina Mullion had to be Mary's sister.

By mid morning on Friday, Chark was convinced that Lovedean was still in the United States. He waited impatiently for a break in the series of negatives that had, so far, frustrated him. The break came when the duty sergeant knocked on the office door and handed him a bundle of paper.

"This just came for you, sir." It was a copy of Paul Lovedean's application for a passport with two copies of his photograph. It was a small, grainy, black and white picture of a serious-looking boy with carefully-brushed fair hair, a thin face and dark circles around the eyes.

"So you're Paul Lovedean," said Chark quietly. "Glad to meet you thus. Now, where the hell are you?" He called to Beane who was in the outer office pouring coffee. "Listen to this, Beane." He read out loud. "Dated July 10th, 1941. Paul Godolphin Lovedean. Born at Fairport, Hamptonshire 1932. Height 4' 11" Weight 97 pounds. Fair hair. Blue eyes. Distinguishing marks: Scars on left hand and arm. Destination; Seattle, Washington, U.S.A."

Chark took one of the photographs and carefully slid it into his briefcase. "He's still in the States, Beane. I know it. "I'm going back to Eastchester. Time to report in."

"And leave me in Fascinating Fairport while you wallow in the carnal delights of Eastchester?" complained Beane. "You know we've been down here almost a week now?"

"Weekend's coming up. You can finish off the interviews then leave the rest to Phil Privett's people. How many more ?"

"Two or three for me to do. About the same for WPC Tufnell. She's doing all the retirement homes.

Chark nodded. "Good." To tell the truth, he was sick of the place too and that room at the 'Duke' was giving him claustrophobia. Anyway, he was down to his last clean shirt, his suit was wrinkled and he had worn the same socks for two days. Despite its country solidity, Mrs Smith's cooking, was beginning to acquire charm *in absentia.*

"While I'm in Eastchester, I'll contact the Seattle Police Department," said Chark. His determination to act and conviction that, to find Paul Lovedean, he now had to start at the American end, had given him new energy. "You can drive me over to the Hampton train station after we pick up my things at the 'Duke.'"

"Where is Seattle?" asked Beane as they walked out of the office to the car park.

Chark shook his head slowly. The decline of primary education since his days at grammar school was his pet gripe and its repetition a source of amusement around the police force. Beane, he surmised, was particularly ignorant in general knowledge. The result of too much concentration on the mysteries of computers. And just sometimes, Chark thought, Beane was a little flippant with him.

"It's in the upper left hand corner of the country," replied Chark. "It's where Boeing builds the 747."

"Oh," said Beane. "I thought they did that in California. So they can work on the planes out in the open in all that lovely sunshine."

"No, Beane," said Chark with exaggerated patience. "Seattle's a long way north of California."

"Best pack some warm clothes, Chief," said Beane with the faintest of smiles.

Back at the 'Duke', Chark took a last look around his room while Beane waited outside in the car. The dingy walls seemed to lean in on him and he longed for the comfort and space of Aurora Cottage. The waste basket had not been emptied since he moved in and had toppled over with the weight of several days' newspapers jammed into it. The bed was still unmade and wet towels hung over the door of the toilet unit.

He closed the door gratefully and hurried down the stairs to the street.

Chapter 17

Chark and Beane drove round the harbour to Hampton where they parked in the railway station yard. The fast commuter trains to Eastchester left every thirty minutes and they had just missed one so they sat drinking coffee from a vending machine while waiting for the next one.

"If you find the Lovedean boy, what do we do next?" asked Beane.

"When we find him. We talk to him."

"We? You mean I get to go to Seattle?"

"That's a royal 'we', Beane. Can you imagine Superintendent Russell popping for two tickets to the States?"

"No," said Beane with a sigh. "It was just a dream." Beane sipped his lukewarm coffee, grimaced and poured in more sugar. He stirred it up with a pair of plastic straws. "While I'm over this side of the harbour,

I'll drop by Nora Priddy's place and talk to her. That's Nora Czernowski as she is now. Just her and Ted Hoff the estate agent to see. He's back in Fairport."

"Then back to Eastchester for the weekend?" asked Chark.

"Yeah,' said Beane with a grin.

When Chark's train was called, he picked up his suitcase and shook Beane's hand. "Take care of things over in Fairport," he said. "I'll be back as soon as I can. Don't let Phil Privett get to you. He means well."

*

Beane sat in the car in the station yard while he planned his route to the last known address for Nora Czernowski. He opened the map and ran his finger along the red lines of roads leading north out of Hampton.

It took a half hour to find the suburb where she lived. Its name was Monk's Wood. Any sign of the monks or the woods had long since disappeared under a crustation of flimsy houses, single-story ware-houses and sad little shopping malls. Beane cruised the neighborhood looking for the Czernowski's house. Dirty children played ball in the streets and skinny dogs chased and yapped at his car. Paper drifted along the pavement and broken bottles littered the gutters. Beane drew up outside a flat-fronted house with peeling blue paint and checked the number on the doorpost.

There was a long-dead, wheelless car jacked up over a black smear of oil on the cracked driveway. What was left of the grass in the tiny front garden had not been cut for weeks. Beane rapped on the door with his knuckles. It was opened by an overweight woman with dyed red hair and smudged lipstick. She was dressed in a light blue house-coat with a fuzzy collar and stained cuffs. A cigarette hung from her lips. Ash fluttered to the floor as she spoke.

"Yes? What d'you want?"

"Beane offered his ID. "County police, ma'am. I'm looking for a Nora Czernowski."

Nora's hand flew to her face. "Oh, my Gawd! What's happened now?"

"Nothing wrong, Mrs Czernowski," said Beane putting his ID back in his pocket. "I just need to ask you a few questions. That's all. May I come in?"

Nora stepped out of the doorway and ground out her cigarette butt on the path. She looked up and down the street. The police were regular visitors in this neighbourhood. This one was not in uniform.

"What's it about?"

"Routine questions. About the Duke of York public house over in Fairport. You worked there during the war?"

Nora's eyes opened wide. "You mean those murders what's been on the telly and in the newspapers? I don't know nothing about that. It was years ago and I was only a girl then."

"I know. Just a few routine questions, that's all. I'm getting background information. It's been a long time."

"You'd best come in then," said Nora with a last look along the street where a few sullen children were taking an interest in Beane's car. "But I don't know nothing."

The house was dark, cold and smelled of cigarette smoke and body odour. Nora led him into the shabby front room. There was a painting of a tall, fair-haired and blue-eyed Jesus Christ hanging on one wall. An old map of Poland and yellowing photographs of laughing young men in Royal Air Force uniform standing in front of World War Two fighter airplanes hung over the fireplace.

"Your husband?" asked Beane pointing to a framed portrait of a handsome man in Air Force officer's uniform.

"Yes, that's Michael. You wouldn't recognise him from that picture now. He was shot down a week after the picture was taken. Lost an arm and one eye and got burned, too. Not much demand for a one-armed, half-blind man these days. He gets a pension and I work down at the supermarket. We manage."

Nora offered a seat.

"Where's your husband now?"

Nora stiffened and lit another cigarette. There was something about her. Maybe it was the eyes. A faint glimmer of youth and brightness behind that tough, worn exterior.

"He's down at the Dom Polski," she said after a pause. "Plays darts and drinks vodka with the other old warriors. It's their way of saying "We're sorry we lived and you had to die". Not many survived, you know. Crazy Polaks. He'll be back for his tea shortly" Nora drew deeply on her cigarette. "Now, what were those questions?"

Beane opened his notebook. "Your name was Nora Priddy when you worked at the Duke during the early part of the war. Right?"

"Yes."

"You were there in June of 1941?"

"That's right. I used to help out with the food and serve drinks sometimes when they were real busy." She brushed away a black cat that had jumped on her lap mewing for attention.

"What can you tell me about the morning of the air raid? That was on June 17th."

"I know what the date was. I was working at the 'Duke' that morning. Had to help Charley Frater with the beer pumps. It was his job to make sure the barrels were changed when they got empty. Pipes had to be flushed out regular. Hard work it was, too."

"What time did you get there?"

"Probably about eleven or twelve. Can't be sure after all this time."

"Was Charley Frater there when you got there?"

"Yes, down in the cellar," said Nora letting a curl of smoke drift upwards from her nose. "He was always at work early in the morning. He slept down there. His old mother was a real tartar. Dominated him something awful."

"What was he doing when you got there that morning?"

Nora thought for a moment. "I forget. All I remember is him looking up at me in that creepy kind of way he had when I went down the stairs to the cellar. Then there was an almighty loud noise. Took my breath away and I couldn't breath for ever such a long time."

"The bomb blast collapsed your lungs," said Beane.

"I suppose so. I remember it hurt real bad and there was a lot of dust. Then I was upstairs in the bar and the wall was gone. Somebody must have carried me up there." Nora's face took on a softer, older look. "Those poor people. It was horrible. All those people."

Beane pretended to write as she regained her composure. "So, you don't know how long Charley was in the cellar before you arrived that morning? Or even if he left it before the air raid?"

"No, I suppose not. He was in the cellar when the bombs dropped. I'm sure of that."

Charley Frater was beginning to interest Beane. He leaned back in the hard chair and tried to shift to a more comfortable position. "Tell me about Charley."

"Not much to tell, really," said Nora thoughtfully. "He was a loner. I think he supported his mother on his wages and the tips he got. His wages was real small, him being only the pot boy. We girls used to slip him a few shillings when business was good and the soldiers gave him something when they felt extra generous. I think he fancied me in those days but he used to look at me like I was a specimen in a bottle."

"Did you see him after the bombing?" asked Beane.

"Yes. A bit later. He got a job in the dockyard keeping records of some kind. They said he was good at figures." Nora shook her head in mock disbelief and laughed unkindly before continuing. "I met him in the grocers in the High Street. And you know what? He asked me to marry him. Right there in the shop in front of everybody. I just laughed at him. Thought he was kidding me. Then he went real quiet and said that one day I'd be sorry I turned him down. Kinda scary. Then he walked off and I never saw him again."

Nora lit up again and Beane could hear the ticking of an alarm clock through the thin walls. "You have any idea what happened to him?"

"They said he went abroad. Years later, he came back and took over the old 'Duke'. I was married to Michael by then and had the kids."

"So you married Michael when?"

"1943. June 27th. Met him at a dance at the air base. He was shot down in 1944."

"You said you had family."

"Four. Why?"

"Just routine. Fills in the blanks in the report."

"Two boys and two girls. The girls write but the boys don't any more. Michael spends most of his time down at the Dom Polski now. It's not like the war. We all had fun then. At least, some of the time." Nora looked up at the young faces in the photographs and smiled faintly. "They were full of hate when they flew. Real lovers on the ground. You know that, when they ran out of ammunition, some of them tried to chase the Germans down and ram them?"

"Heard about that," said Beane. "You ever hear of the Lovedeans?"

Nora screwed up her eyes. "Sounds familiar. They from Fairport?"

"Yes," said Beane. "Family lived close to the 'Duke' when you were there."

"Oh, yeah. I remember. They got killed didn't they?"

Beane nodded. "You hear what happened to the boy, Paul Lovedean?"

Nora thought for a moment. "No, can't say as I did. Why?"

"We're trying to find him." Beane looked at his watch and stood up. "Thanks, Mrs Czernowski. You've been a great help. There might be more questions later, OK?"

Nora heaved herself out of her chair and led the way to the front door. "Next time you can call me Nora." She opened the front door and looked both ways along the street as Beane got back into his car. As he pulled away from the curb, Nora went into the kitchen and poured herself a large gin.

Beane left Monk's Wood and drove the motorway around Hampton Harbour towards Fairport. He took the exit to the Harbour Marina where he bought a cup of coffee and a sandwich at the restaurant and settled down into a booth to put his notes together. There were two more names on his list; Ted Hoff and Charley Frater. He knew where to find Charley, he'd be at the 'Duke' all day. Ted Hoff was likely to be out and about the town on business. He used the payphone in the lobby and called his office.

"Mr Hoff's office," trilled his secretary.

"Mr Hoff there? This is sergeant Beane, CID. County police."

There was a long pause during which Beane could hear a muffled conversation.

"I'm sorry, sir," she said with a little audible smirk. "Mr Hoff is not available right now. Can I take a message?"

"Yes," said Beane. "You tell Mr Hoff I called. Police business. I'll be there in twenty minutes. Tell him to be there." Beane hung up and finished his sandwich and coffee. Then he paid his bill and walked leisurely back to his car. He would make Ted Hoff sweat a little. The pompous little shit.

Beane parked behind the cream Jaguar outside Hoff's building forty minutes later. He walked past the secretary's cubicle and pushed open the door to Hoff's office. Hoff was seated at his desk pouring a large measure of a single malt scotch into a cup of tea.

"Join me? Sun's over the yardarm."

Beane shook his head. Only an Englishman would treat a fine scotch that way.

"I was forgetting," said Hoff. "This is police business. You're late." His face was damp and blotchy and the scotch bottle was three quarters empty.

"Where were you between six and nine o'clock this morning?"

Hoff stared at Beane through watery eyes. "The locals already asked me that. Thought you were working on the air raid shelter murders."

"Answer the question. Please."

"OK," said Hoff. I was in bed 'til seven thirty. Had my breakfast and walked to the office at nine. My wife and secretary will confirm it."

"You walked?"

"Yes. It's only a mile from home and I needed the exercise. My wife took the Jag over to Hampton for shopping. She came back this afternoon. Anything else?"

"Did you walk through the churchyard on your way here?"

"Yes," said Hoff suspiciously. "But I didn't hit old Purvis. Why would I? I told Privett's people that too. They believed me." He poured more scotch in his cup. "You want some?" His voice was slurred. Beane switched the subject.

"Where were you between the hours of ten o'clock and twelve o'clock on the morning of June 17th 1941?"

"Christ Almighty!" gasped Hoff splashing tea down his shirt. "I didn't kill them either. Why would I?" Fear widened his eyes and he shrank back in his chair. Beane leaned over the desk on his knuckles and pressed home his advantage. This was going very nicely. Police College stuff.

"I didn't say you did, Mr Hoff. But to answer the question you only have to remember it was the morning of the big air raid on Fairport. You were in town that day were you not?"

"Yes, I think so."

"In the shelter counting your black market cigarettes and silk stockings? Were the victims dissatisfied customers or something?"

Hoff went pale. "No, no. I told you before, I never met them. I swear." His face sagged and he turned away. His voice softened to a whine. "Look, I did my time in jug for the black marketing. Two years without remission. I did store the stuff in the shelter." He looked up at Beane pleading. "If this gets out among my clients, I'm as good as done for in this business. I didn't kill them, honest."

"Where were you that morning, exactly?" continued Beane.

"Working." Hoff spat the word out and took a swig at his tea. "Why don't you sit down for Christ's sake? You're making me nervous."

"Where were you working, Hoff?" Beane was smiling.

Hoff retreated deeper into his chair. "At the radar site down on the marshes. We were putting roofs on some barracks. You can still see the concrete foundations."

"We?"

"Me and two labourers and some army people."

"Did you leave the site at any time that morning?"

"Yes, damn it, I did," said Hoff petulantly.

"What for?"

"Because I needed a bloody drink at the 'Duke', that's what for. It was hard work. You got any more damn fool questions?" Hoff was becoming angry. Good.

"What time did you get to the 'Duke'?"

Hoff was shouting now. "I didn't. The bloody air raid started just as I reached the south side of the horse pasture."

"Did you go to the shelter?" There was a long pause before Hoff answered in a little, distant voice.

"No, I did not. When the bombs fell I ran back to the radar site. I was scared shitless if you must know." He reached for his bottle. "Satisfied now?"

"Did you see anybody in the horse pasture or near the shelter?" asked Beane.

"No."

"Sure?"

"No. I can't remember. Leave me alone, you bastard!" The last vestige of Hoff's composure vanished. "I didn't kill nobody." The words were a whisper now and tears filled his bloodshot eyes as he slid lower into his oversized chair.

"I didn't say you did, Mr Hoff," said Beane as he stood back from the desk. "But if you think of something we might be interested in, you'll let us know won't you?" He opened the door. "We'll talk again, soon."

The sun was setting and the High Street lights were flickering as Beane opened the door of the 'Duke'. The last of the afternoon customers had left and the chairs were stacked on the tables ready for the cleaners to sweep the floors. Charley Frater looked up from the till.

"You want a beer?"

Beane nodded and took a cold boiled egg from the bowl on the counter. "You got a few minutes, Charley? Need to ask you some questions."

"What about? I need to get ready for the evening business."

"Yeah, I know. We can do it now or over at the station tomorrow. Please yourself."

Charley tore off the long strip of paper from the till and started washing glasses in the sink behind the bar.

"What do you want, copper?" There was a coldness about Charley.

He was a gray man approaching seventy. Gray hair, gray eyes, gray skin. His open-necked shirt was nearer gray than white.

"Where were you between six and nine this morning?"

"Ask Mr Privett over at the station. I already told him."

"I'm asking you.""I was where I always am at that time of the morning."

"Where's that?"

"Here in the 'Duke'. I work here. I live here". Charley held up a glass and peered through it looking for water spots. He hung it on the rack above the counter.

"So you didn't leave the Duke all day?"

"That's right," said Charley. "Except to pick up the bread from the bakery. Took about fifteen minutes. You can ask the baker." He turned away from the bar and dusted the liquor bottles with a damp rag. Their eyes met in the mirror.

"Did you go into the churchyard?"

"No. And I didn't bash the old geezer over the head either. What do I care about old Purvis? Never did nothing to me." Charley turned, flipped the wet cloth straight and hung it over the beer pumps to dry. "Now. If you're through, I've got things to do around here." He leaned over the bar on hairy arms as Beane took another egg and peeled it slowly.

"Nice pub the 'Duke'," said Beane. "Must have cost you a bundle."

Charley hesitated for a moment before answering. He spoke quietly and Beane sensed his effort to control himself. "Yes, I did. You can find out how much I paid for it by checking at the Town Hall."

"Already did."

"Paid for it in cash," said Charley with a mixture of venom and pride. "Cash I earned in Canada by working and saving and scrimping for a lot of years so I could come back here and buy the Duke. But you already knew that too, didn't you, sergeant?"

Beane nodded. "The Toronto police were very helpful. Got the fax this morning. Seems you were in the insurance business."

"That's right. Insurance."

"They say you sold insurance against broken arms and legs."

"I sold all kinds of insurance," said Charley with a sneer. "Legitimate business. Nobody proved otherwise."

"You must have liked the Duke a lot to come back from Canada to buy it," said Beane.

Charley's face contorted into a narrowed-eyed look of hate and spite. "You're wrong, copper," he hissed. "Cleaning urinals and washing rancid beer mugs for a crowd of beer-swilling drunks was not my idea of a life's career." He rolled down his shirtsleeves and buttoned the cuffs. "Now I got my own pot-boy. Pays him regular wages."

"Then why come back to Fairport and to the 'Duke' of all places if you hated it here?"

"To show these small-town hicks that I am as good as they are."

Charley covered the bowl of eggs with a towel. "Anything more?"

"Yes," said Beane. "You remember the big air raid on Fairport back in forty one?"

"Yes, of course. Why?"

"Where, exactly, were you that morning?"

"In the Duke. Down in the cellar, working"

"All morning?"

"Most of it."

"You have a good memory. It was a long time ago."

"Some things you never forget."

"What were you doing?"

"Usual chores. Changing barrels, flushing pipes stacking the bottled beer."

"Anybody with you?" asked Beane.

"You know there was. That's why you're here. Nora Priddy was there. She came in later in the morning."

For a minute Beane and Charley looked at each other. Charley poured himself a glass of water and sipped on it.

"That all?" asked Charley.

"You were fond of Nora?"

Silence. Beane could almost feel sorry for this bitter, emotionally-stunted little man.

"She was just like all the others," said Charley. "Used to make fun of me. I warned her about going around with soldiers but she didn't listen." He gave a little humourless laugh. "Wound up marrying a Pole and had a housefull of kids."

"Four," said Beane. "So you kept in touch?"

"No, but gossip spreads fast around here. 'Specially in the bar."

"Was it you who carried Nora up from the cellar after the bombs fell?"

"Yes. You been asking her about that?"

"Saw her today. Got her side of the story. She doesn't remember much except the dust and noise. She believes it was you that got her out. She sounded grateful."

"Well now, how about that?" said Charley with the faintest of smiles.

"What happened to you after the bombing?" asked Beane. "There wasn't much left of the town as you knew it."

"Called up into the army. Discharged after six months. Underweight. Got myself a job in the dockyard. It lasted until the end of the war. Then I was laid off and went on the welfare."

"How come you went to Canada?"

Charley's eyes narrowed and he half-turned to leave. "You keep on about Canada. You got something you want to know, ask me. I got nothing to hide."

Beane looked at him for a moment and waited.

"My old mother died," continued Charley. "God rest her poor old bones. Then they took back the cottage, the miserable socialist bastards. Tried to put me in one of them concrete chicken coops they call council flats. They were offering British immigrants passages to Canada for ten pounds so I took a chance and signed up. I had nobody here"

Charley switched off the bar lights and picked up his jacket. "Now. If there's no more questions, I want to rest up before the evening rush."

Beane followed him out through the darkened bar. Without a word, Charley climbed the stairs and was gone.

It was late when Beane finished entering the day's interview notes into his computer. He walked down to a fast food restaurant and bought a hamburger. Then he watched television for an hour and lay on the bed listening to the rumble of noise down in the bar. Tomorrow he would be home in Eastchester. He fell asleep and dreamed of old soldiers, mutilated airmen, embittered old men and the sad women of a forgotten age.

Chapter 18

The electric commuter train between the South Coast and London was fast and quiet. Chark walked out of the Eastchester station in the early afternoon, got into a waiting taxi and was in his office in minutes.

Mrs Godfrey bustled in with sweet, hot coffee and cream crackers."Good afternoon, Chief Inspector. How was it down in Fairport?"

"They don't make coffee like yours, Mrs Godfrey."

She smiled and pointed to his in-tray. "I've sorted out the routine stuff and given it to Inspector Lee."

"Then what's all this?" said Chark pointing to the stacked in-tray.

"That's for your personal attention, sir."

Chark stared at it with distaste and handed the tray back to her. "Give this to Lee, too. I won't be staying long."

Mrs Godfrey gave a resigned shrug of her shoulders. "Will that be all, sir?"

"No. Please call the Superintendent's office and make an appointment for me to see him as soon as possible."

Mrs Godfrey sighed again and closed the door behind her.

Chark looked out of the window at the familiar rooftops. Only a few days earlier he had disliked the confining walls of his office almost as much as he had grown to hate that little hotel room down in Fairport. Now it felt positively homey. He picked up the phone and pressed the long-distance digit. In a few minutes he was speaking to someone in the Seattle police department. The voice was slow and deep."Lieutenant Larson. Can I help you?"

Chark introduced himself and explained his need to speak to Paul Lovedean.

"How long ago did all this happen?" asked Larson. "Forty years?"

"I know it's a long shot," said Chark apologetically. "But, if Mr Lovedean is still alive he's our only material witness." There was a brief silence at the other end of the line and Chark could hear someone talking in the background.

Larson came back on the line. "OK, Chief Inspector," he said. "We'll give it a try. It's eight in the morning here here. What do you say I call you back at eight o'clock this evening our time? Give me your number."

Quick calculation. Eight o'clock Seattle time, four in the morning in Eastchester.

"I'll be waiting," said Chark. "Thanks for your help."

Chark pushed open the door to Chief Superintendent Francis Makepiece Russell's office and was waved through into the inner sanctum by his secretary. It was Friday but Russell had his Monday morning face on. Tight, shiny pink skin with little beads of sweat on his forehead. He was decidedly overweight and nearly bald with strands of white hair plastered over his skull. His shirt collar and tightly-knotted tie seemed to be strangling him. Acid white wine and too much fatty food, by the look of him.

"Ah, Chark," he grunted as Chark walked in and took a seat. "How much longer do you need down in Fairport? Got a damn lot of work here that needs your attention." Russell dropped his rimless glasses down his nose and looked over the top of them at Chark.

"You've read the reports, sir?" asked Chark.

"Yes,"

"We may have a material witness. Man named Lovedean."

"The devil you have!" roared Russell leaning back in his leather-covered chair. "A witness, no less. Well done, Chark. Well done. Questioned him yet?"

"No, sir. Not yet."

"What are you waiting for?"

"We believe he lives in the States. Seattle to be precise." Chark pulled a file from his briefcase and started to open it. Russell waved it away.

"You believe? You don't know?"

"The Seattle police department is helping. They'll call back tonight."

"Tell me about his involvement," said Russell. "Briefly, Chark. Briefly." Chark explained.

"Can we get his deposition by phone or fax?" asked Russell.

"It's a bit delicate, sir. I'd rather talk to him personally. As you know from our reports, there were two bodies. The one he saw may have been his father."

Russell was silent for a while. "Yes, yes of course. I see what you mean. So you want to be off to Seattle?"

"Yes. As soon as Seattle confirm that Lovedean is still living there."

"How long?"

"Three, four days at the most. Beane can handle things down in Fairport."

Russell chuckled to himself and picked up the phone. "A material witness, eh? Just wait 'til the Chief Constable hears about this...Hullo? Travel? Superintendent Russell. Chief Inspector Chark needs travel documents. Usual arrangements please. My budget."

Russell put the phone down and reached out to shake Chark's hand. "Good work, Chark."

*

Back at Aurora Cottage, Chark dumped his laundry in the hamper and took a long, leisurely bath. Then he checked the refrigerator. Mrs Smith had left the usual stock of eggs, bacon, cheese and frozen bread. There was some limp lettuce and three sad tomatoes. He made a Dagwood sandwich, poured a generous scotch and water and settled down in a comfortable chair to watch TV and wait for the call from Seattle.

The telephone woke Chark at a few minutes after two in the morning. He fumbled for the handset. "Chark."

"Lt. Larson here. Seattle P.D. We've located your Paul Lovedean for you. Lives on one of the islands in Puget Sound".

Chark was immediately wide awake. He clamped the phone to his ear with a shoulder and reached out to turn off the flickering TV. "Can you arrange a meeting for me?"

"I can try," said Larson. "When will you be here?"

"I'll catch the next British Airways flight. Leaves this afternoon." Chark looked at his watch. "Gets in at four thirty your time."

"We'll have someone meet you at the airport. Have a good flight," said Larson. "And by the way, we had a little difficulty finding him because he's changed his name. Had to go to Immigration and Naturalization to find the records. Goes by Mullion now. Thought you ought to know."

Chark thanked Larson and hung up. Mullion. Of course. Should have thought of that. Natural enough he should become a citizen and take his aunt's name.

Chark rechecked his flight schedule in the packet containing his passport and tickets. Then he repacked his suitcase and went to bed to get a few more hours of sleep before leaving for the airport.

Chapter 19

At Heathrow Chark used his American Express card to upgrade his coach class ticket to first class and checked in. He waited in the lounge for his flight to be called and then spent the nine hour flight reading, dozing, watching the movie, sipping champagne and having an excellent dinner.

He slept after dinner and woke as the British Airways 747 broke through the clouds over the lakes and forests around Seattle

The plane passed over Lake Washington and descended low over a golf course. The wheels scuffed the runway with squeal and the captain was on the address system welcoming his passengers to Seattle-Tacoma International Airport "where it is slightly overcast and the temperature is sixty degrees".

After the crowded, noisy inconvenience of Heathrow, Seattle-

Tacoma Airport had an airy, casual air about it. Chark joined the line at Immigration.

"What's the purpose of your visit to the United States, Mr Chark?" asked the officer at the desk.

"Business."

"You with Boeing?"

"No, police business."

"Oh, really?" said the officer with raised eyebrows. "An English cop. We don't get many through here." He stamped Chark's passport and handed back to him. "Welcome to Seattle, sir. Have a good visit."

Chark collected his bag from the carousel and walked through the "Nothing to Declare" gate. People pressed against the barrier in the arrivals hall. Children ran forward to embrace elderly relatives, hands were being shaken and cries of welcome rang out.

He dropped his bag to the floor and stood looking around. A man wearing a brown sport coat and gray slacks attracted his attention by raising a card with 'Chark?' printed on it in large capitals. He looked at Chark and pointed to his card questioningly. When Chark acknowledged him he stepped forward and held out his hand.

"Chief Inspector Chark?"

"That's me."

"Welcome to Seattle, sir. Name's Larson. Lt Dale Larson. We spoke on the phone earlier. Got a car waiting outside. Hope I spelled your name right? Chief wants to meet you as soon as you get in. That convenient?"

Chark nodded and Larson picked up his bag and led the way out of the terminal to the car park.

Lt Larson was a broad man with thick, black wavy hair and a round face with bright blue eyes. He carried Chark's suitcase as though it weighed nothing.

On the way up the Interstate 5 freeway towards Seattle, Larson made small talk about Chark's flight and pointed out the sports stadia and the busy waterfront where containers were being unloaded. Chark asked him about Paul Lovedean. What did he do? Was he married? Any children? But Larson either didn't know or was being evasive.

"Sorry, sir. All I did was find him. I know nothing of his personal life. You'll have to ask Chief Narvik about that."

The evasion about Lovedean rang a little alarm bell in Chark's mind. He would have to be careful.

Larson parked the car in the underground police garage and escorted Chark in the elevator up to Narvik's office. He introduced him and left.

It was a corner office with a view over Elliott Bay and Puget Sound. Police Chief Stephan Narvik rose from his desk and extended his hand. He was a tall, angular man with thinning, blond hair and deep blue, eyes. He wore a dark gray suit with a white shirt.

"Welcome to Seattle, Chief Inspector. Have a good flight over?" Chark had answered that question several times now and was beginning to feel very welcome to Seattle.

Narvik motioned him to a chair and offered coffee from a vacuum jug. Somehow, Narvik seemed uneasy. Chark drank strong coffee as he waited for the reason to emerge. They slipped into the inevitable small talk about police work and the differences between British and American procedures. After a while they dropped the formality and used first names.

"You're wondering why I asked to see you as soon as you arrived, David." Chark nodded. "Perhaps you should come over here and look at this. It will explain things better than I can."

Intrigued, Chark got up and joined him at the window. Narvik waved a finger along the view."You see all those high-rise buildings and bridges and things? Most of them have been built in the last twenty or thirty years. A good portion of them have been built by the Mullion Corporation."

Chark began to understand. "And Edwina Mullion owns the Mullion Corporation?"

"You got it. Your Paul Lovedean is a pricipal stockholder, president and chief workaholic. You know Mrs Mullion?"

"No. Her name came up in the investigation. It was she who brought

Paul to the States in 1941." Chark thought for a moment. "Did Edwina never marry?"

Narvik nodded. "She did but it didn't last long. After Paul finished college in Vancouver he was groomed to take over the Mullion business. He changed his name. They've been very successful. Lot of city and state contracts went to Mullions."

"And," continued Chark, "You want me to remember that I have absolutely no jurisdiction here and to be careful not to antagonise or otherwise inconvenience Mrs Mullion or Paul?"

Narvik grinned and relaxed. "Yes. The Mullions are a powerful force in this town." They sat down again and Narvik offered more coffee. "Now tell me in a hundred words or less about your case."

Chark described most of the events leading up to his visit to Seattle and the reasons for wanting to talk to Paul Lovedean. When he was through, Narvik gave an admiring laugh.

"Quite a story, David. We've got one or two unsolved murders in this town but I don't think any of them are forty years old. At least, not to my knowledge."

"Then I can rely on your help?"

"Of course. Within my ability. In fact, I've made an appointment for you to see Edwina Mullion tomorrow. Larson will pick you up at your hotel at ten. He's assigned to you while you are here."

*

The Pembroke Hotel overlooks Lake Union on the north side of downtown Seattle. Chark leaned over the railing of the narrow patio of his sixth floor room and watched the colourful crowds walking among the restaurants and shops that line the shore among the marinas and shipyards. In the evening sunlight Seattle was bathed in pastel colours. Like the south of France. A beautiful city. Across the lake, the lights of the condominiums on the side of Queen Anne Hill twinkled in the clear evening air and were reflected in the still water of the lake. Chark was tempted to find a seafood restaurant down there but jet lag had drained his energy and he chose his bed instead.

*

Edwina Mullion lived in the penthouse of a block of condominiums above the Pike Place Market and overlooking Elliott Bay. To get to it, Chark had to take two elevators and pass an armed security guard at the tenth floor lobby. The door was opened by a butler dressed in a black suit and a white, collarless shirt. Edwina was dressed in a white, very thick, toweling robe. She sat in a leather chair surrounded by newspapers and books.

It was large room full of light from a wall of windows looking out over the bay towards Alki Point. Outside the window, on a red brick patio big enough to play basketball on, rhododendrons and azaleas grew in terracotta pots. There was a steaming hot tub with a gazebo. The condominium was not what Chark expected. The walls were hung with bright, modern paintings and impressionist works. Pissaro, Degas, Monet, Yamagata and Delacroix were mixed with cubist and art-deco. The furniture sparkled with white leather, glass and tile.

Edwina rose stiffly from her chair with the aid of a stick and held out her hand to Chark. Her fingers were fragile and deformed by arthritis. Her heavy gold ring hung loosely. He took the hand gently and returned it. She was a short woman, thin with old age and with thick gray hair. But her eyes were dark and inquisitive.

"Good morning, Chief Inspector."

"Good morning, Mrs Mullion. Thank you for seeing me at such short notice."

She motioned Chark to a seat and lowered herself back into her chair. "I think I'll call you Mr Chark if you don't mind. Chief Inspector Chark is such a mouthfull, don't you think?"

"Yes," said Chark. "That would be nice."

Without a word, the butler entered and placed a tray with a silver coffee pot and chocolate cookies on the table beside Edwina. He poured a cup for each of them. Edwina watched Chark's eyes flick around the room.

"You like my little apartment?"

"It's wonderful," said Chark. "Such a view."

"I'm lucky. All made possible by my nephew Paul," she said with a smile. "He's the one you really came to see isn't he?"

"Yes," admitted Chark. "I need to talk to him about something which happened a long time ago in his childhood. During World War Two."

"That was a long time ago."

"It happened about the time of the air raid on Fairport. When he was hurt and his parents were killed and you went down to bring him back to the States with you."

Edwina looked intently at Chark for a while as she sipped on her coffee.

"That's why I wanted to see you first," said Edwina. "Before you talk to Paul. He will see you, of course. In fact, you have an appointment this afternoon. But you must be forewarned about Paul. He still suffers from the trauma of those days in Fairport. It's not generally understood that the children of those war years underwent extraordinary stress. There are fancy names for it nowadays. Post Traumatic Stress I think they call it. In their later years, the children still have an array of psychological problems which are manifested in all kinds of ways. In Paul's case, he has great difficulty with personal relationships." Edwina stopped for a while and looked out of the window at the clearing sky over the Bay. "I'm afraid that dredging up the memories of those days will set him back. He's been married twice and divorced twice. Has no real close friends."

"Except you," said Chark.

Edwina nodded. "Except me. The converse of all this is that he has tremendous powers of concentration and works too hard and too long. It's his way of blocking out the past. You see the results all around you. Mullions is a very successful company." She turned her attention to the coffee pot and refilled their cups.

Chark got the message.

The conversation turned trivial after that and when the butler reappeared, Edwina Mullion extended her hand. "You must excuse me now, Mr Chark. I have more appointments this morning."

Chark took the delicate hand again. "Thank you for talking to me."

Lt. Larson was waiting in the restaurant on the first floor of the building when Chark stepped out of the elevator.

"How'd it go?"

"Alright, "said Chark. "But I got the word to go easy on him. Don't upset the great man."

"Glad it's your problem, sir," said Larsen downing the dregs of his coffee. "Chief Narvik told me to take you there and bring you back. I'm not to sit in on the interview under any circumstance." He looked at his watch. "Just got time to make the next ferry."

The ferry terminal was a few blocks south on the waterfront. Larson bought a ticket at the pay booth and joined the line of trucks and cars which were headed for Bainbridge Island. With a deep-throated hoot of its horn the ferry slowly moved away from the dock

The appointment with Paul Lovedean was for one o'clock. They had plenty of time to reach the address in Chark's notebook. Once aboard the ferry, they left the car on the lower deck and climbed the stairs to the passenger deck. Larsen bought coffee and doughnuts at the concession counter and they sat looking out at the sparkling water of Puget Sound. It was one of those days that Seattleites love to brag about. The snow-topped Olympic mountains had "popped up" above the clouds and everything looked fresh and green as though washed by the rain and dried in the sun.

Larson drove off the ferry at the Winslow dock and headed north up the tree-lined highway to where the map said they would find the Mullion Estate. Chark referred to the map several times as they searched for the exit from the highway and Larsen had to double back twice but they eventually found a carved wooden sign reading simply "Mullion" pointing down a narrow road running west towards the sea. They stopped at a massive wrought iron gate set in a brick wall. Larson pressed a button and spoke into a metal grille. A tinny voice greeted them from somewhere inside the wall.

"Your name, please."

"Lt Larson. Seattle P.D. and Chief Inspector Chark from England. We have an appointment with Mr Paul Mullion."

There was no reply but the gate swung open with a gentle hum of an electric motor and they drove through into the landscaped grounds. Asian gardeners wearing wide-brimmed hats were watering and weeding the flowerbeds in the sunshine. Another rode a tractor cutting acres of bright green grass.

As they moved slowly along the asphalt driveway towards the house, a white Mercedes convertible turned a bend in front of them. Driven too fast by a young man wearing wraparound dark glasses and a multi-coloured windcheater. Larson braked and pulled sharply off the drive as the car swept past them.

"Sonofabitch! He nearly hit us!" yelled Larson as he pulled back onto the asphalt. He left deep wheel grooves and several mashed rose trees in the soft earth of a flowerbed. The Mercedes disappeared through the gate they had just entered.

The Mullion house was long, low and startlingly white. It had a many-angled roofline and big bay windows. A backdrop of tall evergreens waved gently in the breeze off the water. In the west, beyond the Sound, the snow-draped Olympic mountains shone pink in the morning sunlight. Larson parked the car outside a four-car garage between a dark green Jaguar and a midnight blue Mercedes sedan.

"I'll wait for you here, Inspector. Got a book to read and the radio to listen to. Take your time."

Chark walked up to the large double-entry door and looked around for a bell push. By the time he found it, the door was already opened by a tall, thin woman. She was dressed in a black business suit, black Italian shoes, a white silk blouse and a polkadot scarf masquerading as a tie. Her straight black hair was smoothed severely back from her dark face. A beautiful woman who had watched him in her little TV set somewhere inside as he approached the door and fumbled for the bell. He held out a business card.

"Chief Inspector Chark. I have an appointment with Mr Mullion."

She nodded and stepped back to let him in. "Good morning, Chief Inspector." The voice was soft and well-modulated. Confident. "I'm Prudence Whitehorse, Mr Mullion's administrative assistant. Will you follow me, please?" As they walked through the airy, carpeted rooms of the house, she glanced at her wristwatch and notebook.

"Mr Mullion has another appointment in an hour and a half, sir."

Hello and goodbye don't mess with my schedule. Chark dutifully followed her into a large, thickly-carpeted room where three bay windows looked out onto the front lawn. Sunlight poured into the room from skylights high up in the vaulted ceiling. A tanned man dressed in light brown slacks and a green casual shirt was practicing his short game with a putter on the carpeted floor. He was shorter than Chark and a little overweight. Hair approaching silver white and broad shoulders. His face was round and strong with deep lines from nose to the corner of the mouth. Prudence Whitehorse had vanished.

A golf ball curved across the white carpet towards Chark and he moved to avoid it.

"Look out for the lumps in the carpet," called out Paul Mullion as he approached with his hand out. His handshake was firm and brief. "I put golf balls underneath the carpet to add some spice to it. Makes it more realistic. Name's Mullion, Mr Chark. Paul Mullion. Or rather, Lovedean, if you prefer. Aunt Edwina called so I know a little about you."

The eyes were Edwina's, dark and penetrating. Paul Lovedean peeled off his golf glove and dropped it with the putter on the floor.

"I've been expecting you. Must say I am curious to know why a policeman from England would come all the way out here to see me." He waved Chark to a seat in one of the bay windows and sat oppposite him. "We'll have some drinks in a moment."

There was a residual Englishness in the voice. Sharper consonants. But Paul Lovedean exhibited none of the other characteristics of the people in the English town he had left so hurriedly as a boy. Chark studied him carefully as they made small, introductory talk. Chark paid particular to shoes. During his days as a beat cop in the London streets he had learned from the street vendors and petty criminals how to to distinguish the tourists from the natives by the style and quality of their footware. How to tell a German by his heavy-soled walking shoes, the Frenchman by leather shoes as delicate as dancing pumps and the Americans by their laceless slipons and heavy, wingtip brogues. Paul Lovedean's shoes were custom-made in New York or London.

"On the way in we had a problem with someone in a Mercedes and ran over some of your rose bushes," said Chark. "I'll be glad to pay for their replacement."

Lovedean dismissed his offer with a wave of his hand. "It's nothing. You had an encounter with my oldest son, I suspect. First wife's child. Lousy driver. Comes around once in a while. Doesn't stay long."

"It's good that your children live close by."

"No," said Lovedean sadly. "He lives in Los Angeles. The only reason he comes here is for money."

Paul stood up and opened a cabinet full of bottles and glasses. He gestured to Chark. "Scotch? gin?"

"Scotch for me," said Chark. "A small one with a little water."

Paul handed Chark a full Waterford glass and they sat beneath a window in deep leather chairs. 'Small' was a different dimension to Paul Lovedean.

"Now, Chief Inspector, what can I help you with?"

"You are Paul Godolphin Lovedean, formerly of Fairport, England?" asked Chark feeling slightly foolish with the formality.

"Yes," said Lovedean. "Although, as you are aware, I changed my name to Mullion when I became a U.S. citizen many years ago."

"Yes," said Chark. "I'll try to remember." He paused. "There are two reasons for my coming here. First, to tell you that your father's body has been found and identified."

Lovedean's face became still. He held his glass motionless between his lips. He appeared to stop breathing. "Found?" He repeated. "How can that be? His ship blew up and his body was burned in 1941."

"No," said Chark. "I'm afraid that's not so. His ship did burn and many of the crew with it. But your father had already left the ship and was on his way home when he died."

"My God! Where was he found?"

"In the horse pasture behind the Duke of York public house in Fairport."

"But that's very nearly at the house where we lived!"

"True," said Chark. He slowly and carefully described how the bodies were uncovered. "The second thing I have to tell you is that it has been determined that he was murdered."

"Murdered," whispered Lovedean. "By whom?"

"We don't know. Yet."

"But who would murder my father? He was a gentle man. A man without an enemy. Unless it was a German submarine captain. What possible motive was there?" Lovedean rose and walked over to the cabinet and poured two more drinks. He gave one to Chark and drank deeply from the other before looking at him again.

"Motive? Robbery?"

"No motive that we can determine," said Chark.

"Not robbery?""No. There was money found on both bodies."

"There was another one?"

"Yes."

"Who?"

"We don't know. A soldier, we think."

As the news sank in, Lovedean's face reflected shock and disbelief followed by anger. His colour changed from brown to mottled red as he sat drinking. He looked up after a while and studied Chark.

"If I show less than the expected grief, Chief Inspector it's because I'm more angry than sad. Relieved, too, I suppose. You know how long it is since my mother and father were killed? More than forty years. Now they can rest in peace and I can stop wondering just how and when my father died. There's more involved. Isn't there? That's why you're here."

"Yes," said Chark. "The murderer."

"Or murderers."

"Quite," said Chark. "The apparent lack of motive suggests that we are dealing with a deeply disturbed person who may well be dead by now."

Lovedean nodded. "Something else bothers me, Chark."

"Oh, what's that?"

"Did you really come all this way to tell me that my father's body has been found and that he was murdered? I can't believe the British taxpayer would look kindly on the expense of your visit here when a letter or telephone call or a visit from someone in the consulate would do as well. Not that I don't appreciate you're coming here. I do. But is there something else on your mind?"

Lovedean was walking around now and his colour had returned to normal. He put down his glass and turned to look out of the window.

"Yes," said Chark. "You're right. I had two reasons for coming here. The first you already know about. The second is to ask you some questions about an incident that happened a long time ago in Fairport. On the day of the air raid to be precise."

Lovedean turned to look at Chark and rubbed his arm. Chark saw the scars and for the first time, noticed that his left arm was different from the right. A little twisted.

"Souvenir of the war," said Lovedean as he noticed Chark's eyes. "Trapped in the house for the best part of the day. Sometimes messes up my golf swing." He sat down again. "I'll be frank with you, Chark. I spent a lot of time and money with psychiatrists over the years." He grimaced and spoke as if to himself. "What do they know about that kind of fear and pain? They said I should face down my memories and learn to live with them. Bloody fools. Bloody fools."

Chark waited until Paul looked at him. "What I am going to ask you may trigger off more old memories," he said. "You have no obligation to answer me, of course, and I'll understand if you decide not to. I have no jurisdiction in this part of the world."

Lovedean sipped on his drink as he studied Chark. Then he put the glass on the coffee table and crossed his arms on his chest. "OK, go ahead," he said. "What is it you want to know?"

"There's an entry in the Fairport police station's day book for June 17th 1941 written by a Constable Walker. It describes you reporting seeing something in the air raid shelter in the horse pasture. Do you remember what it was about?"

Lovedean uncrossed his arms and looked intently at Chark. "You mean old Walker actually wrote it down?"

"Yes,"

"I'll be damned! And nobody believed me when I told them what I had seen. All they had to do was look in the book."

"Not exactly," said Chark. "Walker was killed within minutes of writing it down. The police station was hit but the book survived and they put it in a little museum. Go on, sir."

Lovedean spoke slowly and clearly, picking his words carefully. "I remember the day very well. There were three of us, me, Joe Mishkin and Michael Ford. We all went to the local grammar school and you know how it was with English school holidays those days; six weeks off with damn-all to do except join the family in the obligatory week in a bed-and-breakfast in Brighton."

Chark laughed at the memory. "Yes. Except we went to Southend and stayed in a cheap hotel on the front. My parents sat in a pub all day drinking wine and eating oysters. If it wasn't for the fun fair and the penny arcades I'd have died of boredom. Was almost glad to be back at school."

"We played a game in that air raid shelter," continued Lovedean getting more serious. "Ran down the ladder at one end and out the entrance at the other. Yelling and screaming our bloody heads off. I was scared to death but too proud to admit it." He stopped and started rubbing his arm again.

"What did you see that day that made you run away?"

Lovedean grimaced at the memory. "By chance, the sun shone down the shaft as I stepped off the bottom rung of the ladder. I saw a body. The others hadn't seen it because the sun shone only for a second or two. Then it was pitch black again. There was blood on the man's head and coat. It dripped on the floor." Lovedean paused for a moment and looked at Chark with a puzzled expression. "I can tell you one thing for sure. It was not my father."

"The soldier," said Chark. Thank heaven for small mercies. "How can you be certain it wasn't your father?"

"Come on now, Chark." said Lovedean impatiently. "I would know my own father even in that light. The man I saw wore khaki and army boots, my father was in the navy and had dark, thick wavy hair. The soldier's hair was thin and straight." Lovedean thought for a moment. "I suppose my father was down there too?"

Chark too a deep breath and stood up. "I believe so. It's very likely that the murderer was nearby, probably down in that shelter in the dark watching you boys run through. One more thing, sir. You say the blood dripped? You're certain of that?"

Lovedean folded his arms and lowered his chin to his chest. "Yes, I'm sure. Then it wasn't all a dream," he muttered to himself. "I tried to tell people what I saw. The adults. The other kids. They told me it was all hysteria. Childish games gotten out of hand. I rationalised it by pretending the soldier was sleeping. Lot of them did that in the shelter after drinking too much in the Duke of York." Lovedean lapsed into silence deep in his chair.

But Chark had accomplished one thing. If the blood was still dripping from the dead man's head he had been dead only a short time, with the time of the air raid established and with Walker's report, the time of death was established at between 11 and 12 0'clock on that awful day.

Lovedean remained silent as Prudence Whitehorse walked in with her notebook and pencil poised. "Mr Mullion? Time for your next appointment."

"Huh?" he grunted and levered himself out of the chair. "Oh, yeah."

"My time's up," said Chark getting up from his chair. "One last thing. You mentioned two other boys. Any idea what happened to them?"

Lovedean nodded briefly. "Heard that Joe left home to get away from his old man. Joined the army and got killed in Korea in 1951. Michael was killed in the air raid."

They walked together to the front door followed by Prudence Whitehorse and stepped out into the sunshine.

"Thanks for your help," said Chark handing Lovedean a business card. "Oh, I almost forgot. There's to be a memorial service for your father and the soldier a week next Sunday. That's the 4th. Any chance you can be there?"

Lovedean nodded "I'll make it."

"Good," said Chark "I'll look forward to meeting you again." He turned to Prudence and gave a little bow of respect. She returned it with a smile.

"I'll be at the Pembroke Hotel if anything more comes to mind."

They shook hands and Chark walked away. He opened the door of Larson's car and woke him up.

As they drove towards the gate there was the whap-whap-whap of a helicopter on the front lawn. Chark saw the door open and a diminutive figure, walking stiffly with a stick, got out with the help of one of the Asian gardeners.

"Get what you want, Chief?" asked Larson stiffling a yawn as he drove out through the gate. The damage to the rose beds and bushes had already been repaired.

"Most of it," replied Chark. Mr Mullion's had a shock, I think. We'll leave him to think for a while. He might remember something else when his mind settles down. Often happens that way."

At three o'clock they drove down the ramp of the the state ferry "Hyak" onto the dock in Seattle and made their way downtown. Larson parked under the blue canvas canopy of the Pembroke Hotel.

"Thanks for the ride and the company," said Chark as he slid out of his seat and stood on the sidewalk.

"My pleasure," said Larson. "How about a drink later? I'll check in at the precinct and join you when I get off duty. About six?"

"Fine," said Chark. "Look forward to it."

Chark collected his room key. No messages. In his room he showered and changed into casual slacks and a roll-necked cotton sweater. He relaxed in a chair and looked out over the city trying to fit all the facts of the case together into some sort of cohesive story. Motive was the key. Or was it the lack of an apparent motive? The traditional approach of motive, opportunity and means somehow didn't fit.

Chapter 20

At six o'clock the Pembroke hotel's lounge bar was full of well-dressed people sipping mineral water or white wine. Earnest conversations punctuated by discrete laughter were being conducted around tables along the walls and in the secluded booths. Chark sat at the bar on a tall stool and caught the bartender's eye.

"Evening, sir. What'll it be tonight?" He put a place mat in front of him.

"Gin and tonic?" asked Chark tentatively.

"English?"

"Fresh off the plane."

"Name's Harry," said the bartender as he left to make the drink. He set the drink down and watched as Chark took his first sip.

"Good?"

"Good," agreed Chark. "Where did you learn how to make one of these?"

"Worked at the London Hilton for a couple of seasons a few years back. "Jigger of gin, two of tonic water, one olive and no ice. Absolutely no ice."

Chark raised his glass in salute. "Right."

Larson arrived at six thirty looking tired and rumpled.

"Sorry I'm late." He sat heavily on the barstool next to Chark. "Another drive-by shooting. Half the neighborhood standing around watching and nobody saw anything. How's your drink?"

"Fine," said Chark. Go ahead. My tab tonight."

Larson leaned over the bar and called out to Harry who was talking to a waiter at the other end. "Hey, Harry! Bring me a nice cold Bud will ya?" He scooped up a handfull of peanuts from the bowl on the bar, tossed one into the air and caught it in his mouth. He was not having a good evening. "You Brits still drinking your beer warm?"

Chark had answered that one a hundred times before. There was only one acceptable reply. "Yes."

"Ugh," said Larson. "Can't imagine drinking warm beer."

"You get used to it."

Harry brought Larson's beer and he swallowed half of it before putting the glass down. "That's better. You ever drink warm beer, Harry?"

Harry winked at Chark. "Yeah. Like I was telling your friend, I worked in London for a while. They're funny about their gin, too." A waiter called a drink order and Harry left.

"What's on for tomorrow," said Larson "You want me to come over and pick you up? Run around town a little? See some of the sights? Maybe take a run up in the mountains. Great place for breakfast up at Snoqualmie Falls. Salish Lodge."

Chark was tempted but decided not to take advantage of the offer. "No thanks," he said. "Got to get back to Fairport. I'll get the hotel bus out to the airport in the morning."

"Suit yourself."

After two more beers and a gin and tonic, the happy hour crowd began to leave and the shrill bar noise diminished to a rumble. Larson drained his beer and spun around on his stool to scan the stragglers.

"You sure you don't want me to drive you to the airport tomorrow? No problem. Chief Narvik has assigned me to you for as long as you're here. Might as well make use of me."

Chark shook his head. "Tell Chief Narvik not to worry. I'll be gone tomorrow."

Larson laughed. "OK. I'll tell him." He dismissed Chark's thanks with a slap on his shoulder. "Call me again anytime if I can help." Then he walked out of the bar leaving Chark to his gin and tonic.

Chark was hungry. The gin had sharpened his appetite and the thought of a well-done steak made his mouth water. But he was casually dressed and not knowing the formalities for dressing to eat out in a strange city, he went up to his room and ordered room service. A half bottle of wine and a thick steak with french fries and asparagus arrived on a trolley fifteen minutes later and he settled down to enjoy it. The lights of the city were blinking outside his window and dark clouds billowed up over the rooftops.

After dinner, Chark made up his notes for the day, snapped the book shut and put it away in his suitcase. Not a lot to show for a six thousand mile trip. But at least, he had found his only material witness so far. He'd confirmed the time and date of death for the two victims as a result of Paul Lovedean's story. He could justify the visit but he was no nearer to identifying a suspect. There was a nagging feeling in the back of his mind that somebody, somewhere had a piece of information that would begin the process of unraveling the case despite all the years that had passed since the murders. Or was it a lost cause and all the information had died with its owners? He was about to undress for bed when the phone rang.

"Chark here."

"Paul Mullion. Lovedean. You want to meet? Got something I want to talk about."

"Yes," said Chark. "Of course. Where are you?"

"I'm home. Be there in a half hour. I'll use the company chopper since it's over here. Meet me in the bar." Paul hung up leaving Chark looking at the handset in surprise.

It took Paul forty five minutes to get to the bar. He sat next to Chark at a table in a corner where they could talk in comparative peace. Harry walked over and asked if they wanted a drink.

"Brandy. Large one," said Paul.

"Beer, Harry," said Chark. "A cold one, please."

Paul stared into his drink for a while before starting to talk. "After you left today I took a long walk on the beach. Trying to put some perspective on this whole business. I've been suppressing a lot of memories most of my life but some keep coming back. There's one that repeats more than the others and I think it might have some bearing on the case. Don't know how but you might make some sense out of it, Chark." He put down his glass and looked at Chark for a long moment.

"Something to do with the air raid shelter?" said Chark.

"No. Not really. It has to do with those two other boys we spoke about earlier."

"Joe Mishkin and Michael Ford?"

"Right," said Lovedean. "You've a good memory."

"I'm a policeman. Go on."

"You remember that I was pinned under the stairs when the house was hit?"

"Yes."

"Did you know my mother was also trapped?"

"Yes," said Lovedean. "I know she died there."

Lovedean was silent again as he twirled the brandy. When he spoke it sounded like a confession to Chark. "For years my analysts have been trying to get me to remember what happened at the time so I can resolve it and get on with my life. I've been successful in not doing what they wanted. But now you come along and the memories are coming back in clear perspective. Maybe I was wrong. It doesn't seem so bad to talk about it. I've been all over the world in the past forty years but never back to Fairport. Not even to my mother's grave. A florist puts flowers there every Sunday." Paul smiled and finished his drink. "That's why I'll go back to the memorial service."

"That's good," said Chark as he signalled Harry for more drinks. "I plan to be there myself. But there was something else you wanted to talk about?"

"Yes," said Lovedean. "Michael Ford, Joe Mishkin and I were friends. Lived close to each other in Fairport. Went to the same school together. There wasn't much to do in those days and we didn't travel far from home because of the war. We made up silly games like the one where we ran through the shelter. Something else happened the day of the big air raid. Earlier in the morning. It always bothered me but now it seems to make sense after you explained about my father and the soldier."

"You remembered something else that happened on the day of the air raid?"

"Yes," said Paul. "It was before we ran down the shelter and I saw the body. We had built a campfire among the trees and pulled vegetables from the gardens and were trying to boil them in an old saucepan. Made a lot of white smoke. Then this soldier suddenly appeared. Scary son of a bitch. Asked us what the hell we were doing. He was real angry about something. He kicked over the pot of water and put out the fire. Then he gave us a lecture about stealing food when there were kids starving in Europe. Scared the shit out of us."

Chark started to write. "A soldier? Can you describe him?"

"Not very tall. Of course I was only nine at the time but Michael was nearly as tall as he was so I would guess he was average height or a little less. Hair was cut real short. I remember distinctly that he had shiny black boots and his uniform was clean and had sharp creases."

"Army battledress?" asked Chark.

"With a black beret."

Chark looked up from his notes. "Was he the soldier you saw down in the shelter?"

Paul shook his head slowly. "No, I'm sure about that. Hair was all wrong and he didn't have a topcoat. The soldier down the shelter had a coat and longer hair which hung down over his face. His tunic was buttoned up to the neck. The scary one in the trees wore a tunic with those little collars which didn't button up all the way to the neck and his hair was too short to hang down."

"How about his face?"

"Don't remember much. Only that he was angry about something. Had bushy eyebrows and a long nose. Not big. Long. But what I noticed most were his eyes, big, brown and staring."

"Anything else? Badges or rank markings like stripes?"

"No," said Paul. "Nothing that I can remember." He gave a little laugh. "Funny thing, though. He was wearing a red tie and a white shirt."

"Red tie and white shirt? With an army uniform? You sure?"

"Yeah. I'm sure. Joe Mishkin remarked on it later in the day."

"What happened then?" asked Chark.

"We ran away and hid in the trees. The soldier started laughing and walked off."

"In what direction?"

"Don't remember."

"You said he laughed," said Chark. "Was it a humourous laugh like he was playing a joke on you? A loud one?"

"It's hard to describe it, really. Kinda loud, yes. But hollow too. No humour in it. As if he was crying when he laughed. This make sense?"

"Maybe," said Chark as he wrote quickly. He looked up. "That's all?"

"That's it, Chark. The rest of the memories are little things about being in the hospital and Aunt Edwina coming to see me. Oh, yes. There was a real cute little nurse who sat with me. I never did get her name so I could write to her from Seattle. Any chance you could track her down?"

"I'll try," said Chark. "Anything else?"

"No, that's all. If anything else comes to mind, I'll call you. Got your number on your business card at home."

They sat for a while and relaxed with their drinks and salted peanuts. Then Paul checked his watch and looked like he was about to leave.

"You think there is any chance of finding the bastard who killed my father?" he asked. Chark pondered the question. Then he shook his head.

"Chances are slim to none. He's most likely dead by now."

Paul nodded. "At least I'll know where he is buried. That helps. You've done a good job, Chark." There was no trace of patronage in the words.

Paul shook Chark's hand and signalled that he was ready to leave to a man dressed in a leather jacket who was waiting in the bar at a discrete distance. Then he was gone. Leaving Chark to mull over this new piece of information on his way back to his room.

It was eleven o'clock Seattle time. With the eight-hour time difference, Beane would be back in the Fairport police station to start his day in an hour. Chark rang the room service number and got a recorded apology. Damnation. After all the alcohol that evening he needed some coffee. There was instant coffee and fake cream in the bathroom next to the electric kettle so he made a cup and settled down to wait for the time when he could call Beane's number.

Chapter 21

Hume Beane was enjoying a cup of hot, sweet tea and a sugary pastry filled with improbably red jam and yellow custard when the phone rang. At the sound of Chark's voice he dropped it sticky-side-down and watched as a gory mess spread across the sports page of the Eastchester Chronicle

"Morning, Chief. Yes, I've got pencil and paper. Go ahead." Beane held the phone to his ear with his shoulder as he listened and wrote. Briefly, Chark told him about his meeting with Paul Mullion and when he finished, Beane drew in a deep breath and gave a low whistle. Chark continued.

"Now here's what I want you to do." Beane started to write again as Chark gave him his instructions. "And one more thing, Beane. Find out the name of the nurse who attended young Lovedean when he was in the hospital."

"Yes, I've got all that down. What's all this about a red tie? Seems improbable. Was Lovedean dreaming that one up?"

"No," said Chark. "He was quite positive about it. Might be something in it. Check with the military and see if there is any record of a uniform like that and who might have worn it. Now, what's new in Fairport? You through with all the interviews?"

"Yes, Chief. All those on the list are done and entered in the computer. I want to see Nora Czernowski again. See if she can add some more about Mrs Walker. I started sorting and comparing yesterday. No results yet but there's been a development that'll surprise you. The old man who was attacked."

"Purvis," said Chark impatiently. "What about him?"

"He's recovering. Done so well he's been able to talk to the locals and tell him who hit him. Guess what? You won't believe this. It was Mrs Walker."

"What!" yelled Chark loud enough to make Beane pull the handset away from his ear.

"No shit, Chief. Purvis is adamant it was her."

"Is she denying it?"

"No. Keeps smiling at Inspector Privett and muttering something about it being the Lord's will. Don't think he has any idea how to cope with her. You want me to talk to her?" Beane switched the phone to his other ear and rubbed the other one back to life. He dipped his finger in the mess on the Chronicle and licked the jam.

"No," said Chark. "I want to talk to her myself. Find out some more of her background. Especially her life before she married Walker. Be discrete about it if you talk to Phil Privett."

"OK," said Beane.

Chark yawned into the phone and shook his head. "I'm going to get some sleep now. The BA flight gets into Heathrow at eleven in the morning. Can you pick me up?"

"I'll be there." Beane waited until he heard the buzz which indicated that Chark had hung up. Then he peeled the pastry off the newspaper.

Phil Privett knocked on the door of the office and looked over Beane's shoulder at his notes.

"Good God! Your handwriting is worse than mine. Can't make out a thing. Heard from Dave Chark?"

"Yes," said Beane through his sagging pastry. "That was him just now. Called to let me know when to pick him up at the airport."

"Took a hell of a time to say that. Anything new in Seattle?" said Privett pretending to be more interested in the pile of paper in the in-basket.

"No," lied Beane. "He didn't say." This was one time when Privett's loose tongue was of no advantage.

At lunch time, Beane walked into the Duke of York. He fancied a cool pint of bitter and a ploughman's plate of fresh bread, cheddar cheese and sliced beef. He was two sips down the beer when a figure loomed in his peripheral vision. It was like Sam Gilkicker had a private line into Chark's head. Sam dropped onto the seat next to Beane and called out to the barmaid.

"The usual, love!" As though this was his local pub. But she had a good memory and indulged him by bringing a pint of foaming bitter.

"So what brings you back to Fairport, Sam? said Beane with a mouthful of cheese and pickles. "Thought the fourth estate had lost interest in this case. Nothing new to tell you."

Sam smiled. "That's the point. No news for several days. Chark is over in the States for some reason and Mrs Walker's gone potty and been charged with beating up on old Purvis in the churchyard. Stuff good stories are made of." He reached for a cigarette. "Mind if I smoke?"

"Yes, I'm eating."

Sam reluctantly replaced his packet of Craven 'A' in his pocket. "So when's Chark coming back?"

"Tomorrow."

"What's he been over in the States for?"

"Business and pleasure."

"On public expenses?" Sam took out his notebook.

"Look, Sam. Before you rush off to the telephone," said Beane. "Mrs Walker's only being questioned. She's not being charged with anything yet. Inspector Privett is handling it so why don't you ask him? He's been handling the questioning, not me or Chief Inspector Chark." He emphasised the 'Chief Inspector'.

"So, any revelations from her?" persisted Sam.

"Revelations? Revelations? Since when did you use three-syllable words, Sam? You been promoted to the sports beat?"

"Very funny, Beane."

They sat quietly while Beane finished his lunch and then looked at his watch. Chark's question about the red tie on the soldier had been in his mind and the prospect of the tedious routine of finding the answer bothered him. Maybe he could divert Sam with it.

"Say, Sam," he started. "You're old enough. Were you in the army?"

"Yes, National Service. Did two years in BAOR, Berlin. Why?"

"Ever heard of an army uniform with a white shirt and a red tie? World War Two?"

"Regular uniform like khaki? Officer or ranker?"

"Probably a private soldier although we're not sure."

"What's the angle?" asked Sam.

"None," said Beane casually. "Came up somewhere. Just curious."

Sam thought for a moment. "Never seen it myself."

"Just a thought," said Beane as he got up from his seat and made for the door. "See you around."

Sam Gilkicker nodded slowly and drained his glass. Then he reached over for the bar phone and dialed.

*

The drive to the Czernowki's home in Monk's Wood was familiar now and Beane pulled up outside the house a little before one o'clock without having to check the street map. There was a shuffling behind the door and it was opened a few inches. Nora peered out suspiciously through the gap.

"Inspector, you came back."

"Yes, ma'am. But it's detective sergeant, not inspector. I have a few questions. May I come in?"

Nora opened the door and invited Beane in with a wave of her cigarette. She looked tired and her feet dragged a little in her fuzzy slippers as he followed her into the familiar living room.

"Sorry about the mess. Haven't had time to clean up yet this morning. You should have called first. We're on the phone, you know."

The house smelled of stale food and unwashed clothes. A man's jacket and shoes were thrown on the sofa and a vodka bottle and empty glass stood on the table.

"Looks fine to me," lied Beane as he moved the shoes to sit down. "You're husband home?" He could hear rhythmic snoring through the thin walls.

"Yes, he's sleeping now. He's had a tough day. Know what I mean?" said Nora lowering herself into a chair and reached for another cigarette.

"Look, Mrs Czernowski. I don't want to disturb him, it's you I want to talk to. Why don't we go out somewhere? There's a restaurant out on the Hampton road. Saw it as I drove over. We could go there and have some coffee while we talk. It'll not take long. I'm buying."

"You mean it?" said Nora brightening and stubbing out the cigarette.

"Yeah. Could do with a coffee myself."

Nora went to the mirror. "God! I look a mess. Haven't been in a real restaurant for ages. Give me a minute to freshen up?"

Beane nodded and picked up the morning newspaper. It took Nora more than a few minutes but when she returned the transformation was remarkable. She wore a black skirt that was only a little tight. A frothy, white blouse with a huge bow at the throat and patent leather high heeled shoes. Her hair was brushed into a mound of red held in place by a liberal coating of hair spray. He got up and smiled approval as he helped her on with her raincoat.

The theme restaurant was the same as all those that grow like mushrooms along any motorway. A large, littered car park, plastic ferns and brass decorations with framed hunting scenes hanging on the walls. Beane followed Nora inside. Her heels clacked on the tiled floor and as she wriggled her ample hips in the black skirt, Beane got a glimpse of the young Nora of wartime fame.

A hostess greeted them with an exaggerated, insincere smile and showed them to a booth. The restaurant was dimly lit and full of heavy dark furniture. The waiter pulled out her order book.

"What can I get you?"

Beane pointed to the menu. "Pot of coffee for two and a plate of cakes, please."

"That be all?"

"That's all."

She left and Beane looked across at Nora.

"Mrs Czer " he began.

"Call me Nora?"

"Nora. When I spoke to you last, you mentioned a Mrs Walker. Can you tell me something about her? What was she like? Where did she come from. That sort of thing."

Nora leaned over and spoke confidentially. "I was very young in the war. A lot of what I know is second-hand stuff from my mother or the other ladies of the town."

Beane held up his hand reassuringly. "That's alright. whatever you can tell me. Go on."

"Her name was Hunt before she married constable Walker. Family from up country. Farmers they say." Nora paused as the coffee and cakes were delivered. "Seems she got religion after her husband, Walker, got killed. Then she moved into the vicarage as housekeeper to Dr Tweed. He was the vicar before Reverend Batley came."

"Yes, I know. Go on," said Beane passing a cup of coffee to Nora.

"Well, rumour is she had a boyfriend before Walker came along and her old man didn't approve so he threw her out of the house and put her in service somewhere. This boyfriend got himself into trouble or something and took off."

Nora sipped her coffee and nibbled on a cake.

"Took off where?"

"Who knows? Things around Fairport were pretty bad at that time. There was unemployment. Only places for the young men was the army or the navy. Maybe some labouring job in the dockyard." Nora took another, bigger bite from a cream cake. "You should try one of these," she said. "They're good."

"Who was this boyfriend?"

"No idea. Came from out in the county I think. Leastways, the women said he was a foreigner. Which means he wasn't from Old Town. Good-looking boy, according to mother. But then they all were to her." Nora gave a loud cackle of laughter and clamped a hand over her mouth as several people turned to look in her direction.

"Sorry, sergeant."

"You said she got religion. How do you mean that?"

"Mother said it was the shock of losing her husband. Mrs Walker was shopping in Hampton when the bombs fell on Fairport. The ferries stopped because the dock was burned and the buses weren't running because the streets were blocked with rubble. So she was stuck over there for a day or two. When she got back she found that Walker was dead. That's probably what did it. Poor old girl." Nora eyed another cream cake and placed it delicately on her plate.

"You're sure Mrs Walker was in Hampton on the day of the air raid?" asked Beane.

"So far as I know, yes. I remember it well because she stayed at our house after the bombing. We was lucky. Only a few roof tiles and windows gone. She arrived in a police car and stayed with us because she couldn't stand being alone. Mother, God rest her soft old heart, made me give up my bed for her. I had to sleep on the floor for a week." Nora giggled as a squirt of cream shot out of the end of her cake onto the tablecloth as she bit into it.

"I'm still not sure I know what you mean by her getting religion," said Beane.

"Cut herself off from the rest of the town. Social suicide in a small place like Fairport was then. Spent all her time in the church and the vicarage. Really weird she was to us kids. It was like she didn't want to see anybody. Only people she spoke to was Charley Frater at the 'Duke' because she bought the vicar's wine and whiskey there. Oh, but he loved his wine and whiskey! And then there was that shyster Ted Hoff and old Purvis and Colonel Ford before he died."

Beane wrote rapidly in his book and sipped his cold coffee with a grimace. Nora continued.

"Reverend Tweed gave her the job and she lived in so she gave up the police cottage that came with Walker's job. There was his pension and life insurance from the county so she didn't hurt for money too much. Didn't spend a penny on herself. Tight as a drum with money, they said. She bought all her clothes from the church bazaar every year. Some of the old women used to laugh at her about it because they saw her wearing old clothes they had donated. Lousy bitches."

"And Reverend Batley kept her on after Reverend Tweed died?"

"Yes. She's been housekeeper there for over forty years now I reckon." Nora eyed the last cream cake and forced herself to refrain.

"Forty one, to be exact," said Beane. "Can you think of anything else?"

"No," said Nora "I think that's it. If I think of anything else, I'll call you. Maybe come out for coffee again?" She smiled at Beane and turned her wrist over to look at her watch. "My God! Look at the time. I really should be going home. Michael will be awake looking for his tea. When he drinks he gets pain in his arm. The one that's gone. Doctors say it's something to do with his brain. I must get back to him."

Beane felt a wave of sympathy for Nora Czernowski. A gray sadness had come back into her face. She laid her hand on his arm.

"Thanks for the talk and the coffee and cakes. It's been really nice."

Beane paid the bill at the counter and asked for a receipt. Then they walked together to the car and he drove her home. On his way back to Fairport Beane mentally eliminated one of his suspects. Mrs Walker was in Hampton at the time of the murders. He would ask her about that.

Chapter 22

Chark slept for several hours during his flight back to London from Seattle. Breakfast was served above rippled, gray clouds somewhere between Iceland and Scotland. The landing at Heathrow was made on time at eleven o'clock under overcast skies with a glimmering of recent rain on the runway. He strode along the moving walkways and unending corridors of terminal 3 and showed his passport to a surly officer at the immigration gate. He picked up his suitcase at the carousel and walked out into the crowds beyond the green "nothing to declare' light.

Beane was waiting at the barrier waving a copy of the Daily Mirror at him. "Morning, Chief. Good flight?"" he asked as he grabbed Chark's suitcase and led the way out through the crowded building into the fresh air and the covered car park.

"Let's get back to Eastchester," said Chark. "You can tell me about the interviews on the way."

Beane smiled broadly at the prospect of rejoining big city civilisation. He unlocked the car and threw Chark's case in the back seat beside his own.

They drove onto the motorway and headed south for the next hour exchanging details of their respective conversations with Paul Lovedean and the residents of Fairport. Chark listened attentively as Beane retold the surprising story of Mrs Walker's confession to having attacked Purvis and the tough old man's remarkable recovery. He perked up when Beane relayed the story of Mrs Walker's sojourn in Hampton during the war at the time of the air raid. All the while something was stirring in the back of Chark's mind. Was there a connection between Mrs Walker and the events surrounding the murder in the air raid shelter? He told Beane of Lovedean's experiences with the soldier in the horse pasture and then fell into a reflective silence for the rest of the journey to Eastchester.

They pulled into the Eastchester County Constabulary Building parking lot just after one o'clock. They sat in Chark's office and drank Mrs Godfrey's strong coffee and decided on their strategy for the next week.

"We'll meet down in Fairport tomorrow morning," said Chark after a few minutes. "Those rooms still available at the Duke?"

"Mine is. I can get yours again if you want it."

Chark nodded and pointed to the door. "See you tomorrow, Beane," he said. "And make an appointment for me to see Mrs Walker tomorrow."

With obvious haste, Beane left the office and went to his desk where he dialed Fiona's number and leaned back in his chair with his feet on the desk and a grin on his face.

As usual, Superintendent Russell's secretary was immaculate in her white and blue regulation uniform. She eyed Chark coldly.

"I see you're back, Chief Inspector." Chark was tempted to deny the visually obvious and perpetuate their animosity towards each other but was irritatingly polite instead. Miss Peel did not approve of Chark's methods. His frequent trips to exotic places at public expense were in strict contrast to her annual two-week excursion to a popular Spanish resort among loud English families who lay on the crowded beaches drinking and burning in the hot sun. "Superintendent Russell said you are to go right in as soon as you arrive."

She opened the polished mahogany door and announced him.

"Sit down, Chark. Tell me all about this Seattle trip."

Chark sat in one of the guest chairs facing Russell and gave his detailed report without referring to his notes. He watched with apprehension as Russell fidgeted and looked beyond him at the rows of autographed, framed photographs of himself with smiling dignitaries.

"So that's it?" said Russell. "You went all the way to Seattle to confirm the time of death and get some story about a soldier who scared a bunch of kids forty years ago? Not much is it?"

Chark had to agree with the facts. "That's it, sir. I won't know how important this information is until we've questioned some more people down in Fairport." Chark started to rise and take his leave. "I'm going home to get some clean clothes and a shower then get back down there." But Russell's chubby finger made him sit down again.

"Chark. I want you to finish with this business down there as soon as possible. Get back to your duties here in Eastchester. Christ knows what mischief is going uninvestigated up here while you're dabbling in ancient history and archeology in Fairport." Russell leaned on his elbows and touched his fingers together. "Have you a suspect, Chark? One I can tell the powers-that-be?"

So that's it. The carnivorous politicians have got to him.

"I need more time, sir. Another week at least."

"I want you back here. Now."

"A few more days," said Chark. "If I can come up with some kind of closure before the memorial service on Sunday we will all look good."

He watched as Russell weakened.

"How do you mean?"

"You. Me. The whole County Constabulary will benefit. Look, we could use some success now. We're not doing so well with the drug traffic in the town and the burglary rate is up."

186 | HOLMAN SMITH

"Especially up on the Ridgeway," said Russell.

"Right. Give me until next Monday morning and I'll give you something to go with."

Russell adjusted his tie for the third time. "You really think you can conclude this thing?"

"Maybe," said Chark. And get you another framed, autographed picture for your 'bring and brag' wall you snobby old bastard.

Russell eyed him for several seconds. "That new man still with you?" What's his name?"

"Beane, sir. Detective Sergeant Hume Beane. Good man for the details. Keeps everything in a computer. I need him if I'm going to finish this case."

Russell tapped the desk nervously. "Alright, Chark. But I want you back here early Monday morning without fail. I'm getting hell about the drug and hooligan problem at the soccer stadium. Got to show visible results there. You understand?"

Chark understood political pressure. And private interests. And budgets, too.

"Yes, sir. I understand."

Russell snapped open the Police Gazette and swiveled his chair away from Chark. He had been dismissed. Chark walked out past the baleful eyes of Miss Peel and gave her one of his best smiles on the way.

Chapter 23

In the morning, Chark and Beane drove down to Fairport separately. Beane in an unmarked car and Chark in his classic, black 1956 Morris Minor station wagon.

They settled back into their rooms in the 'Duke' before walking over to the vicarage for the interview with Mrs Walker.

She had been driven from the county hospital to the vicarage so that she could be in familiar surroundings. When Chark and Beane arrived at the vicarage she was already seated primly in a straight-backed chair in the parlour. The room was cold and the dim lights cast shadows on the walls. She wore a flowered cotton dress and woolen cardigan which hung loosely on her spare figure. Her straight gray hair was pulled tightly back into a bun at her neck. The vicar, dressed in a black suit and white dog collar, sat at her left. A stocky, uniformed policewoman stood behind her, legs apart, military fashion. Chark took a seat in front of Mrs Walker with his arms crossed and studied her for a few seconds.

"Good morning, Mrs Walker," he said softly. "Do you know why I'm here?"

No response.

"Tell me, Mrs Walker. Why did you hit Purvis with his garden rake?"

Mrs Walker looked round at the Reverend Batley. He nodded his approval.

"You want to know why I did it?" she asked.

"Yes, please."

"Tell me, Chief Inspector, are you a Christian?" She looked intently, unblinking, into Chark's eyes. He closed them and swore silently. He had forgotten her but she must have remembered him from all those years back. "You were one of the evacuees from London weren't you?" she said. "Used to sing in the choir. In a Christian church. Saw you there on Sundays. Never forget a face."

"Yes," said Chark. "That's true. But it has nothing to do with why we're here."

Mrs Walker leaned forward and hissed at Chark. "You're not a Christian. That has everything to do with it."

Chark shook his head. This was getting out of hand and he was losing ground. No wonder Phil Privett had trouble with her. The policewoman and the others shifted their weight and eyes in embarrassment.

"My father was a Jew, Mrs Walker," said Chark. "My mother a French Roman Catholic. I guess that gives me a choice. I'm not a particularly good member of either faith. Why does it matter to you?"

"Because you cannot understand why I did it, that's why."

"So. You admit assaulting Mr Purvis."

Mrs Walker jutted out her chin and looked around at the others in triumph. They remained silent.

"What did you do, Mrs Walker?"

"The Lord told me to strike down that man. He was defiling a holy monument. He appeared to me in the church and commanded me to pick up the rake and smite him."

"Defiling a monument?" asked Chark. "What monument?"

"The plaque in the wall, of course. The War Memorial. Walker's name's on it with all the others. He was scrubbing at it. That's my job, not his." She looked round at the vicar with a smile.

"I think you were afraid of something and acted compulsively," said Chark pointing an accusing finger at her. The police woman glared at Chark and placed her hands on the back of Mrs Walker's chair.

"No!" screamed Mrs Walker and Chark blinked as she jumped up and struggled against the brawny arms of the policewoman who was taken by surprise at the vehemance of the outburst and nearly let her go. "No! It was the Lord told me to do it. It was His bidding!" Her face suddenly transformed into a fury of hatred as a lifetime of repression and bigotry surfaced. Spittle sprayed as she fought to escape. "You have no right to judge me. Unbeliever. Jew!"

The vicar sat helpless and open-mouthed at the scene until Mrs Walker sat down again and resumed her demure posture. She clasped her hands in her lap.

"What was it you wanted to talk to me about." The fury was spent. She looked up at Chark with unblinking, child-like eyes. The police-woman shook her head at Chark. He persisted.

"Your fiancee. The one before Walker. He went away?"

"Yes, but he came back to me." There was a note of pathetic pride in Mrs Walker's tiny voice.

"He came back," said Chark quietly. "When was that?"

"After Dunkirk."

"Was he hurt?"

"He was in the hospital. They let me see him there. I was married to Walker then."

"What hospital was he in?"

Mrs Walker hesitated.

"Really, Chief Inspector," said Reverend Batley who was now stand-ing and pacing the room. "Is this really necessary? Can't you see the poor woman is disturbed? Why keep on with this questioning?"

But Chark ignored him and looked at Mrs Walker. "What hospital was he in, Mrs Walker?"

"Don't remember."

"What was his name, Mrs Walker?"

"Enough!" exploded the vicar. "You go too far. I want Mr Privett here." He turned to leave but Chark held up his hand and pointed to the chair.

"Sit down, vicar," he said coldly and politely. "Almost over."

"What was his name, Mrs Walker?" he continued. "You remembered me after all these years. You must remember him. Where is he now?"

The rage and spittle rose again and incoherent words poured from the little woman's lips. The policewoman leaped and Chark knew the interview was over. Obscenities and accusations filled the echoing room and there was confusion as everybody but Chark started talking at once. The policewoman patiently calmed Mrs Walker from rage to tears and led her away to the waiting ambulance. The white-faced vicar turned on Chark shaking with anger. Chark spread his arms in a gesture of defeat and gestured to Beane to join him.

"Sorry, Chief," he said. "Didn't get all that down. Went too fast for me."

"No matter," said Chark. "Her evidence will be useless in court anyway. Any competent lawyer would see to that."

As they left the parlour, the trembling vicar stopped them at the door. "You haven't heard the last of this, Chark. You had no business treating that poor woman that way."

Chark looked at him with measured indifference. "This *is* my business, vicar. Mrs Walker's guilty of a serious offense. Assault. If that old man had died she would be facing a more serious charge." Chark's voice took on a harder, more authoritative tone. "And now we would like to see Mrs Walker's room if you have no objection, sir. We've not had time to get a warrant yet so we need your permission. Is there any reason why we shouldn't see it?"

"For what reason?""Curiosity?"Batley stood back and pointed up the stairs. "Second door on the left."

Mrs Walker's room was bigger than Chark expected. It had a bay window overlooking the vicarage gardens and a fireplace laid with kindling and smokeless fuel pellets. The floor was thickly carpeted and the furniture soft and comfortable. A television set and VCR occupied an alcove beside the fireplace and a large bookcase was filled with video tapes. No books except a stack of women's magazines on a coffee table in front of the sofa. Somehow this room did not fit the austere lifestyle professed by Mrs Walker.

Beane took of his coat in preparation for the search. "What are we looking for, Chief?"

Chark didn't answer for a moment and stood looking out of the window at the carefully-tended flower beds and manucured lawn. It reminded him of Paul Lovedean's place on Bainbridge Island. He turned around to face Beane.

"There were two things in common between the three victims, Beane. What were they?" Beane looked puzzled. "Three? I thought we had two victims. Who's the other one?"

"We have three. Remember the German airman the children found in the pasture in the early part of the war? It was in your file records."

"Yes," said Beane. "I remember. But that was months before the others were murdered."

"Seven weeks to be precise. Everybody assumed he had been killed when he parachuted from his plane and they buried him in almighty haste."

"Right," said Beane. "But I still don't get the point."

"What was his name?"

"The headstone says 'Unknown German Airman.'"

"Right," said Chark. "Which means somebody removed his ID. A German airman dressed in Luftwaffe uniform would carry identification if only for the obligatory 'Name, Rank and Serial Number' if he was shot down and taken prisoner. This one had nothing at all. Not even a photograph on him." Chark sat down on the bed.

"So what do we have, sergeant?"

Beane counted off on his fingers. "Three victims. All in uniform. None of them with ID papers. All killed in the same way in the same general location." He paused. "Then we are looking for their IDs?"

"Right, " said Chark standing up. "Get on to Phil Privett and get a search warrant and some experienced help over here. This could take some time."

"But why here?" asked Beane. "What makes you think we'll find it here?"

"I don't know. Intuition perhaps."

*

Chark, Beane and two detectives from the Fairport station worked quickly and efficiently on Mrs Walker's room. When they had done with the drawers and closets they took up the loose floorboards and moved the furniture. Beane stood in the chimney and shone a flashlight above him in to the sooty blackness. Chark opened all the video boxes. After two hours of systematic searching they found nothing. Then they repeated the process in the bathroom and bedroom with the same result.

Chark called a halt to the search and gathered the team together in the bedroom. "Where else would Mrs Walker spend her time?" he asked.

"The kitchen," said Beane. "She spent a lot of her time in the kitchen."

They searched the kitchen. Every cavity and crack in the place. Nothing. It was clear to Chark that they would find nothing in the vicarage. He was running out of time. Reluctantly, he thanked the two detectives and sent them back to the station.

"Time for a drink, Beane. All that dust has me parched." They pulled on their jackets and walked down to the parlour where Batley stood with his back to the unlit fire.

"Find what you want?" asked Batley, his eyes glowering at them from beneath his white eyebrows.

"Oh, yes, Reverend," lied Chark. "Thank you."

They made a gloomy pair as they sat in the bar at the Duke drinking their beers. Chark watched Beane as he attacked a large cheese and onion sandwich. At the other end of the bar Charley Frater eyed them coldly as he talked to his customers.

"Why is it you don't get fat?" Chark asked as Beane started on the second half of the sandwich. Beane shrugged and grinned. The Chief was depressed.

A bartender with a punk-rocker's haircut nonchalantly put two more beers in front of them, sloshing some of the beer on the table, and left without a word. Chark turned to watch him leave. "Think it's worth checking him out?" he asked. "Looks too young to be serving alcohol."

"Nah," said Beane. "Comes in every day to help out. Twenty five if he's a day."

Chark grunted and turned back to his beer. He was about an inch down the glass when he suddenly straightened up and grabbed Beane by the sleeve.

"What was Purvis doing when Mrs Walker hit him?"

"He was cleaning the memorial plaque on the wall of the church. He probably didn't know it was dirty until you tried to read the names on it that time. Likely you're the first person in years to want to read it."

"Why?" said Chark.

"Because it was corroded and the names were hard to read."

"That's not the question," said Chark. "Why would Mrs Walker, an elderly and relatively weak woman react so violently. Was it Purvis' cleaning it or did the fact that someone was reading the names on it that alarmed her? Or something else?"

Beane laid down his sandwich and listened carefully as Chark thought. He'd heard that silence before. Chark had reasoned something out and was surprised at the answer.

Chark leaned back and smiled. "Come on, Beane. More work to do. I think I know where those IDs are." He pushed back his chair and hurried towards the door. "Come on, Beane. Hurry it up."

Beane dropped the remains of the sandwich and looked longingly at his beer. That's why I never get fat. Always running around behind Chark and leaving most of my food on the table when we eat together.

As they hurried along the High Street towards the church it started to rain. A steady drizzle had set in. The kind that soaks your clothes without you knowing it. Beane turned up his collar and hunched miserably down into his jacket. Chark strode on, oblivious of the wetness, and didn't stop until he stood in front of the plaque. He pointed at the plaque as Beane stamped his feet to shake off the water and wiped his face with a handkerchief.

"So. What do you see," asked Chark.

Beane scanned the plaque for a moment. "Bronze plaque. Approximately two feet wide and three feet deep. Names in eight columns. Weighs at least a hundred pounds. Bronze finials at each corner shaped like Tudor roses."

"That all?"

"Yes,"

"Look again. This time at the bottom where all the credits are written."

"Yes," said Beane crouching down lower. "Something about the money to buy it being raised by public subscription and the thing being dedicated by the mayor in 1946. Says they sealed a time capsule at the same time." Beane stood up. "There's a cavity behind the plaque."

"Yes. Purvis mentioned it."

They both felt around the edges to find a handhold which might help to pull it away from the wall but it was firmly fixed.

"Assuming that the IDs are in the cavity. Mrs Walker was trying to prevent Purvis from finding them and telling me about it," said Chark. "She obviously knew about them."

"Right," said Beane. "How do we find out what's behind the plaque?"

"We remove it."

"Maybe we don't have to remove it," said Beane. "With some kind of mechanical advantage, like with a lever, we could loosen one of the finials and rotate it to expose a part of the cavity."

Chark gave a hoot of triumph and embraced Beane by spreading his arm around his surprised shoulders. "Of course! Who was it said 'Give me a long enough lever and I will move the world'?".

"Archimedes," said Beane as he crouched down and felt carefully along the lower edge of the plaque with his fingers looking for dents in the soft metal where some kind of lever would have been placed.

He found them. About half way along. And there were corresponding chips on the lip of the limestone flower box underneath the plaque.

"Now, Beane," said Chark. "What could we use as a lever? Something close by. A common object you'd find in a churchyard."

"A spade?" Beane was already on his way towards a little hut against the churchyard wall where Purvis stored his tools. It was unlocked and he returned with a spade to find Chark trying to unscrew the finials.

"Corroded tight," grumbled Chark. "We're going to need a wrench of some kind."

"There might be one in the shed," said Beane. "But first let's see if the spade theory works." He experimented with the spade and the dents and chips. "Yeah," he said after a few minutes. "That's how it could have been done. The marks fit close enough. I'll go get that wrench."

The untidy, oily interior of the shed was full of rusting cans, bits of wire, discarded metal flowerpots and gardening tools. After rummaging about in the boxes on a shelf, Beane found an ancient adjustable wrench of suitable size.

Back at the plaque he fixed it on one of the finials and gave it a jerk. He skinned a knuckle and his blasphemous yell echoed off the consecrated walls. At the third or fourth attempt, the finial moved with a screal and he was able to wind it off. Carefully, Beane moved the other finials until all four were in a pile on the ground and the plaque hung heavily on its four bolts.

"What now?" asked Chark.

"Lever it forward away from the wall and off the bolts until it's suspended by only one bolt at the top. There's enough slop in the holes to do that." Beane slipped the shovel blade under the lower edge and began to jiggle it. With a clang the plaque finally fell and hung on one bolt. It rested on the stone flower box exactly where they had found the chips. There was a small triangle of blackness in the bottom right corner and Chark took a pencil light from his pocket and shone it into the hole.

"There it is," he whispered. "The time capsule. Shiny. probably chrome-plated."

"Nothing else?"

"Wait a bit." Chark rolled back his sleeve and gingerly inserted his hand into the hole. He felt around and stiffened. "Something else." Delicately, he pulled out a dark object and cupped it in his hands. A bundle of small, rectangular books and papers tied together with rotting string. Soft, limp, damp and fragile. With reverence, Chark put them in a plastic evidence bag.

"These are army paybooks, Beane. Let's get back to the station," he said. "Privett's people can fix up the plaque again."

Back at the station they closed the office door and threw their coats over the radiator. Chark swept the desk clean of papers with his forearm.

"Get some paper towels from the men's room, Beane. And get that high-wattage bulb again."

Beane went down the hall to the toilets and cranked out several feet of paper from the dispenser. He returned and spread it over the desk. He put the high wattage bulb back in the desk lamp and switched it on. Chark carefully placed the bundle under the lamp, cut the string and lay the thin paybooks on the paper to study them carefully. There were several kinds. Green, blue, yellow. All damp and faded but the insignia of the country of their former owners could be made out. The top one showed the lion and the unicorn.

With patience, Chark separated each book and lay them out individually on the paper sheet where their delicate condition was evident. He tried to separate the corner of the pages of one of them with the broadest blade of his silver-handled pocketknife but the page ripped soggily. He tried another and succeeded in separating a page far enough to see the smeared blue-ink signature but the page collapsed again. He stopped and looked up at Beane. "This won't work. They've been in that sandstone for too many years." He put away his knife and carefully placed the books in a plastic envelope and sealed it up. "A job for the forensics people up in Eastchester. They'll know how to get inside these things without destroying them,"

Chark picked up the phone and dialed. "I'll get on to McVicar up at the lab and let him know we're coming. Hurry it up, Beane. Time's running short. Go bring the car around. Hullo? Forensics? Chark here "

Beane put the packet of books on the back seat of the unmarked car and drove round to the main entrance to the station. Chark hurried out carrying the plastic envelope containing the books and got into the passenger seat. "Eastchester, Beane. Don't spare the horsepower."

They drove to Eastchester through afternoon traffic made easier by the car's flashing blue light and warbling siren. Beane expertly forced his way through the lines of cars and trucks onto the Eastchester exit from the motorway. They pulled up outside the County Constabulary Building, raced up the steps to the lobby and down the shining corridors to the double doors marked *"Forensics-authorised personnel only"* and pushed them open.

Angus McVicar stood up from his paper-strewn desk and reached for the plastic bag which Beane held out to him. McVicar was a tall, lean, taciturn man of about sixty with red-white hair swept back from his forehead and half-glasses perched on the end of a long nose from which hair grew in abundance. He wore a stained white jacket and oversized running shoes.

"What kept you, Chark? This it?" He pushed his glasses up and held the plastic packet up to the light. "You didn't try to dry this out or any other foolish thing, did you?" His Highland Scot's accent was more pronounced than Beane's.

"No," said Chark. "They're just the way we found them except for a little damage to the corners where we tried to open one up."

McVicar clicked his tongue. "I've told you people before. Don't mess with the evidence. That's our business."

Chark nodded impatiently. "Can we get to work, Doc?"

McVicar glowered at Chark for an instant. Then, without a word, he led the way through a series of double doors with small, circular windows set at eye level. The last doors swung open with a rush of outgoing air. They were in a brightly-lit room filled with benches covered in expensive-looking, complicated scientific equipment. A young technician dressed in white coveralls and sporting the beginnings of a red beard was seated watching a large glass belljar filled with nothing. He was emptying it with a gurgling vacuum pump.

"Ready to go Dr McVicar," he said reverently. "I was testing the seals before we start. Just as you said."

McVicar explained. "We are gong to place the wet books in the bell jar and suck all the air out. As the air leaves, the water will evaporate and dry out the books. That way we don't have to add heat to drive off the moisture. It's the heat which does all the damage."

"Will we be able to read the contents?" asked Chark.

McVicar looked at him over his glasses. "Of course. That's why you came to me wasn't it?"

McVicar took the plastic evidence bag and carefully laid the contents on the white porcelain counter top. The technician picked up each one with tongs and put them in a giant stainless steel toast rack. He placed it in the bell jar and turned on the vacuum pump. The belljar filled with steam as the pump growled and strained. The the books disappeared in the mist. The technician smiled. "Don't worry, gentlemen. It will soon clear."

In a few minutes the steam was sucked out and the pump motor began to labour as its gauges flickered uncertainly.

"Done," said the technician. He switched off the pump and let in dry air with a hiss. "Now let's see what we've got."

McVicar removed the bell jar and then the toast rack. He laid the first book gently on the counter and with delicate fingers, carefully opened it up with blunt-ended tweezers. The pages were still very fragile but they separated without tearing. It took an agonizing fifteen minutes to open all the books to their first pages where the names and signatures were written. Names and ranks appeared one by one. Some had irregular brown stains. When Captain Lovedean's faded and water-stained name was revealed, Chark and Beane gave a simultaneous gasp and clasped each other's hand.

"Well done, sir!" said Beane. "Well done."

Chark nodded his appreciation. "Let's get the details down."

Some of the other names were of soldiers of the Hamptonshire Regiment. There was a yellowed page with German words and insignia. Beane stopped writing and leaned forward to read it aloud. "Klaus Rintzenhelfer. Pilot Officer. Luftflotte 3, Cherbourg, France." He looked up at Chark. "Now we have a name for him. Maybe even find some family?"

Private William Brown's decayed and water-stained army paybook lay open. The metal staples that held it together had corroded away into a red stain but the name was clear. Beane's hand tightened on his pencil as he wrote. The image of an empty cot in the abandoned farm on windy Salisbury Plain flashed into his mind together with the pathetic little pile personal belongings of that other William Brown abandoned in the colourless hospital.

"That's him," said Beane quietly. That's the soldier in the shelter. I know it's him." Beane tried to cover up a shudder of emotion.

"We can't be certain," said Chark. "There's nothing to directly connect this book to that particular William Brown. According to the medical examiner's report, our William had had no treatment by a regular dentist for his dental caries. Except for two extractions which were probably done by one of those army butchers. How many William Brown's did you find in army records? Same with the German. Chances are you're right. But it's not conclusive."

They counted up the books. "Eight," said Chark. We may know something of three of them. You want to make a guess at what happened to the others? Where they are now?"

Beane shook his head. He hadn't thought about that. "We going to dig up the rest of that horse pasture to find out?"

"No," said Chark. "No time for that. We'll leave that to Privett's people. Right now we've got until Monday to finish up here."

McVicar and the technician were gently laying out the books ready to store them in the refrigerated evidence safe.

"You want a thorough analysis of all this stuff, Chark?" he asked.

"Yes please," said Chark. "We'll need as much information as you can get. Usual material analysis. Especially blood. There should be blood on some of them. Call us back in Fairport when you get something?" He turned to Beane. "You got all you want from the books, Beane?"

"Nearly done," said Beane hurrying with the last entry in his notebook.

They took their leave of McVicar and the technician and Beane drove them back to Fairport in a late afternoon sun which dipped rapidly behind the dark clouds on the horizon. As they turned off the motorway into Fairport, Chark sighed. "One more day, Beane. One more day. What can we learn from all this in one more day?"

"Then it's true, Chief? The Super has given us until Monday morning to finish up this case?"

"Yes."

"Jesus," said Beane. "That's a rough assignment. You want to jack it in now?" The prospect of getting out of Fairport and back to Eastchester's relative civilisation and the voluptuous Fiona was welcome news. Leaving a case of murder unfinished when snippets of information were beginning to add up was disappointing. But orders is orders.

Chark crossed his arms and buried his chin in his chest. "Paul Lovedean should be in town now. He's going to the memorial service tomorrow. Let's get back to the 'Duke' and make sure Charley Frater hasn't sold our rooms to someone else."

"OK," said Beane.

"And we'll have another word with our Mrs Walker, I think."

Beane looked at Chark and wrinkled his brow. Now what was he up to?

Chapter 24

Mrs Walker sat upright in her hospital bed supported by piles of snowy white pillows. Like an aged empress surrounded by her court of doctors, nurses, policemen and policewomen. The last rays of the sun washed across the dustless furniture. The doctor stood at the foot of the bed with his arms folded across his chest. A nurse in a starched uniform sat stiffly on the opposite side of the bed to Chark. Beane took a chair against the wall behind Chark and opened his notebook.

Chark looked into Mrs Walker's bright eyes. Her face seemed older and more lined, her body more frail. She looked back at Chark with a hint of challenge.

"You can have five minutes, Chief Inspector. That's all." The doctor checked his watch. "From now."

"Where did you get the soldier's paybooks, Mrs Walker?" Chark asked gently. There was silence as he waited for a response. Mrs Walker smiled and folded her blue-veined hands on the skin-tight bed cover.

"From my boyfriend." Her voice was light and breathless. Like a little girl's. She lowered her eyes.

"Look at me, please," said Chark. She complied slowly.

"Who was your boyfriend?"

"None of your business," she snapped. Her eyes scanned around the room for support. Chark leaned back in his chair and searched through his pockets for nothing in particular as he bought some time while Mrs Walker relaxed.

"I don't believe you had a boyfriend except for Walker. You made him up didn't you?"

Mrs Walker's eyes searched the room. Chark leaned forward and spoke confidentially.

"Are you looking for someone?"

"I told you I had a boyfriend. I don't lie. You're trying to trick me. He used to meet me at the back of the churchyard. Strong as a horse he was in them days. Went away to the war and left me."

Chark paused again and then spoke casually and kindly.

"But he did come back to you after the war?"

"Yes."

"After Dunkirk?"

"Yes."

"Did you take the paybooks from him then?"

Mrs Walker smiled up at him, her eyes dreamy and distant. "There was blood on them. It was dried blood and I hid them. Had to." She became agitated and her eyes rolled as she frantically searched the room about her. Chark continued to press his questions as the doctor and nurse closed in on him.

"Why did you have to?"

"Because I might get in trouble."

"No. That's not the reason, Mrs Walker. Why did you hide them? You could have burned them."

"He would have left me again!" she screamed. "That's why!"

The doctor moved quickly to stand between Mrs Walker and Chark but he was pushed aside.

"Who is your boyfriend?" Chark stared into her eyes. "Was it Charley Frater? Ted Hoff? Colonel Ford? Somebody else? Somebody who should be here now. Somebody you keep looking around for?"

Laughter. Shrill, crazy laughter and spittle. "You'll never know! I'll never tell!"

Then the doctor pulled Chark aside and motioned the nurse to restrain her patient. "The interview's over," he said angrily. "You'll have to leave. I'm going to report your behaviour to the authorities."

Chark walked quickly out of the room, down the corridor and out of the hospital followed by an embarrassed Beane.

"Thought you had her that time, Chief," said Beane as they stood beside the car. "Tough luck. Pity to come away with nothing when you got so close."

"Not quite nothing, Beane my old mate. Remember what she said? 'Strong as a horse he was in them days'. What does that phraseology suggest to you?"

Beane thought for a moment. "That he's still alive?"

"And she can compare him to what he was forty years ago," added Chark.

"Which means she could have seen him recently."

"Right," said Chark. "It's a possibility."

"And you think she was blackmailing whoever it is with those hidden paybooks? But surely not for money. The woman lives like a pauper except for that free room at the vicarage."

Chark was silent for a long while. Then he turned to Beane with a quizzical look. "No. Not blackmail for money." He said quietly. "Maybe for obsessive love. So long as she had the paybooks, whoever he is has to stick around."

"After all these years?" asked Beane incredulously. "They must both be in their seventies."

"And what does age have to do with love?" said Chark. "Come on, Beane. Let's get back to the office and give that computer of yours another chance to redeem itself. We've still got the greater part of a whole day left."

The police station smelled of stale cigarettes, food and the accumulated dust of years of paperwork. More familiar than the sharp smell of the hospital. There were empty teacups, their saucers filled with cigarette butts on the filing cabinets. It was six in the evening and Chark was tired. The interview with Mrs Walker had drained him.

Beane lifted the cover from the computer and brought up his menu on the screen. "Where do we start, Chief?"

"At the beginning. Just keep going. Somewhere in there is something we passed over." Chark took off his tie and crossed his feet on the desk.

"There's more than hundred and forty files in here," said Beane distantly. "You want to see them all?"

"Yep. All of them."

For two hours the blocks of words moved up and down the screen. An untidy heap of printouts piled up on the desk. Chark pondered on them momentarily or impatiently waved Beane onwards to the next file. Word images of Nora Czernowski, Ted Hoff, Charley Frater and the others appeared. Descriptions of the crime scene and stories of the day the bomb fell on the town. But at the end of the one hundred and forty-fifth file Chark sighed and buried his head in his hands.

"Nothing," he said. "Do it again."

"Again?" Beane stared at him. "All one hundred and forty five?" His voice was about an octave higher than usual. "You have any idea what we're looking for?"

"No. But there's an anomaly there somewhere. We are taking something for granted."

Another two hours produced nothing and Beane gratefully turned off the computer and lay his head on the desk for a moment. Chark yawned, stretched his arms high in the air and looked at his watch. "It's ten o'clock," he said. "You want to eat? There's just time to get dinner at the 'Duke' or at that Italian restaurant." He looked into Beane's stubbly face with its puffy, half-closed eyes and decided not to pursue the matter of food. "Just making conversation. Let's get some sleep. It's back to Eastchester and the old routine for you and me."

Beane squinted at Chark. The dull routine of the Eastchester crime scene would come as a relief from nearly two weeks in Fairport.

As they stepped out into the cool night air of the police station car park the duty sergeant called them from the doorway.

"Chief Inspector Chark, sir? Phone call. Says it's urgent."

Chark walked back reluctantly, expecting it to be a call from Eastchester reminding him to be back at work on Monday. But it was Sam Gilkicker.

"Dave Chark?"

"Yes, Sam. What do you want?"

"Got something for you. Not much but it might help. Want to meet me for a cup of coffee? There's that all-night place on the motorway about five minutes from the station. The Cormorant. I'm there now."

"This had better be good, Sam. I'm in no mood to be fucked about tonight. What is it?"

"Remember that question Beane asked me? About the WWII uniform with the red tie? Think I've got the answer."

"Well, what is it?"

"See you at the Cormorant, Chark. Five minutes." Sam hung up.

Chark walked back to the parking lot where Beane was leaning against the car yawning. "Gilkicker says he has an answer to the question about the red tie and white shirt that Lovedean told me about. We'd better hear him out. The Cormorant. Know it?"

Beane nodded and they climbed into the car.

"What the hell," said Chark as they accelerated onto the empty motorway. "Maybe we can, at least, get a good cup of coffee. That stuff in the 'Duke' gives me heartburn."

They drove in a starry night where the moon raced behind small black clouds. The yellow streetlights reflected off the still water of the harbour and a few farm trucks rumbled their way along the slow lane to the city markets.

The Cormorant was one of those islands of noise and light created by the motorway in an otherwise peacefull rural setting. There was a large car park where headlights flashed and horns honked as late diners said their goodbyes. Beane pulled into an empty stall near the door and they walked into the restaurant looking for Sam.

They found him seated in a booth nursing a schooner of beer. The thin strands of black hair that were normally brushed carefully to cover his bald head had fallen over one ear. He raised his hand as though expecting a 'high five'.

"Hi, Guys."

Chark winced at the greeting. Sam was prone to using Americanisms from the TV police shows.

"Hello, Sam. What have you got for me?"

"Drink?"

"Coffee. Strong with cream and sugar."

"Me, too," said Beane.

"So? What have you got?" demanded Chark as the waiter took their order.

"Beane, you remember asking me about that weird WWII uniform? The one with the white shirt and red tie on a soldier?"

"Yes."

"Turns out there was such a thing back in the 40s. Friend of mine got wounded in the war and was in the hospital for a time. When he recovered enough where he could take care of himself, you know, walking wounded or something, and go into the town for a beer or check out the girls, they had to give them some identification. So the MPs wouldn't hassle them."

"A white shirt with a red tie?" asked Chark, his tiredness evaporating.

"Exactly," said Gilkicker. "So if somebody saw one of those uniforms in Fairport in 1941 it was probably worn by some soldier from a local military hospital."

Sam sucked noisily at his cigarette and squinted through the smoke at Chark. Chark studied Sam over his coffee cup while Beane searched his memory for the file about the soldier in the horse pasture. Then Sam leaned forward, stubbed out his cigarette and lit another.

"Well, Dave? What do you think?" he asked through the smoke "We got a story or not?"

Chark thought for a few seconds before answering. "There were a lot of military hospitals around here during the war. The British and Canadians had several. Americans too. Most of them were temporary and built of Quonset huts." He drained his cup and tried to avoid the smoke pouring from Sam's nostrils.

"But not in 1941," said Sam. "Those temporary ones came after the Normandy invasion."

Chark agreed. "Right. There must be records somewhere of those hospitals taken over by the military after the Dunkirk evaccuation."

"Three," said Sam triumphantly. "I already checked. Got their locations on the map here." He reached inside his jacket, pulled out a creased large-scale Ordnance Survey map of the Hampton area and laid it on the table. There were three rough circles drawn with a red pencil. Two in the light green patches north of the town where the country areas lay and the other in the jumbled black and gray which was the old and new parts of Fairport. Beane spun the map around and studied it closely. He hit the table with the flat of his hand.

"Remember what Lovedean said about the soldier that scared the boys in the horse pasture? He said his uniform was clean and creased and his boots were polished and shiny. When he kicked over the saucepan they were cooking in over the fire he got ash on them."

"Yes," said Chark. "What about it?"

Beane returned to the map and traced the lines which were the roads. "If he walked to the horse pasture from the hospital, he didn't come far. If he did, his boots would have been dirty or at least, dusty."

"Unless he got on a bus," said Sam licking his pencil as he wrote.

"It was a Sunday. No country buses on a Sunday then," said Chark.

"Taxi?"

"Unlikely," said Chark. "It was a small town. He would have had to call for one and there weren't many around in the war. Anyway, if he came from one of the hospitals out in the country, the cost would be out of reach of a British private soldier's pay."

The lights were going out in the bar as the last of the customers left. "You boys going to have another drink before we close?" A plump and tired waitress picked up their empty cups and glasses.

"Just leaving," said Chark. "We'll be out of here soon."

"Suit yourself," she sniffed as she wiped down the table and left.

The three men huddled over the map in the diminishing light.

"The one in town looks the best bet," Beane pointed at the red circle. "That's the Fairport Memorial Hospital. Where Mrs Walker is."

"What's this one?" Chark pointed to the one farthest away from Fairport.

"Institution for juvenile delinquents. Fifteen miles away. Too far to walk."

"And this one?" Chark looked up as he pointed at the third circle. A black square on the map surrounded by the pale green of open country. Sam turned back his notebook pages. "That's the old DeCourcy estate. Family donated the house and grounds to the county. The house was converted into a hospital in 1916. It's a maternity hospital now. Nice place."

"And only three inches from the centre of Fairport. Straight road all the way with a sidewalk as I remember," said Chark. "Easy walk for a soldier if he's fit." He took the map up and put it into his pocket. "Mind if I keep this, Sam?"

"Sure. But I go with it. I'm part of the deal. It was me who gave you the info, don't forget." Sam peeled off a banknote and put it under the paper napkin caddy. "Fair deal, Chark?"

"You know I don't make deals, Sam. But thanks for the information. We'll take it from here."

The restaurant was dark as they picked their way between the tables and went out into the parking lot. Sam Gilkicker padded along behind them complaining loudly and falling over the chairs.

The cold night air was refreshing and there was a slight salty, seaweedy smell coming in off the harbour. Chark buckled himself into his seat and watched Sam saunter over to his own car and start the engine.

"Where to, Chief?"

"Fairport Memorial Hospital. That's where all the county records are kept. And lose Sam on the way. Head off as though we're going to the DeCourcy place, then double back."

Beane grinned and burned rubber as he pulled onto the motorway. Chark looked up into the rear view mirror. No sign of Sam.

"Take the next exit," said Chark and he leaned heavily against the door as Beane swung the car up a narrow ramp over the bridge to the westbound lanes and on past the Cormorant again towards Fairport.

Beane parked in the hospital staff parking area. They walked up to the receptionist's desk in the bright lights.

"Oh, shit," said Beane with a giggle. "He's here."

Sam was already at the desk talking to the receptionist who was adjusting her cap and smoothing her straight blond hair.

"Hi, Chief," said Sam smugly. "Thought you might show up here. I was just asking this beautiful young lady where we can find the records department."

"It's this way," said Chark with a shrug of resignation and led the way down the polished hall to the familiar varnished door.

The clerk was not the helpful volunteer woman he had spoken to the first time. This one was a short, pudgy man wearing a shabby black suit, blue tie and a dirty shirt.

"Yes?" he asked suspiciously over the stained teacup from which he was drinking. The spoon was still in it and he chewed as he drank. Chark took a breath and framed his question with care.

"I would like to see the county medical records for 1941. The military patients of that time. Please."

The clerk eyed the three of them. "Why?"

Chark took another breath and stood closer to the desk. "Because I am on police business and I need help in making my enquiries. My name is Detective Chief Inspector Chark of the County Constabulary CID. Do you want to see my identification? And what's your name?"

The clerk put down his teacup sullenly. "It's Arthur. Arthur Bottomly. It's late and I'm on my tea break. Union insists we take our breaks. Can't you come back in the morning?"

"Show me the military records, dammit," growled Chark who did not suffer the indifference of public servants easily, including policemen. His voice was heavy with menace and it was not lost on Bottomly who took refuge behind his teacup.

"Not here," he said.

"What's not here?"

"Military records. Moved years ago to the archives. Old Pritchard takes care of them now. Does it for free. Stupid old scab. You'll have to talk to him." Bottomly slurped his tea and looked up warily at Chark.

"Well, where can we find this Pritchard!" roared Chark who was about to reach over the desk and grab Bottomly by the collar. Beane restrained him. "I don't have time to squeeze every little bit of information out of you, you useless little bastard!"

Bottomly's eyes widened and his jaw dropped as his cup rattled back in its saucer. He pushed his chair back against the wall away from Chark's anger. "I can call him if you like? Lives in Fairport."

Chark nodded as Bottomly reached for the phone and dialed. Keeping his eyes on Chark. After a few moments he handed it to him. The voice at the other end was soft and quiet.

"Pritchard here."

"Chief Inspector Chark, County Constabulary. I need your help with some enquiries, Mr Pritchard. I understand you have charge of the military medical records for the district?"

"Not exactly in charge," said Pritchard. "The records are a matter of history now although I get questions from relatives and insurance companies. Writers sometimes looking for stories. I'm the honorary historian." Pritchard's voice was precise and well modulated. Chark figured him for a retired teacher or lawyer.

"I need to know about military patients who were here in the Fairport area around the time of the big air raid on Fairport in early 1941," said Chark. "Can you help me?"

"The time of the big raid? I remember it well. Yes, I think I can help. Shall we meet tomorrow? At ten?"

"No, Mr Pritchard. Now. I need help now."

"Oh," said Pritchard. "How exciting. Sounds awfully important. The records are kept in the DeCourcy hospital and I don't have a car. Can you pick me up?"

"Of course," said Chark. "Give me the address."

Pritchard's house was a tidy, ivy-covered cottage close to the Memorial hospital in the old part of Fairport. Beane was back at the hospital with him in ten minutes. Chark had left the records clerk to his teapot and was standing on the forecourt with Sam Gilkicker as they drove up. The night was getting colder and he shivered as he opened the car door to get in.

"Thanks for the help, Sam. We can take it from here."

Sam rolled his collar up against the chill wind. "Oh, come on, Chief. Be reasonable. Be a lot less trouble to take me along with you than have poor old Beane try to give me the slip again. All I ask is an hour's start on the story."

"If there is a story," said Chark. Sam had the rear door open now and was standing looking as appealing as he could.

"Get in, Sam."

Chark sat in the front of the car with Beane. Sam squeezed in beside Mr Pritchard in the back. Cursory introductions were made and the car rolled out of the hospital forecourt and headed north out of town. Beane looked in the rear-view mirror at his passengers who were rearranging themselves on the back seat. Pritchard was a scholarly-looking man of average height with a perpetual look of surprise on his face. Sixty five years old or more with a pink, round face and colourless eyes. He appeared to be completely bald but there was a fine down of fuzz on his pink, shining head.

"I should warn you, gentlemen, that I often get car sick," said Pritchard as they rolled along the deserted street.

"This a police car or a golf cart?" asked Sam as he pulled his packet of cigarettes from his pocket. "Can't it go any faster?"

"You light that thing in here," said Beane looking into the mirror. "And I'll stick it up your nose. Lighted end first."

"Oh, dear," muttered Pritchard mildly.

A flashing blue light attached to a police motor cycle closed in from behind. "Oh, shit!" said Beane as he braked..

"You going to a fire?" The traffic cop ceremoniously peeled off his gauntlet gloves and took out his ticket book. Chark leaned out of the window and opened his wallet.

"Sorry, sir," said the cop recognising the warrant card. "But you were doing forty in a thirty mile an hour zone. Just doing my job, sir." "That's alright, constable. So are we. Well done." They had traveled about a mile. The motorcycle cop waved them on.

One mile later, as they crossed a bridge out into the blackness of the countryside, Mr Pritchard clamped a handkerchief over his mouth and started to heave. "Oh, dear," he said between clenched teeth. "I fear I am going to be sick."

"Stop the car! Stop the car!" yelled Chark. He flung open the door before Beane brought it to a slithering stop on the gravel shoulder. He leaped out to open the rear door. Sam gave Pritchard a push from behind. He fell out and disappeared down the bank. There was a howl of pain followed by the sound of uncontrolled retching. The others got back into the car and waited. Beane leaned wearily on the steering wheel and Sam sank back into his corner while Chark fulminated in front. Soon, Mr Pritchard opened the door and collapsed into his seat.

"Can we go now?" asked Chark.

"Can I sit up front with the driver?" asked Pritchard feebly. "I don't get as sick if I can look through the windshield."

There was a moment's silence followed by laughter led by Chark who, with exaggerated patience, exchanged places with the apologising old man. Sam studied his nails and wished he had a cigarette.

"What was all that yelling about, Mr Pritchard?" asked Chark as they drove off again down the dark road. "Did you hurt yourself?"

"No, Chief Inspector," said Pritchard. "I fell into some nettles. Got my hands all blistered. I'm allergic to nettles." Sam and Beane exploded in laughter as Chark threw up his hands.

*

The DeCourcy Maternity Hospital lay in a hundred acres of rolling parkland. The oaks and elms in the park were outlined in sharp relief on the horizon against a moonlit sky. Lights shone from every window. A red and white barrier stopped the car at the main gate and Beane sounded the horn. He showed his ID to the guard and the barrier was lifted noiselessly. As they drove through the gate the guard turned to his desk and lifted the phone.

The four men presented themselves at the reception desk and waited until the gray-haired, overweight woman receptionist looked suspiciously at their tired, unshaven faces and rumpled clothes.

"Is it always this busy at night?" asked Beane as a tinkling trolley full of glass bottles and tubes pushed by an energetic orderly bore down on the group and scattered them. The receptionist bristled.

"Young man, this is a maternity hospital. Babies don't care what time of day it is. Now, what do you want? Which one of you is the father?"

They looked around at each other until Chark produced his wallet again. "We're not new fathers, Nurse," he said testily. "On police business." They shuffled their feet in embarrassment until Pritchard stepped forward and introduced himself.

"Hullo, Polly."

"Oh, it's you, Mr Pritchard," she said beaming up at him.

"I'm with these gentlemen on police business today," he said grandly. "We are going down to the archives to do some research."

"Really? Since they're with you, I suppose it's alright." She waved them off and the four walked through a maze of corridors, down a flight of wooden stairs into the cold confines of the basement. Pritchard snapped on the lights. The vaulted, redbrick cavern was illuminated by harsh, white strip lights. There was an outsized "NO SMOKING" sign.

"The deCourcy's wine cellar. No wine left now, unfortunately. Just me and a lot of other old relics."

Pritchard led the way around the room through metal racks filled with books and cardboard boxes. There was a large collection of guns, uniforms, flags of all nations and maps.

"My research department," said Pritchard proudly. "Going to take me a few more years to catalogue it all. Trouble is, people keep bringing more. Mostly from the estates of WWII veterans." He lapsed into thought and looked around the basement. "Lots of boys died around Fairport during the war. British, Free French, Poles, Norwegians, Canadians, Americans."

Chark put down the Webley revolver he was admiring. "You were here during the war?"

"Yes. I've no night vision. Bright lights make me blind so they called me up in 1940 and classified me 4F and sent me home. But I volunteered for the Medical Corps and they sent me here to the DeCourcy. I was only twenty then." Pritchard took off his rimless glasses and polished them with a silk handkerchief. "I suppose you saw the military cemetary in Fairport?"

Beane looked up from a case full of regimental hat badges. "Yes. One of the murder victims is buried there."

Pritchard's face hardenend. "They were all murdered," he said quietly, looking away into a corner of the room as if talking to someone else. "You know how they trained those American boys? Made them crawl on their bellies through barbed wire. Fired machine guns over them. Six feet the first day, five feet the next day. Down to one foot. Some of them got shot accidentally, some of them panicked and ran. They're the ones buried in the cemetary. Just kids from the slums and the farms. Treated like WWI cannon fodder. There's a hundred or more buried out there. And damned few of us left to remember them."

There was silence as Pritchard took a deep breath and recovered his humour. "But that's not why we're here, is it? You want to see the records. Can you give me the name?"

"Sorry, no," said Chark. "Only the date. Say March and April 1941 to start with. Bring us the files and we'll work through them."

"Oh, God," muttered Beane. "Here we go again."

In the cold and deep silence of the wine cellar they pored over old records until the names and dates numbed their brains. Nothing. Not one familiar name or event. The hours passed into early Sunday morning, the last day of Chark's investigation and the final episode in the Fairport murders case—the memorial service.

"Well, that's it," said Pritchard as he dropped the last file onto the broad table top. "That's all the DeCourcy hospital records for January through September of that year."

Beane was asleep at the table, his head on his arms, Sam was sprawled in a chair out of cigarettes and getting nervous.

Chark turned to Pritchard with one more desperate question. "Is there anything you remember about those days? Anything. An unusual occurrence. Something out of the usual routine."

Pritchard shook his head slowly. "No, nothing. Of course, everything was unusual in those days. Patients came and went. Some stayed for months. Others died. Most got well and went back to their units. Keeping track of them was a major task and we made a few mistakes and lost people altogether. Some just wandered off into town and most we picked up quickly and brought them back."

"You said 'most', Mr Pritchard," said Chark. "What does 'most' mean?"

"We only lost one." Pritchard looked thoughtful. "It was the day of the big air raid on Fairport. I remember now. He never showed up after we missed him at roll call. I haven't thought about that for forty years."

"Go on," said Chark. "What happened?"

"We had a lot of AWOLs. Mostly, they just walked off for a beer in town and decided not to come back. Sometimes they got all the way home."

"What happened to the one you lost?"

"Never found him. Gave up looking after a few weeks. They assumed he was killed in the raid and his body was never found." Pritchard began sorting through a pile of files. "It's in here somewhere."

"You said 'they' assumed he was killed. Who's 'they'?" asked Chark shaking Beane awake.

"Military Police. MPs. They wanted to talk to him about something that happened over in France. They were really upset that he had gone missing." Pritchard pulled a file and waved it.

"What was his name?" asked Chark eagerly as Pritchard read through the papers.

"Here it is. Private Benjamin Stewkley H964804. Hamptonshire Regiment."

Chark felt the disappointment like a blow. There was nothing about Benjamin Stewkley that rang a bell in his memory."You remember anything about him?" he asked Pritchard

"Vaguely. Long time ago. As best I remember he was a loner. Not liked by the other patients. Kept to himself. There were the usual rumours after the MPs left after the doctors said they couldn't interrogate him. 'Battle fatigue' they called it in those days. The MPs hung around for a few days trying to get their hands on him but they left after a while. The other patients invented all sorts of crimes for him from black marketing to murder and rape."

As Pritchard spoke, Beane read the file. When he came to the last sheet he found an envelope stapled to the back cover. He opened it and pulled out a black and white photograph with Ben Stewkley's name and serial number written on the back. He stared. Then he handed the photograph to Chark.

"Chief, look at this."

"Holy Christ," said Chark and he sat heavily in a chair looking at the picture. It was a young man with dark hair cut army fashion. The face was thinner and unlined but there was no doubting the eyebrows and ears. No doubt at all. Chark was looking at a photograph of the Reverend Dennis Batley.

Chapter 25

Chark sat back in his chair and smiled to himself. All the events of the past week now took on a different perspective. Here was the anomaly he had known was there from the beginning. The one thing Chark had taken for granted, the word of that ecclesiastic. That plausible, benign old man he had first met in St Ethelred's church. The bondage created for so many years by a strong-willed, possessive woman had become a safe haven for the Reverend Batley who, like a prisoner lacking other human companionship, calls his jailer his friend.

"You alright, Chief?" Beane leaned over and took the photograph from Chark's hand.

"It's the vicar alright," he said in a loud whisper. "No mistaking that face."

Mr Pritchard was looking from one to the other in bewilderment. "Something wrong?"

Sam Gilkicker was frantically calling for a telephone.

"You found what you're looking for?" asked Pritchard.

"Oh, yes," said Chark as he got stiffly up from his chair. "What I wanted but not what I expected."

"Where's the damn phone?" bleated Sam. "I got to call the paper."

Chark turned to Sam as if he had just noticed him. "Can you wait a little longer, Sam?"

"Why?" he asked suspiciously.

"Because I don't want to lose this one. We've got one more interview to make before we go back to Fairport." He looked at his watch. "There's time before the memorial service. It'll be worth it."

"You promise?" said Sam.

"Cop's honour."

"That and a packet of cigarettes will make me feel a lot better. Can we stop on the way and get some?"

"No. No time. Come on. Let's get moving. You feel like you can drive?" The last question was aimed at Beane who was still looking at the photograph and shaking his head in disbelief.

"Just give me directions. Where are we going?"

"Hampton Theological College. To check out Batley's college career. Anybody know where it is?" Three heads shook at once.

"Damn," said Chark. "We'll have to ask the receptionist for a phone book and look it up."

She was on the phone. Chark looked at his watch and drummed his fingers on her desk. Finally, with an imperious "Yes?" she laid down the handset and looked up at him.

"Can you look up the number for the Hampton Theological College for us and find out where it is? We need to get there in a hurry." He looked at his watch again. It was already five past eight and the memorial service started at ten.

"No," she said holding up her hand to stifle Chark's next words. "I can do better than that. If you give me a lift I'll take you there. It's close by where I live. I can get there without going through all that down-town traffic."

She stood and stomped out from behind her desk on thick legs, wrapped her dark blue cape around her and hoisted a canvas bag onto her broad shoulders. Then she led the way out into the morning light. Like Margaret Rutherford's Jane Marple.

"Come on," she called. "My shift was over five minutes ago. You going to give me a lift or do I have to walk to the bus stop?"

"Of course, madam," said Chark with a generous sweep of his arm. "Please come with us." He led the way to the car followed by a grinning Beane, a suffering Sam and a confused Pritchard. Sam, who was now in the middle stages of acute nicotine deprivation, opened the rear door of the car and got in first followed by the nurse and Chark. It was a tight fit and after they had to fence with their elbows for space. She won. The two men were wedged against the doors separated by the nurse who laid her beefy arms across her bosom and pinned them back against the seat.

As Beane drove through the backstreets and unfamiliar neighbourhoods of Hampton he received a barrage of peremptory commands from the woman in the back seat. "Turn left. Turn right. Watch out for the children. Slow down for the crosswalk. You're supposed to be a policeman, you should know better. You're swinging the back of the car around too much. Stop here!"

The car squealed to a stop and she glared at Sam and Chark as they strained forward against their captor.

"Is this the college?" asked Beane looking around at the rows of red-brick houses with well-kept gardens.

"Certainly not," she barked. "This is where I live. College is around the corner. Next left. Can't miss it." With a hearty slap on Chark's thigh, she pushed him out of the car and followed heavily as he held the door open for her.

"Thanks for the lift." When she was gone, Sam took a deep breath of relief. Beane drove around the corner and parked. Chark instructed Mr Pritchard to wait in it with patience until they returned.

Hampton Theological College's architecture was of the Victorian

Ugly Period. Massive, grimy granite blocks piled on one another until they terminated in a squat, crenellated bell tower. Narrow, deep-set clerestory windows with tiny glass panes prevented the light of ordinary day from penetrating the cloistered interior. There was a weathered wooden door opening directly onto the sidewalk. Beane pressed the brass doorbell. The door was opened by an elderly man dressed in the faded livery of a hotel bellhop. He enquired of their business.

"We want to talk to the principal or whatever you call the administrator of this establishment." Chark offered his warrant card and the man stepped back in surprise.

"Police?" he stammered. "I'll have to talk to the master of the college. Just a moment, please." He started to close the door on them but Beane placed a size ten shoe against it. They pushed their way in and filed through into the dim interior.

"We'll wait here."

The doorman protested briefly and then scuttled off. He returned a few minutes later and beckoned them to follow him deeper into the building. The party walked down uncarpeted wooden floors dimly lit by yellowing glass globes set in brass pillars from another era. From somewhere came the rumble of an organ and voices in a monotonous recital. Chark's initial impression was being confirmed at each step. Hampton Theological College may once have been a successful institution. Not now.

Their conductor stopped outside a door shaped like one of the windows and tapped on it.

"Enter"

They were ushered in reverently and greeted by the Master of the College. He rose from behind a heavy oak desk with grotesque, bulbous legs and a Tiffany-styled desk lamp.

"Welcome, brothers. I'm Doctor Hunter. Please take a seat." The man was tall and very thin. He wore a well-cut, belted tweed jacket of ancient style and a Roman collar. His head was bald or clean-shaven and he sucked noisily on a Holmesian pipe clenched between long, yellow teeth.

Chark accepted a handshake and introduced himself and the

others. They sank gratefully into the soft cushions of overstuffed chairs.

"And what can I do for you, Chief Inspector?" asked Hunter through his pipe. "None of my students in trouble with the law are they?" He guffawed as though the idea were completely laughable. Chark had keen ears for local dialects. He detected a trace of London Cockney. South of the river. He'd bet a month's salary on it.

"No, sir," said Chark. "Nobody is in trouble to my knowledge. I need information about one of your earlier students. A Dennis Batley. He entered your college sometime in 1940s." Chark watched as Hunter refilled his pipe from a greasy leather pouch.

"1940s eh?" said Hunter. "That's a long time ago. May I ask the reason for this request?"

"We are investigating a case of murder. Mr Batley may have been a witness. That's all I can tell you at this stage."

"And you think this Dennis Batley had something to do with it? A member of this college?" Dr Hunter leaned back in his chair and stared incredulously at Chark.

"We won't know until you answer the questions," said Chark evenly. "Of course, you are not compelled to answer my questions right now. We could do it under more formal conditions if you want to consult a lawyer, Dr Hunter."

Hunter waved his hand and dismissed the idea. "Forties you say? Before my time, of course. During Dr Dent's tenure. Fine man. Good Christian scholar. Published several books on the early Greek biblical writers. I remember-."

Chark interrupted him as Beane rolled his eyes upwards. "Yes, Doctor, but what about Dennis Batley? We don't have much time."

Hunter stopped his reminiscence and put the pipe back in his mouth. "No problem there. We have all our records going back to the beginning of our beloved college." He pressed a button on the desk. The door was opened by a mousy little woman dressed in a pleated tweed skirt and a gray woolen sweater.

"Our secretary," said Hunter as an introduction. "Miss Hammond, these gentlemen wish to see the scholastic records of one Dennis Batley. He was a student in 1940 or thereabouts. Please bring the file in?"

Miss Hammond nodded and was gone.

As they waited while the minutes passed and the time approached nine o'clock, Hunter lit and relit his pipe. Beane's eyes flicked across the room looking for something of interest among the dusty pieces of porcelain and the array of old religious prints on the walls. Sam watched enviously at the blue smoke which rose from Hunter's lips.

After a few minutes, Miss Hammond reappeared carrying a faded red-covered file tied with a black ribbon. On the outside, written in large, black letters was the name "Dennis C. Batley. D.D." Dr Hunter opened the file and read the contents. "Dennis Conway Batley. Came to us in September of 1941. Highly recommended. An orphan. Parents killed in an uprising in Africa where they were missionaries. No immediate family. Brought up in one of those free schools run by the masons. Joined the army in 1939. Here is his letter of recommendation."

Chark took the letter, read it and passed it on to Beane.

"And how did they verify his identity when he was admitted to the college?"

"Verify?" said Hunter, aghast at the idea. "There would be no need to. He was from a very good Christian family. Carried a fine letter of recommendation from his school and had excellent grades. Anyway, his fees were paid in advance for the first year and were never in arrears.

"How were Batley's fees paid? Cash, cheque, money order?" Hunter took the pipe from his mouth and took the file. "Funny you should ask that, Inspector. From the records it appears his fees were paid in cash. First of the month. Not by Dr Batley. The receipts were made out to someone called Jones."

Chark took the book and passed it over to Beane. "We'll need this for evidence, sir. We'll write a receipt of course and you will get it back in due course." Chark instinctively knew who Jones was. Mrs Walker had used her savings and meagre pay from the vicarage to put Batley through the college.

"One last question, Dr Hunter," said Chark consulting his watch again. "Do you have a picture of Dr Batley?"

Hunter stood and walked to the wall opposite his desk. It was covered with framed photographs from ceiling to wainscoting.

"Yes. They're all here. Let me see. Ah! Here it is." He pulled a group photograph from the wall and handed it to Chark. It was the same one that hung in the Fairport vicarage. Hunter pointed to the man standing in the back row. Chark placed the other picture of Ben Stewkley from Pritchard's collection beside it. The hair was a little longer and the face smiling instead of dour. But they were undoubtedly the same person.

Chapter 26

Chark, Beane and Sam Gilkicker raced out of the College and piled into the car. Mr Pritchard was sleeping in the back seat , his pursed lips vibrating softly. He woke with a start as Beane started the engine. With a grinding of gears they pulled rapidly away from the curb and headed for Fairport.

"The vicarage, Beane. Make it fast. We've got thirty minutes before the memorial service starts at the church. Get us to there before Batley leaves for the service."

"Oh, my goodness," whispered Pritchard in anticipation of the wildest ride he had had for many years. Beane turned on the blue flashers and wound his way through the traffic out of Hampton and on to the motorway around the harbour to Fairport. As Pritchard rolled around in the back seat hanging on to Sam Gilkicker's arm, his car sickness disappeared and he gave little whoops of joy as they passed other cars.

Beane honked impatiently at an obstinate beer truck pulling slowly up the incline at the exit to Fairport. He passed on the wrong side and roared through the town to the vicarage. The car skidded to a stop in the gravel outside the vicarage. Sam sprinted for the tobacconist's shop and a telephone. Chark and Beane ran up to the front door where they were greeted nervously by a church warden dressed in a black cassock. He was just leaving and closing the door behind him.

"The vicar?" he answered to their panting question. "Gone over to the church. Service starts in ten minutes. You've just missed him."

"Church," yelled Chark as they tumbled into the car again. Sam stood on the sidewalk sucking deeply on a cigarette with a look of sublime satisfaction on his face. At the sight of Beane's car, he turned and trotted towards the church.

Beane threw up a cloud of gravel as he made a U-turn and drove off to the church. The tree-lined streets were full of parked cars and jaywalking pedestrians dressed in their Sunday finery. An elderly lady stepped into their path and waved her umbrella at them as though it were her shield against mortality. The nose of the car dipped as Beane braked to avoid her. Chark threw up his hands and admitted defeat as Beane slowly moved among the pedestrians to find a place to doublepark. A uniformed constable started forward to remonstrate with him. Chark leaned over and let his glowering face be seen. They left the car in the middle of the street and walked into the church.

*

Sunlight poured through the stained-glass window above the flower-decked altar. The congregation filled the nave and flowed over into the aisles. Arguments grew over real or imagined ownership of places in the pews.Places that had been worn down and polished by the ample backsides of generations of Fairporters. In the balcony above the west door, a TV team were busy setting up their cameras and microphones. Before the altar, two flag-draped coffins lay on trestles hung with purple cloths. They were oak coffins with brass fittings. Placed on one was a Naval Officer's cap resplendent with gold badge and trim. On the other, a soldier's simple, plain khaki cap with a brass regimental badge. Flowers cascaded down from the altar to frame the coffins. No expense had been spared by the Fairport Town Council for their new-found war heroes.

The crowd in the aisle pressed in on Chark and Beane as they tried to reach the vestry to the left of the altar. Mr Pritchard was holding court with a few older men and giving an animated description of his day's work.

A persistent voice kept calling "Sergeant! Sergeant!" Beane looked over the heads of the people about him. Nora Czernowski ploughing her way towards him. "Sit by me?" she signaled. But Beane shook his head and pointed at Chark who had stopped to speak to a gray-haired man dressed in a dark suit and tie sitting in a pew towards the front of the church. A beautiful, dark-haired woman sat next to him. Chark turned to Beane as Paul Lovedean stood and held out his hand.

"Detective Sergeant Hume Beane. Mr Paul Lovedean," he said. "And this is Prudence Whitehorse. Also from Seattle."

Beane was impaled on those bright, black eyes as he took her hand. Old Chark hadn't mentioned this one. Sly old bugger!

Chark and Beane squeezed in among the complaining occupiers of the pew behind Lovedean. The organist struck a rumbling vibrato and the choirboys in scarlet cassocks and white lace collars stopped their giggling and punching to remain angelically silent. Chark looked around and identified the faces of Charley Frater and Ted Hoff sitting over to his right. Around the church he saw familiar faces from the interviews. There was no sign of the Reverend Batley.

The high, sweet voices of the choirboys soared to the ceiling. The congregation stopped its foot-shuffling and coughing. Children were shushed. The elderly deaf sternly signaled to stop talking. All eyes were fixed on the raised pulpit.

The door behind the pulpit opened and the vicar of Fairport stepped out. He raised his arms and eyes heavenwards as if he were the Pope at St Peter's. The white lace of his surplice fanned out below his arms like the wings of a bird. The purple hood of his doctoral gown framed his white hair. He intoned a blessing on his flock and dropped his eyes and hands. The choir sang a hymn and ended on a high, ringing note.

Chark leaned forward and peered between Lovedean's and Prudence Whitehorse's heads. The vicar beamed energy and warmth as he leaned over the pulpit with his hands on the rail to address the overflowing church.

"My dear, dear friends," he boomed out over their heads. "We are gathered here today to pay homage to two lost heroes of that distant but glorious conflict of two score years and more ago. To lay their bones to rest at last in that hallowed ground reserved for those citizens of Fairport who gave their lives in the two Great Wars of our century-" The rhetoric was like warm water from his lips and the people responded with a splattering of "Amens" and "Hallelujahs". He spoke in strong theatrical phrases that left the congregation looking at each other, mystified. Was this Boring Old Batley? Is this the vicar of Fairport? He, who for decades, had rarely expressed a controversial opinion on any subject except the selection of hymns for the service. What had caused this remarkable change? Chark knew. The incapacitation of Mrs Walker had released him from his fear of discovery. He felt safe at last. Confident.

Paul Lovedean stared at the coffins, his mind racing back over the years trying to place the voice that flowed from the pulpit. As the vicar's voice rose higher, the characters of the victims under the flags grew to saintly heights. Then, in a grand gesture, he pointed a quivering finger at the coffins and roared a finale.

"We who survived., salute you!"

There was silence in the church and Chark suspected that some of the congregation wanted to applaud. The vicar mopped his brow and beamed down at them. "Now," he started in a softer voice. "We will sing hymn number-." But he was interrupted. Paul Lovedean stood amid the silence and pointed a finger at the pulpit.

"It was you," called out Lovedean. Two hundred pairs of eyes were fixed on him. "You were the soldier in the horse pasture. I remember your voice."

The vicar backed away from the pulpit rail. "Who are you?" he quavered.

Lovedean turned his finger to the coffins. The congregation took a breath and started to whisper. "Those are my father's remains. And you kicked over our cooking pot." Lovedean began walking down the aisle towards the pulpit.

Beane reached out to restrain him but Chark took his arm and stopped him.

"Not yet, Beane, not yet."

Lovedean continued down the aisle with his finger raised. As he stood below the pulpit, he stopped. In a ringing voice that echoed off the walls he called out. "You killed my father! It was you!"

There was pandemonium in the church. The congregation rose to its feet and the TV crew swung the cameras.

"No!" shouted the vicar. "No, I tell you! No!" But Lovedean was on the first step up to the pulpit and Beane was in the aisle ready to join him.

"Wait, Beane. Wait," said Chark above the noise. The noise stopped as the vicar, his face contorted with anger and fear reached for his long-handled crucifix with the heavy brass cross.. He pointed it down as Lovedean took another step up to the pulpit.

"One more step and I'll split your fucking skull!" growled the vicar. At that, the church broke into unrestrained clamour as the vicar disappeared through the door behind the pulpit carrying the crucifix with him.

"Now, Beane. After him," called Chark. "He's making for the roof. That's the only way out."

"You crafty old bastard," said Beane as he struggled out into the aisle against a sea of people. "You knew this would happen."

"No, I didn't," said Chark. "I didn't plan it this way. But I did hope a confrontation would work. It's our only chance to get a confession. We still don't have enough evidence to convict, so be careful up there."

Beane pushed his way through the mass of people in the aisle and joined Lovedean who was wrestling with the door behind the pulpit. It was bolted from the inside. Together they battered at it with their shoulders until the ancient, dry wood splintered and they could ran up the narrow stairs towards the roof. By now, Chark had shoved his way down the aisle through the excited crowd in the opposite direction. He stood in the dark space behind the font.

His childhood memories served him well. There was another way up to the roof from above the west door and if he could make it, they would have the vicar trapped. A small door was set in the wall adjacent to the main door.It opened with a creak as Chark lifted the heavy latch and peered into the darkness beyond. He climbed the narrow, circular stairs through the accumulated cobwebs and dust until he reached the door onto the roof. It was weathered shut and took several pushes with all his weight to open it. Finally, it swung open on sagging hinges and Chark stood looking out across the flat church roof at Beane and Lovedean in the breezy sunshine. No sign of the vicar. Below them in the churchyard the crowd looked up and pointed at the figures on the roof.

For a moment, Chark felt the nausea of failure and fatigue well up inside him. How could an elderly man dressed in such restrictive clothing have got away in the confines of a church? Chark rested against the door frame as he reran his memory of those wild childhood chases through the old church. Beane and Paul Lovedean were walking across the leaded roof towards him. Then he remembered. The space between the flat roof they stood on and the upper side of the vaulted nave. A dark, unlit and uneven space filled with bats and the nests of thousands of spiders. A forbidden place that only the bravest of the boys had ventured into. Chark waved Lovedean and Beane back.

"He's in the attic!" he called. "There's a door in the wall of the belltower. About ten feet down the stairs."

Beane hesitated for a moment before he understood and then with a wave of acknowledgement, ran back across the roof to the belltower. Chark stepped back through the roof door and carefully made his way down the steps in the dark, feeling the wall for the door to the attic as he went. A few seconds later he felt the handle and pulled it open. The doorway was narrow so he had to turn sideways to get through it. He stood on the narrow catwalk that extended across the roof of the nave like the keel of an upturned boat. Beane opened the door at the other end and a shaft of sunlight lit up the scene.

In the centre of the catwalk, standing stooped and fearfull was the vicar. He was outlined in the light from behind him. He leaned on his crucifix, panting for breath. The old, decayed catwalk swayed and shifted under Chark's feet as he stepped forward. He signaled to Beane and Lovedean to stay where they were. Above them, the low, blackened timbers of the roof created eerie patterns in the shaft of light. Chark stepped forward and Batley retreated one tentative little step. Chark stopped and spoke in a clear voice so that the witnesses could hear.

"Is your name Benjamin Harold Stewkley?"

There was silence. Then, as though from far away, the vicar of Fairport answered.

"It is."

"Did you, on the morning of June 17th 1941, with a blow from a shovel, kill the soldier and sailor in the horse pasture behind the Duke of York public house in Fairport?"

Again a silence and Chark had to repeat the question. The vicar's voice was scarcely audible as they all stood motionless on the catwalk.

"Yes, God help me, I did."

Chark waited for a second or two and then spoke in a more kindly tone. "Was Mrs Walker blackmailing you with those paybooks she hid, Mr Stewkley?"

The vicar looked up at Chark in astonishment. "You know about that?"

"We know all about it."

"Then it's over," said Stewkley. "It's over at last." He tried to step forward but the catwalk swayed a little. He stopped. "She found me when I was in the hospital and I gave her back her half crown. Then she took me from the hospital one day when I was let out and she looked after me until I got better. Said she couldn't marry me, you see, because they never found Walker so she said she was still married to him. She found those books in my kit and kept them."

"And you took the identity of Dennis Batley?"

"Yes. It was easy. It was her idea. Batley was killed in France. They made me take the paybooks off the bodies There were letters in his pocket when I took his paybook. One was addressed to the college. I used it to get in."

Stewkley made an effort to move away from Chark.

"Don't move!" called Chark. "I'm going to help you. I'll come to you." He inched forward with his eyes on Stewkley.

"What happened over there in France?" asked Chark as he shuffled forward on the catwalk.

"Sergeant Major made me do things I can't talk about. After a while I couldn't tell who was on our side and who wasn't. Then I walked in the mud and the sand and water and woke up in the hospital."

"Go on," said Chark. He was closer to him now.

"They let me out one day. Said I needed some fresh air and exercise. And I saw those men in uniform near the air raid shelter and I was confused again. There was a shovel laying on the ground. I don't remember much else. There was an air raid."

"The German too?"

Before Stewkley could answer, the door behind Chark was flung back noisily on its hinges and a beam of light from a powerful flashlight illuminated the scene. Phil Privett stood there in his dress uniform and peaked cap pointing a leather-covered swagger stick at Stewkley.

"You need help, David?" he bellowed into the silence.

"Not now, Phil! Not now!" called out Chark, half-turning. But it was too late. The sight of Privett and his swagger stick brought a scream of rage and fear from Stewkley. He hoisted the crucifix above his head to bring it down on the nearest target. Chark's head. Chark was speechless as he watched the brass cross rise in a shining arc and hang poised above him. He was unable to move back or forward on the unstable catwalk.

The blow never fell. The massive brass cross at the end of the long wooden shaft of the crucifix was too much for Stewkley. He leaned sideways under its weight, gasping and struggling to stay upright.

"Let it fall, man," called Chark. "Let it go!"

But the weight of it overpowered Ben Stewkley. With a great cry somewhere between triumph and fear, he tumbled down the curving slope of the nave roof after the clattering crucifix.

Stewkley's body bounced twice before he slid to the darkness of the eaves. He was dead when they climbed down to him. The first bounce had broken his neck.

Chapter 27

On the following Tuesday morning, Superintendent Russell called a press conference in the Eastchester Constabulary Building. Chark walked in to the crowded room to find Russell dressed for the occasion in his immaculate black uniform with the silver buttons and badges. He was talking to the mayor who looked as bored as all the other politicians there under suffrance to applaud someone other than themselves.

As the mayor listened to Russell, his eyes wandered around the room until they fixed on Chark who was standing among a knot of newspaper men at the hors d'ouvres table. He gave a wan smile and winked at him.

The reporters were pecking at Chark with questions and everybody seemed to be talking at once. A reporter dressed in a corduroy

jacket and suede hush puppies was eagerly taking notes as a city councilman spoke vehemently about the epidemic of hooliganism in the
town and saying that it was a good thing that Eastchester had such a
fine police department. He had, of course, voted for the appropriation
of funds for the crime lab which had featured so prominently in the
Fairport murder case.

Across the room, Sam Gilkicker stuffed shrimp sandwiches into
his mouth and waved a hand at Chark. There was no use trying to to
get to the food, the politicians seemed to have cleaned off the more
savoury items and the press were devouring the rest. The coffee was
cold. Chark edged his way towards the entrance and freedom. He was
six feet short of the door when Russell waved an imperious hand at
him.

"Ah, there you are, Chark. Come and be introduced."

Chark shook the mayor's hand and several others attached to people
he didn't know and said his *how-do-you-do's* politely.

Russell took his place at the podium and called for silence. The
crowd slowly went silent as they prepared to pay the price for their
attendance at the conference.

"Allow me to introduce Chief Inspector Chark. He has worked
under my direction in Fairport to bring this remarkable case to a successful
conclusion."

Russell's speech rambled on for five minutes. There was a flutter of
applause at the end and the gathering returned to the feeding tables as
Russell took Chark's arm and guided him to a tray that everybody else
seemed to be avoiding.

"Try these sausage rolls, old boy. The lady wife made them 'specially
for the occasion."

Chark stiffened at the "old boy" routine and smiled his thanks to
the absent Mrs Russell through clenched teeth. Patronizing old bastard.

A reporter closed in on Chark with pencil poised and Chark eyed
his escape route. Taking the greasy roll from his mouth and gesturing
in mock pain to his lower abdomen, he pointed to the Superintendent's
rest room and told the reporter to wait right there. Once in the rest
room, he dumped the roll and sneaked out through the back door. On

his way to the main entrance he was still muttering to Solomon about pompous Superintendents and carnivorous politicians when he passed the front desk.

"Beg your pardon, sir?" asked the receptionist.

"Nothing," said Chark. "I just strangled a Superintendent with his damn tie and poisoned the mayor with a sausage roll."

"Good," said the receptionist with the faintest of smiles. "I'll send in the cleanup crew."

Chark pushed open one side of the door as Prudence Whitehorse walked in the other. She smiled at his confusion.

"Do we go up to the press conference or are you going to invite me out for lunch?" she said.

He took her arm and steered her back out of the door into the car park. "Lunch with champagne and fresh-caught trout."

"Fine," she said as Chark opened the door of the Morris Minor and helped her in. "Then you can be my guide for a week. I've heard so much about England these last few weeks, I want to see it for myself."

"What about Paul?"

"Oh, Paul's gone back to Seattle in a huff," said Prudence. "Your sergeant Beane found out that the nurse who took care of him in the hospital is happily married. She and her husband are retired. They have four children, seven grandchildren, play Bingo for entertainment and are perfectly happy not remembering the least thing about him."

Chark and Prudence laughed together as they left the car park and drove out into the countryside.

*

Paul Lovedean returned to Seattle directly after the memorial service and set to work building hotels and roads and a new relationship with his family. Fairport held no attraction for him. Few of the villagers remembered him or his family.

Captain Charles Lovedean and Private William Brown were buried

with full military honours in St Ethelred's churchyard. The bishop re-
fused a dispensation to bury Ben Stewkley there and he was laid to rest
near the German airman in the plot set aside for the war dead. His
simple granite headstone read:

Pvt. B. H. StewkleyThe Hamptonshire Regiment
1940